Elton Hall Chronicles:

SECOND SNOWFALL

By Sarah Fischer

Elton Hall Chronicles: Second Snowfall

Limitless Publishing, LLC
Kailua, HI 96734
www.limitlesspublishing.com

Formatting: Limitless Publishing

ISBN-13: 978-1-64034-138-8
ISBN-10: 1-64034-138-2

Dedication

This book is dedicated to anyone fighting what seems like a hopeless battle. There is an end in sight if you allow those who care to help.

Also, this book would not be possible without my twin brother, Jacques Fischer, and his help with some of the darker aspects of this book.

Chapter 1

Any minute, my best friend, Violet, was going to walk into my dorm room and tell me all about her trip to England with her boyfriend, literature professor David Berneli. I was dying to hear about how they were doing. We talked almost every day over video chat but it wasn't the same. Besides, I needed to talk to her about Jason. Until now, I wasn't able to talk about it. But that was over. I couldn't keep this a secret anymore. I needed my friend.

The waiting was too much for me, so I decided to start unpacking my bags. I really needed to exchange some of my summer clothes for winter clothes. There definitely was not enough room in my closet for half the things I wanted to wear. Thankfully, I had brought several more containers to shove in the limited remaining space under my bed.

I was under the bed, trying to rearrange things, when I heard a hard knock on my door. I quickly slid out, careful not to hit my head, and rushed to

1

answer it. Violet was standing there with a giant package topped with an elaborate bow someone else must have tied for her.

"Hi," I shouted as I tried to hug her around the box.

"Hey, babe." She smiled and forced the box into my arms. "This is for you, since I missed seeing you at Christmas."

"Stop! You shouldn't have." I took the box and we both headed to my bed. It was covered in clothes but I moved a couple piles for Violet to sit down. Then I grabbed a small box out of one of my bags and sat next to her.

"Here, I got you something too." I handed her the present, eager to see her face when she opened it. I absolutely loved giving personalized presents to people.

We dug into the boxes and I pulled out a beautiful tote bag. It was bright yellow and orange with a paisley pattern and thick handles. "This is perfect." She had remembered yellow was my favorite color.

"There's more. You can't give someone a bag with nothing in it," she insisted, putting her present aside to watch me expectantly.

I searched through some of the pockets and finally pulled out a snow globe with the London Bridge inside. The bottom read:

Merry Christmas from Jolly Ole England.

"Aww, I love them both!"
"I'm glad. I was a little worried it would be too

touristy, but I know how much you love Christmas, so I figured—"

"No," I interrupted. "I like touristy, and I actually brought a mini Christmas tree to put up."

"Seriously? Christmas was almost a month ago." She snickered and rolled her eyes at me.

"Don't judge me!"

Violet finished opening her present and pulled out a beautiful leather journal. I had found it in a secondhand bookshop I visited with Jason. The pages were old and there was a thick gold bookmark sticking out of the top. Violet was always talking about how she liked to write her thoughts down, and when I saw this, I knew she'd love it. It was the perfect mix of romanticism and literature, basically Violet's personality in a gift.

"This is the most amazing journal I've ever seen!" I thought I saw a tear in the corner of her eye, but she quickly flipped it away and pulled me into a quick hug.

"Thanks! Jason and I thought it screamed your name when we were doing some shopping."

Violet shifted her eyes from the journal to me and squinted suspiciously. It was always unnerving that she seemed to be able to read my mind. She definitely knew there was something going on between Jason and me, but I didn't think she was aware of the extent of my feelings. Or if she was, she was actually keeping her thoughts to herself.

"So, what exactly happened over break? You more or less refused to talk about him when we Skyped. I didn't get much more out of him when we talked."

"I don't know! Okay, I kept inviting him and Janice to do things, because they live really close to me, but Janice kept bailing. She didn't come out with us once. So Jason and I explored together," I explained, avoiding her eye contact.

"You explored *what*?" Violet was looking at me suggestively, raising her eyebrows.

I rolled my eyes. She had such a dirty mind. "Explored the *area*, like we went to some lesser known shops, the movies, uh…we went to an ice skating rink, and he took me to a hockey game."

"Seriously?"

"I know, right? Who would have thought I'd ever step foot in a hockey arena? But it was actually a lot of fun." I remembered sitting a little too close to Jason because I was cold. He wrapped an arm around my shoulders to help warm me up. We sat like that for most of the game. I tried not to focus on how good it felt to be in his arms, but most nights, I dreamed about what it would be like to be folded up in his embrace. He radiated this warmth from his being and it drew me in. I was constantly cold, but with his arm around my neck, I felt like I'd never be cold again.

"No, I'm more focused on the fact that you went on, like, four dates with Jason."

"They weren't dates," I insisted, but I really didn't put up much of a fight. Deep inside, I wanted them to mean more.

Violet started to protest, but there was a knock on the door. When I opened it, my heart fell into my stomach as Jason stared back at me. His short hair somehow managed to stand on end and his shoelaces, as always, were untied. I shook my head slightly. He needed someone to clean him up, though, for some reason, I couldn't bring myself to do it. Maybe it was part of his charm.

"Hey, Annabelle." Jason walked into my room and then pulled me into a hug. I heard Violet giggle behind me but ignored it, giving her a dirty look over his shoulder.

He let go of me and turned toward Violet.

"Jason," she yelled, and barreled toward him, hip bumping me out of the way so she could hug him.

"Vi," he bellowed into her ear as he looked at me over her shoulder, shaking his head as if to say, "What are we gonna do with her?"

I tried to control the blush creeping up my neck, but it was no use. His blue eyes did it to me every time.

"So, how was England?" Jason asked, making himself comfortable on my bed.

Violet grabbed a pillow and sat at the end of the bed. She gave me a knowing stare, expecting me to sit in between them. Normally, I'd sit between them like it was nothing. My bed was just a place we congregated sometimes. It was probably because I wasn't having sex in it so it was safe. Today, with all the feelings swirling around in my head, I wasn't ready for that, so I sat in my desk chair.

"It was good! David introduced me to his mom, which was terrifying, but it actually went really well." She couldn't keep the smile off her face as she talked about walking hand in hand around Piccadilly Circus, sneaking kisses on the London Eye, laughing too loudly at the movies, dancing in the rain, and eating fish and chips in English pubs.

"But Carina, that's his mom, is convinced she can teach me how to cook. We tried it once and it wasn't so bad."

Jason and I looked at Violet incredulously. We'd heard stories about her trying to cook before and it usually ended badly.

"Okay, so it involved a lot of supervision but David said it was good."

"Of course he did, you're bangin' him," Jason teased.

Violet and Professor Berneli hooked up last semester. She called me on Skype almost every day to update me on her "holiday" with him. Things seemed to be going well. They claimed the relationship was all physical at first, but I thought they'd been in love with each other since she kicked his ass in poker that first night they met.

But their relationship was still against school rules, so they were using covert methods to see each other. That was why the trip to London had been perfect. They finally didn't need to hide their feelings, or their budding relationship. I envied her a little bit. Sure, she was talking a huge risk, but at least she was going for what she wanted.

"Did the professor manage to teach you a few new things while you were there?" Jason raised his eyebrows and winked at her.

Violet looked Jason dead in the eye and a sinister smile spread across her face. "Not as much as the *Kama Sutra* did. Did you know he has a copy in his library?"

We all burst into laughter as Violet stood up and

started to stretch into different positions. Jason got up and tried to copy her, his gangly arms and legs barely bending.

"You might want to practice touching your toes before you try any of those positions," I told Jason when I managed to stop laughing.

"What, you aren't impressed by my moves, Annabelle?"

"Yes, of course. I've always wanted a man like you." I forced a laugh, trying to make it seem like I was kidding. It just slipped out. Actually, things like that were slipping out more and more. I needed some self-control.

"So, how's Janice?" Violet asked Jason, changing the subject. I knew she was trying to be polite, but I couldn't help but feel like she had punched me in the stomach. I couldn't stand Jason's girlfriend, well, Violet couldn't either. We both put on a brave face whenever he talked about her. But we almost never brought her up first. However, Violet was bringing her up more and more often. It was driving me nuts, but the smile on her face made me think that was the exact reaction she wanted.

"She's good. Uh, she had a lot going on during winter break so I didn't get to see her as much as I would have liked." Jason turned to look at me and then smiled big. "Annabelle and I ended up hanging out most of the time."

"I heard that. She was just telling me about your hockey game." Violet snickered again and gave me a little wink.

"Oh man! It was hysterical. She didn't bring gloves, a hat, or a scarf. She didn't realize ice hockey rinks were that cold." Jason laughed and chucked a pillow at me lightly.

"Ha-ha! You didn't tell me, and you knew I'd never been to a game before. I figured we'd be inside so it wouldn't be as cold as it was outside." I tried to defend myself, but they both looked at me with pursed lips and raised brows. "Why don't we go get some lunch? You guys can tease me more then. I'll have better comebacks once I get some food in my system."

Violet and Jason seemed to be fine with my change of subject and we headed to the cafeteria.

Normally, I was not an outdoors person. I didn't really like dirt, bugs, or sweating, so being outside was not my thing. But this campus was so beautiful that I didn't care. The grass was luscious and there were flowerbeds and gazebos dispersed throughout the grounds. It was like walking through the Secret Garden and it actually made me feel at peace. At least it did until Jason put his arm around my shoulders and shattered any semblance of calm I may have been experiencing.

He was the only guy who had ever done this to me. Heck, he was the only guy I'd ever hugged who I wasn't related to. When he stood this close to me, I could smell his cologne. He usually wore a clean scent that reminded me of laundry day. To me, there was nothing better than falling into fresh sheets. He made me think of that, but then I thought about falling into fresh sheets with him and I quickly started to panic and tried to push those thoughts away. But then it dawned on me. I knew that smell. It made me think of the ocean spray from the boardwalk and I could almost hear the seagulls.

"Are you wearing the cologne I got you for Christmas?"

"Yeah, why?" Jason didn't look at me, but rather stared straight ahead. I couldn't see the look on his face, however his ears turned a light shade of red. Could he be blushing too?

"Nothing, I just think it smells good," I replied, trying to keep the ridiculous smile off my face.

"Well, I would hope so. You bought it. Unless you got me something that smelled awful in an effort to stay as far away from me as possible."

"Ah, you have me figured out. I guess they switched the bottle at the store."

"That must be it," he said, and gave me a bright smile, squeezing my shoulder a little with his big hand.

He was wearing my gift and it seemed kind of intimate for some reason. I didn't think it would have this kind of effect on me. My pulse was beating rapidly and I was desperate to calm it before Jason noticed. There was an awkward silence, but I didn't know what to say. Violet, as she almost always did, seemed to pick up on it.

"So, I love my journal. I assume you were a part of that gift?" She gave Jason a little side hug and pulled him away from me for a second. Sometimes it was frustrating that she was so perceptive. But I was grateful for her. I needed those few moments to try to compose my face and calm my nerves.

"Oh yeah, glad you like it. Where's my present, then?"

"Was I supposed to get you a present? I thought

your present was that I came back from England and now you get to be in my presence."

"Eh, Annabelle and I had enough fun without you." Jason gave her a little shove then pulled me close so he could put his arm back around my shoulders. "Right, Annabelle?"

"Nah, I kinda like her. She brings excitement to the group."

Jason pulled Violet back under his arm. "Fine, whatever Annabelle says."

"Your present is in my room. We can get it after we eat," she told him, and he dropped the arm around me and gave her a quick hug. I instantly felt a chill go through my system now that his warm arm was around Violet. He didn't pull me back in for a hug and I didn't reach for it. The three of us just continued to walk while Jason's arm was wrapped around Violet.

The cafeteria was pretty empty so Violet asked Jason a few more questions about his family and the rest of his break as we grabbed trays to get food. Then we separated to grab our favorites. Violet worshiped pasta and Jason basically lived off pizza and burgers. Although, he could only eat burgers when Janice wasn't around. She didn't eat red meat and insisted Jason didn't as well.

My favorite was anything I could throw in a stir fry. Well, that and ice cream. Jason finished getting his food and told us he was going to get our table by the windows while the two of us finished getting our dinner.

I was almost done with my stir fry when Violet basically snuck behind me. I jumped a little, my focus too on Jason to realize she was there.

"You bought him cologne? That's a girlfriend gift." She rested her tray on the counter so she could put her hands on her hips and give me one hell of a judgmental look. Eyebrows raised, head tilted to the side, and lips pursed. Since she'd walked into my room, she kept giving me this look. At this rate, her face was gonna freeze that way, and I didn't think Berneli was gonna like that O face.

I rolled my eyes and flipped the stir fry onto my plate. "I didn't know what to get him and some websites suggested cologne. So, you know, I just found one I liked. Guess he liked it too." In reality, I had spent hours on his gift. I didn't want to get him just anything and I read an article that said cologne could cause a guy to subconsciously think about you throughout the day. Not that I should want him to think of me. It was just wrong, but whatever. I wasn't made of money so it was one of the few things I could get. At least I didn't get him boxers.

"Well, what do you think Janice is going to say when she is hooking up with Jason while he is wearing your cologne?"

"It doesn't matter. He decides when to wear it. It's not my fault if he is wearing it while kissing Janice. Maybe Jason wants to wear it because he likes it."

"Maybe he wants to wear it because he wants you to smell it when you're kissing him?" Violet suggested while nudging me a little.

"Since he is with Janice, I don't think we need to worry about that," I told her, walking across the cafeteria and setting the tray down next to Jason.

11

"We don't need to worry about what?" Jason asked, and then wiped some pizza sauce off his face. He missed some of it and I rolled my eyes. Why was he always such a mess?

"Finding good stir fry. Annabelle was just telling me how much she missed it while on break." Violet didn't even pause to think of the lie.

I took a deep breath and lightly tapped her leg under the table with my foot in gratitude. She was always quick with a response, no matter the situation. Sometimes they were dirty comments, but that made her fun. I never knew what she was going to say.

We were talking about classes when Jason's phone went off. It was a text from Janice. The smile faded from his face almost instantly.

"I was hoping to hang out with Janice tonight, but she said she is driving back first thing in the morning. Her mom wants to do a family night before she comes back to school." He fired back a response and then looked at us with a big grin. "On the bright side, she isn't gonna sneak up on me, so I'm getting a burger." He winked at me and then got up from the table.

Violet and I waited until he was out of earshot to groan. "I don't know why he stays with her. All she does is bail on him," I said, shaking my head.

"Comfort. They've been together for so long, he is probably afraid to be without her." Violet's voice was quiet and filled with despair. She really loved Jason as a friend, and I knew it killed her to watch Janice mistreat him. I was surprised she'd stayed silent this long. It wasn't like her to keep her opinions to herself.

"What should we do about it?" I asked her, watching Jason talk to a couple of guys by the grill station.

Violet slapped at my arm to get my attention and locked eyes with me. "We do *nothing*! Until you're ready to be with him for real, then you do nothing."

"It's not that simple." I didn't know how to explain it to her. For months, Violet had been insisting there was something more between us. She claimed he stared at me with a longing he never showed Janice, but I just didn't see it. Probably because we never really saw the way he looked at Janice since she was never around. But at the same time, I didn't think he looked at me any differently than he looked at Violet, and I knew he wasn't in love with her.

What if he wasn't actually interested in me? What if he was just being nice? He treated Violet and me the same way. He hugged her and hung out with her too. Maybe we were all just friends. He actually found Violet's journal and chipped in, but didn't get me anything. He paid for one of my dinners, which was nice, but it wasn't anywhere near the thought he had for her present.

"I know. But you can't be responsible for breaking them up if you aren't one hundred percent positive you want him." Violet's eyes were stern and all her usual jokes were long gone.

"I want to be with him, but I'm not ready for that. What if he isn't interested and I screw everything up?" I asked, more afraid than positive. No, I wasn't ready for this. Jason needed to give me a sign that he was interested in me as more than a friend. I couldn't ruin the friendship. That, and I'd never been in a relationship before. I didn't know how to be with someone in that way and I wouldn't want to start my first relationship as a homewrecker. What if I was a bad girlfriend and he left me to go back to Janice?

Violet snapped her fingers in my face and then looked at me as if she was reading my soul. "But he does…"

"No, you think he does. Has he ever said it to you? Has he come out and said, 'Vi, I've got feelings for Annabelle'?"

"No, but—"

"Exactly. You two are my best friends, and I'm not screwing that up on ifs. What if he doesn't like me and things get awkward? Then you'll be in the middle and I'll lose my best friend and you will probably lose a best friend and then we all can't hang out. I don't want to screw up what we have. Besides, I'm no homewrecker. If he liked me enough, he'd leave her. I think that's the biggest clue here. He's still with her."

She opened her mouth like she wanted to say something further, but then went back to her pasta. I was glad she didn't press me or insist on talking about it more. She was crazy persuasive and it would only be a matter of time before she talked me into doing something.

Jason came back a few minutes later with a new guy and my mouth went dry. He was gorgeous. His eyes were hazel and they were framed by dark, long lashes. It should be illegal for a man to have such

14

beautiful lashes. I forced myself to look at the rest of him. His straight brown hair was cropped short and his creamy skin held a natural tan. But it was his fierce cheek and jaw bones that grabbed my attention. They were prominent and utterly manly.

He slid his jacket off before sitting down and I almost choked on my soda. His arm muscles were bulging and I knew I was gaping. Normally, lean muscle was my favorite, but his thick, defined form was so overwhelming and hot that I decided I could make an exception for him. In fact, I wanted to make a whole lot of exceptions for him.

"This is Kingsley," Jason introduced us.

"Kingsley? That's an interesting name. Where did your parents come up with it?" Violet asked him as she gave him a little wave.

"My name is Thomas Kingsley III. I played sports forever and they always call you by your last name. Eventually, I just decided to start using it since my mom was tired of yelling for Tom and having two people answer. If my grandpa is there, it's even worse." He smiled, revealing a set of perfectly straight and white teeth. They glistened like a toothpaste commercial.

"Kingsley moved in across the hall after he had some problems with his roommate last semester," Jason told us.

"Yeah, he was just super jealous of me and things got hostile. But I didn't want to force him to move, so I was the bigger person and just changed rooms," Kingsley explained, and then took a bite of his burger. "Shit, they made it wrong again. I only like it medium well and there is way too much pink in this burger. I'll be back." Kingsley grabbed his tray and walked back to the grill station.

"Well, he's a little prissy." Violet snorted.

"Kind of. I heard he hooked up with his roommate's girlfriend and that's why he moved out," Jason informed us.

"Maybe he didn't know," I said, remembering Kenny. I was the other woman with him and had no idea. It still upset me that I had been used like that. Maybe he was in the same position. I just met the guy, so it seemed wrong to just assume the worst.

"I feel like he probably knew," Jason stated.

"But you don't know that, right?" I asked him.

"No, I don't know that. It's just a rumor," he confirmed.

"Well, people were saying crappy things about me after the Kenny thing blew up and that was a nasty rumor too. I think we should give him the benefit of the doubt." I glanced at Kingsley, smiling. I kind of admired how he went back to talk to the cooks. I never had the courage to do it, which meant sometimes I didn't enjoy my meal.

Jason turned his head and followed my glance. "Don't tell me, you think he's hot."

"I sure as hell do," Violet responded, letting out a low whistle.

I laughed with her and Jason rolled his eyes.

"Well, obviously, he's buff," I added, still looking at him. Kingsley took that moment to turn around and made eye contact with me. I quickly looked down, but not before I noticed the giant grin that spread out on his face. He'd caught me but it looked like he didn't mind. Feeling brave for whatever reason, I risked a look at him again and he was still smiling in my direction as he placed his new burger on his tray.

"Looks aren't everything," Jason tried to remind me.

"No, but they don't hurt," I stated, excited he was walking back toward us. I gave him a little wave, like Violet had done, and he gave me a nod, sending shivers of excitement through me. Kingsley sat down next to me and handed me a chocolate chip cookie.

"I grabbed myself one and they were having a deal. Do you want the other one?"

"Thanks, I love sweets. They're kind of my weakness."

"Mine too," he said, but his smile was gone. Instead, he gave me a very different look. I didn't know how to label it, hell, I wasn't even sure if another guy had ever looked at me that way. All I knew was that I hoped he wouldn't look away.

Chapter 2

We were just leaving the cafeteria when Kingsley stopped us.

"Hey, so what are you guys doing tonight? I heard there is an awesome mini golf place not far from here. I don't mean to brag, but I'm pretty amazing at it." He reached out and put his arm around my shoulders. "We could double date."

I bit my lip to try to keep it together. He'd said date.

Violet's hand flew up in the air and she shook her head. "Hold up there, buddy. Jason and I aren't together. But mini golf sounds fun. Maybe we could just make it a group thing."

"Sounds good. What do you think, babe?" Kingsley looked down at me and raised his eyebrows expectantly. He already knew my answer.

"I'd love to," I replied, and looked down. He called me babe. No one had ever really given me a nickname before and I kind of liked it.

"How about you?" he asked Jason, but kept his gaze on me.

"As long as Annabelle isn't on my team," Jason said, putting extra emphasis on my name.

"Hey, I'm actually really good at mini golf!" I was. We played a lot when I was younger. My family had a beach house and we would spend weeks there. There was this mini golf place within walking distance. Sometimes my brother and I would sneak there just to get away from our overprotective mother. Of course, she always knew where to find us, so our reprieve wasn't long.

"Whatever you say. You can just crush Vi and me."

Jason offered to drive, and at first I thought Kingsley was going to sit in the front, but he opened the back door for me and slid in next to me. I tried my hardest not to giggle in excitement as his knee brushed mine.

Luckily, he didn't notice me spaz because his phone rang and he turned to the window to answer it.

"Hey, man, what's up?" Kingsley said. "Yeah, I can switch shifts with you. I have class, but I'm sure they'll let me out. What are they gonna say, 'No, we don't want you to fight fires'?" He laughed a bit and then hung up the phone. "Sorry about that."

"You're a firefighter?" Violet asked from the front seat.

"Yeah, I volunteer right now while I'm in school. My parents insisted I go to school, but when I graduate, I'm gonna do it full time."

I started picturing him in a firefighting uniform and definitely liked what I saw. "Wow, do you actually go into the fire?"

"All the time. It's pretty dangerous, but I have to look out for people. Mom would rather I go into business or law, but protecting people is my passion." He smiled and nodded his head at me. Then Kingsley shifted and flexed his arm muscles.

"That's really impressive," I said, referring more to his muscles than to his job.

"I'm glad you think so. How about you, Violet, are you a fan of firefighters?" He leaned forward and looked at her.

"Who isn't? But I prefer them in my porn."

Jason and I laughed hysterically while Kingsley looked at us, confused. He leaned over to me and whispered in my ear, "Is she kidding?"

I pulled it together long enough to shake my head at him. "To be honest, I'm not sure sometimes," I said, suppressing a giggle. "She likes the shock value that comes with half the things she says but it wouldn't surprise me if she had a crazy porn collection."

"I like my girls a little more subdued."

"Good to know." I was definitely more subdued than Violet, though that was not hard.

We pulled into the mini golf parking lot and climbed out of the car. As we entered the bright red brick building, Kingsley stopped me while Violet and Jason went to the register to pay.

"So, this is really embarrassing, but I forgot my wallet. Do you mind paying for me? I'll get you next time." Kingsley placed his hand on my shoulder and looked into my eyes. "I really want to do this with you and I'd hate to have to wait behind. You want to hang out with me, right?"

I panicked for a second. I did want to spend the day with him. "Yeah, no problem. I'll take care of it."

"Great, you're the best, babe!" Kingsley draped his arm on my shoulder like Jason had earlier. It felt different. I still had butterflies, but they were different. With Jason, I pretty much knew I had no chance. With Kingsley, it could actually be something. I took a deep breath and tried to push the fear away. I wanted to have fun tonight so I wrapped my arm around his waist and we headed to the register.

Once we paid, we grabbed our colored golf balls and joined Violet and Jason at the first hole.

"Move over, ladies, let me show you how it's done." Kingsley stretched his arms and walked up to the tee, nearly pushing Violet out of the way. It was cute how excited he was but he probably needed to calm it down. Violet may actually beat him with her club if he tried that again.

"Dude, ladies first. Come on, man," Jason scoffed, and looked at Violet. They seemed to share a moment, but I didn't understand what the big deal was. Who cared if he went first? It was just a game. It was probably just their competitive sides coming through. We had tried to go bowling as a group and the two of them were ridiculous.

"Yeah, of course. I just figured the girls might like an example of how to line up the putt and how hard they should hit it. I'm just looking out for them. I told you, I'm good at this. I just want it to be fair for everyone." Kingsley didn't move from the tee.

It was almost a straight shot to the hole, which was situated between two rocks. I probably didn't need him to show me how to get it in, but I could let him have his moment. Who did it hurt? It wasn't like we were in a rush or anything.

"No, Jason, let him. I'd like to see what he can do," I said.

Kingsley gave Jason an "I told you so" look with raised eyebrows, a slight smirk, and a tilted head. I thought it looked cute, but Violet snorted behind us, not even bothering to cover it up with a cough. I looked over at her and rolled my eyes. She was probably just eager to play.

Kingsley knocked the ball and it went in, hole in one. He shot his arm in the air and cheered. "There you go! That's how it's done." Kingsley nodded hard and winked at me. "Come on, babe, why don't you come over here and I'll help you out." He beckoned for me to join him.

I walked to him and he stood behind me. As he placed his hands on my putter, he slightly grazed my arms and I felt a shudder of excitement flow through me. Kingsley was so close that I could feel his heart beating against my back and mine quickly synced up with his pattern. I smiled big and looked at Violet.

She had a big grin on her face as Kingsley was giving me putting instructions. Then she turned to look at Jason and I followed her gaze. He didn't look impressed with Kingsley's manners. In fact, he looked pretty pissed. Well, he needed to get over it. I vowed to ignore Jason's sour face and enjoy being this close to Kingsley.

"Think you got it, babe?"

"Yeah, you're a good teacher," I told him, even though I really hadn't heard anything he said. I was too distracted by his strong arms draped around me.

"Great, I'll be right here, watching you do your thing." Kingsley backed up and stood next to Violet, far away from Jason.

I was about to hit the ball when Jason reached out and grabbed my arm. It was a different feeling. Almost as if I was being electrocuted. I wouldn't say that I liked it, but it was kind of thrilling and it really seemed to bring me to life. It was almost like splashing water on your face in the morning to help wake up. You felt a jolt and then it calmed as you began to feel more refreshed.

"Kingsley, get your ball, bro. If she gets a hole in one, then it won't go in because your ball will knock it out."

"I know, man, but I was just giving her some space. I'll go get it." Kingsley rushed down to the hole and pulled his ball out. "You're good to go."

I took a deep breath and tried not to focus on the fact that Kingsley was watching me and just hit the ball. I tapped it with a bit of force and sure enough, it went in. Kingsley cheered and rushed over to me. He gave me a high-five and then looked at Jason.

"I guess it's a good thing I showed her what to do." Then he turned to Violet and extended his hand to her. "What about you, want some help?"

Violet's eye grew wide and I couldn't tell if she was going to laugh or shut him down with a nasty comment. She shook her head for a second and then smiled sweetly.

"That's okay. My boyfriend and I went a couple times over winter break, so I think I'm good." Her pleasant expression was forced, but I was glad she was leaving the extra attention to me. After all, she really did have a boyfriend. Though I was a little surprised she mentioned him. Violet usually told people she was single and not interested in dating anyone.

"Wait, I thought you said that you and Jason weren't a thing. Did you guys just break up?"

"Ah, no. Jason and I were never together. My boyfriend is studying abroad in England this semester."

"Aren't you afraid, being that far away from each other? Seems like a great excuse for him to cheat on you. Guys usually follow the zip code rule."

"What the hell is the zip code rule?" Jason asked, looking at Kingsley as if he had three heads.

"Oh, come on, man! Everyone knows the zip code rule. If the girl you mess with is outside the zip code your girlfriend lives in, then it isn't cheating." Kingsley explained this as if it was the most obvious thing in the world.

Jason laughed, but it was a bitter sound and I didn't like it. It didn't suit him. "I've never heard of that crap. I don't care who you are or where you are, cheating is cheating. I'd never cheat on my girlfriend."

"Hey, good for you. I'm not saying I'd cheat, just that Violet might want to be careful. Not all guys are as noble as we are." It was good to hear Kingsley wouldn't cheat. For a second there, he was sounding an awful lot like Kenny, and I was not all right with that.

Violet crossed her arms and frowned. "Thanks for looking out, but I trust my boyfriend."

"Famous last words," Kingsley sang to her backswing.

Violet didn't respond and walked to the other end of the green where she'd have to hit the ball in since she missed the hole.

Jason lined up and shot. He also missed, so the two of them tapped their balls in and we moved on.

I watched as Jason and Violet walked to the next hole and I couldn't get his words out of my head. He'd never cheat on Janice. Of course he wouldn't cheat on her, and he didn't seem to have any intention of breaking up with her either. I needed to let this stupid crush go. Here I was with this gorgeous man who was clearly interested in me and I was thinking about Jason. I looked up at Kingsley and gave him a bright smile as we headed to the next hole. It was time to focus my attention on the sexy firefighter beaming down at me instead of the guy who had me firmly in the friendzone.

***

We made it to the last hole, and as it turned out, I was winning. Violet was actually really bad at mini golf, so she wasn't anywhere near my score, but she was still a good sport about the whole thing. Jason wasn't much better than her, but he put up a good fight. Kingsley, however, was one stroke behind me. If I got a hole in one on the final hole, then I'd win. I wasn't super competitive but I wanted to impress him.

"Don't mess up, babe!" Kingsley shouted when I swung.

I stopped just before I hit the ball because he had messed up my concentration. I turned toward him and shook a playful finger at him. "Hey, that's not nice." I giggled and turned back to realign my shot. I knocked it off the side and it went straight in. There was no question it was a perfect shot. I dropped my putter and threw my arms up in the air. "Woooo, I won!"

"Really, there's no need to brag. I thought you were better than that." Kingsley walked into the main building without even finishing the last hole.

My smile fell and I looked at Violet and Jason, confused. "What did I do? Was I really that obnoxious?"

Violet walked over to me and placed a hand on my shoulder. "No, he just looks like a sore loser. He probably is a little embarrassed that you beat him."

"Why? I told you guys I was good."

"I know," Jason piped up. "But some guys still like to think they're better than girls at everything. You did a good job. Don't let him ruin the night. We can take him back to his dorm and hang out just the three of us. He doesn't need to be involved in our fun."

"No, it's okay. I knew he was competitive and I pushed his buttons. I'll go talk to him and make this right. I'll meet you guys at the car. Just play your turns." I headed inside, following where I saw Kingsley walk to. He was leaning on the counter and talking to the cashier. She was around my age, maybe older, and really pretty. At the moment, she was laughing hard at something he said. She reached out and touched his forearm and leaned in closer. My heart fell into my stomach. Was he trying to make me jealous? No, he didn't even know I was there. He was actively looking for another option. This was my first real date and it was crashing and burning. Maybe I could still fix this.

"Hey, Kingsley, um, Jason goofed up," I said, walking over to him. He looked over at me, quickly distancing himself from the girl and showing me a different smile. "You were actually three ahead, so you can still win if you play the last hole," I lied as I forced a smile on my face. My pulse was racing and I was terrified he'd reject the idea and leave without me. I'd be back to being alone again. I hoped he'd give me another chance.

"That jerk. I bet he did that on purpose to make me look bad. I don't know why you hang out with that guy, he's kind of an ass." Kingsley wrapped his arm around my waist and we walked back to the hole where Violet and Jason were waiting. Kingsley leaned down and whispered in my ear, "Don't worry, I'm not going to embarrass him and say anything. I'll just knock this in and win gracefully."

"He's been my friend since I came here. He's just super competitive." I felt like I had to defend Jason. After all, he was still one of my best friends.

"I can respect that. I know guys who act like that and they're standup guys all the other times. We just probably shouldn't do anything else competitive with him in the future. I don't want to show him up again and cause problems."

"Good plan." I smiled, staring down at the ground. He'd said in the future. He wasn't sick of me yet.

Kingsley knocked the ball into the hole in one shot. He chucked his putter in the water and threw his arms in the air. "That's right, baby." He pointed his finger at Jason and smiled big. "That's okay, man, I'll let you win next time."

"Don't worry about it. I'm not big into sports."

"Why, are you gay?"

Violet laughed so hard she stopped breathing for a second. I bit my lip to try to keep the giggles at bay, but they ended up coming out as snorts.

"No, I just prefer movies and video games than actual sports. You do know that all guys who don't play sports aren't gay, right? And there are a lot of gay guys who are amazing at sports."

Violet seemed to have stopped laughing and draped her arm around Jason's shoulder. "It's okay. I think he was just kidding. I'm sure he didn't mean to offend anyone." She turned to look at Kingsley and he shook his head.

"Nah, of course not. But you said you two weren't dating and he didn't mention having a girlfriend. I just figured it was a chance. No offense meant, bro." Kingsley extended his hand to Jason.

He looked at it for a second and then Jason walked over and shook it. "Yeah, no stress. I do have a girlfriend, and her name is Janice."

"That's cool."

There was an awkward silence as the four of us just stared at each other. Finally, Jason spoke up.

"Why don't we head back? Violet was telling me that she has a couple things to do back at her dorm." Jason looked at Violet and they seemed to have a silent conversation.

"Right, I have a crazy amount of stuff to unpack from my trip and I'm exhausted from my flight the other night. Jet lag is a bitch." She smiled and nodded her head at me. I could tell she wanted to leave but I didn't think it was because of the unpacking or jet lag. I just didn't know what was wrong.

"I have a little unpacking to do too," I added, hoping she'd tell me what was going on later.

Kingsley agreed and we all walked back to the car.

The ride back was pretty exciting. Kingsley was telling us about this dramatic time that he saved three children from a burning home.

"Everyone else was willing to let them die, but I knew I could get to them. Against the captain's orders, I ran back into the house and carried all three of them out at one time. It didn't matter how unsafe the building was or what happened to me. All I could think about were those kids."

I looked at him with utter admiration. "I can't believe you would risk your life for people you didn't even know."

"Not people, *children*. I just couldn't let them die. I didn't care about my own life, or even my future. Those kids needed me, and I wasn't going to let them down." He reached out and held my hand. "What else could I do?"

"You're an amazing man." Holy crap. Did that

come out of my mouth? I was so embarrassed. At least I *was* until he reached his other hand out and gently stroked my cheek.

"And you're beautiful."

I dropped my gaze and blushed all over. I bit my lip and a smile quickly escaped. "Thanks."

But before anything else could happen, Jason honked the horn. "Okay, Annabelle, we're at your dorm. You and Violet probably want to head out."

"Right." I was about to get out when I realized Kingsley had never asked for my number. I debated asking for his but I didn't have the courage for it.

I looked away from him and went to open the door. My heart had fallen into my stomach again, but for a different reason, and I was desperate for some ice cream. I was going to head to my room and tear into the new carton of rocky road calling for me in my freezer.

"Annabelle, wait!" Kingsley had jumped out of the car and rushed over to me. "I owe you for the putt-putt. How can I repay you if I don't have your number?"

"Oh, right. Sorry," I said, and typed my number into his proffered cell.

"Perfect. I'll text you, babe." He grinned and then turned and walked toward his dorm.

I looked at Violet and squealed a little. We were about to walk into the building when Jason honked his horn.

"Are you really so love struck that you forgot to say goodbye to me?" He stepped out of the car and stood hunched over with his hands in his pocket.

"Oh, sorry, bye." I gave him a quick hug and

rushed inside. Violet and I had a lot to talk about.

Chapter 3

Violet wasn't going to see Berneli, but she still insisted she had a couple things to take care of.

"So what's up?" I asked her when she followed me into my room, making herself comfortable on my bed.

"What do you mean?"

"You and Jason. Didn't you have fun? I saw you guys decide you were ready to leave. There was like a private mental conversation between the two of you."

"We did but…"

"But what?"

"I don't know. Kingsley just kinda rubbed us the wrong way."

"Why?"

"I think it's 'cause he just made a few comments that were a little rude. Nothing too big."

"Well, think about it from his perspective. We're all friends and he's the new guy trying to impress everyone. He just seemed a little nervous to me."

"I think that's a fair thing to say. I'm totally

willing to give him a chance if you like him. I mean, it seemed to me like he was interested in you."

"I hope so. He is gorgeous."

"Yeah, he is definitely good looking, but earlier you were talking to me about how you might have feelings for—"

"No, we're done talking about him. I can't keep pretending it's all gonna change. I'm moving on."

We talked a bit longer about some superficial stuff but nothing got real deep and nothing more about Jason versus Kingsley. Eventually, Violet went back to her room to sleep while I, on the other hand, really did need to continue unpacking.

It took me a lot longer to unpack than I had intended. I spent most of the night reorganizing, hoping that if I played Tetris enough, it would all magically fit. When that didn't work, I took two of the containers to my car and left them in my trunk. At least if I needed any of those clothes, they weren't too far away.

As I was walking back to my room, I heard yelling. The closer to the sound I got, the more I realized I knew that voice. It was Violet. I rushed over to her room and tried the door. Of course, it was locked. I pounded on the door until Violet finally flung it open.

She looked at me with bleary eyes. "What are you doing here? It's, like, one in the morning."

"You were screaming. Is everything all right?"

Violet closed her eyes and took a deep breath. "Come in." We walked over to her bed and sat down.

The tears quickly came as she practically collapsed into my lap. "I'm sorry. I know you can't handle tears but—"

I cut her off. "Stop, it's fine. Just tell me what's wrong." I was really worried about her. The last time I saw her this upset was when the campus police officer attacked her fall semester. He had taken her behind this building and tried to rape her. Luckily, Violet had managed to fight him off, but the incident had left her really shaken.

"I don't know. I spent almost every night in bed with David and he made me feel so safe. Now, he won't be back until tomorrow, and, well, something has been happening that I haven't told you. For the last couple of months, I've been having night terrors." She sat up and wiped her tears on her shirt, finally taking a deep breath and looking up at me.

"What do you mean? Like nightmares? Are there clowns?" My version of hell was filled with clowns.

Violet laughed softly. "No, I wish it were clowns. I'm back behind the dorm and Finn is there. He's on top of me and I can't shake him off. But it feels so real and there is this pressure on my chest. It's like I can feel his hands on me and I can't wake up. It's mostly happened when David would stay up later than me and I was left to fall asleep alone. He'd hear me scream and rush to wake me up."

I hugged her hard and lightly stroked her back while she continued. "David wants me to see someone about it but I don't know if I want to. Will that actually help? Will sitting on someone's couch while I recount the worst moments of my life really make this go away? No, I just need to be stronger.

34

Finn is in jail and I don't need to worry about him coming after me. I'm just being ridiculous. Sorry, this is all pretty pathetic."

"But you slept here for two months after the attack. Why didn't it happen then?"

"It did. The first time was the first night I came back here after spending the weekend with David. I tried to convince myself that I was fine, but fear almost overwhelmed me as I walked into the building. I climbed into bed and fell asleep with the light on. It was okay that night, until around two in the morning." Violet took a deep breath and stared at the door, as if remembering what happened.

"I heard the door open and Lola walked in. But in that split second before I saw her, I thought it was Finn coming back to finish the job. Since then, I really haven't been able to sleep in my bed."

"So why did you come back? I'm sure Berneli would have let you stay at his place or maybe we can see about changing your room."

"This isn't me. I don't run from things like this. Hell, I fought Finn and got away. Now, I'm shrinking away from dreams. I thought maybe I was strong enough to fight this Finn too."

"Okay, so I have an idea. We can talk to Lola. I can sleep in her bed when she isn't here. If you have a terror, I can wake you up and remind you that Finn isn't here. Maybe if we do this, you'll get used to it. You know, you'd be getting the reinforcement from both Berneli and me."

"You don't have to do that. I don't want to put you out." While her words said she was fine, her eyes practically begged me. Violet's face was stark white and her eyes were bugging out a little. She looked terrified.

"Let me go get a change of sheets and I'll sleep in the other bed. Besides, that dating show started up while you were in England and now we're desperately behind."

***

I hardly slept at all that night. Violet didn't have another terror, but every time I closed my eyes, I thought I heard her murmur. It really didn't help that she appeared to have a tendency to talk in her sleep. Nonetheless, I had to get up and get ready for my first class. It was biology and I was really not looking forward to it. There truly was no helping me when it came to math and science. Things had not turned out well when I tried to get a math tutor so I needed to show up to this class. Maybe I just needed a female tutor.

Even the hot water of my morning shower did nothing to improve my mood. It was definitely going to be a long day. I wrapped myself in my robe and started to put a little bit of natural make-up on.

As I was getting dressed, I heard my phone go off. It was a text from Kingsley. After all the drama with Violet, I completely forgot that he never contacted me last night. That was probably for the best, though, since I would have been a wreck of anxiety if I had managed to remember.

Kingsley: *Hey, wanna get coffee?*

Ah, this was the way to my heart. Some women adored food, like Violet, while I worshiped the coffee gods.

Me: Sounds good. Where should I meet u?

I turned to my closet and quickly pulled out my favorite yellow shirt and a pair of skinny jeans. I had just managed to slip my legs into my pants when my phone went off again.

Kingsley: How about now? Look out ur window.

I bit my lip, threw my shirt on, and ran over to my window. Sure enough, Kingsley was standing there with two cups of coffee raised in the air. He couldn't see me, since he didn't know where my room was, but he was smiling in my general direction.

Giggling a little, I stuffed my feet in my shoes, grabbed my bag and coat, then almost ran outside. As I got closer to the door, I slowed so he wouldn't know just how eager I was to see him.

"Hey, babe." Kingsley handed me one of the cups and leaned down to kiss my cheek.

I blushed madly. His stubble was rough as it grazed my cheek, but for some reason, I kind of liked the feeling.

"You didn't have to bring me coffee." I looked down at the ground and took a sip. Hopefully the coffee would help to still my nerves. Though, maybe he would assume the shake was from lack of caffeine. That was partially true.

"I wanted to. Besides, I owe you from last night. Now we're even." He smiled big at me as he took a sip of his coffee. "I hope you like it. You mentioned you liked things sweet, so I took a risk and assumed you liked some sugar and milk in your drink, but if it's wrong, I can get you another."

"No, I like my coffee a little sweet. It's perfect. Thanks for remembering." It was actually way too sweet, but maybe the sugar would help wake me up. I took another big sip and forced a big smile.

We started walking toward the castle, in silence at first, just trying to enjoy our coffee. I looked up at Kingsley through my eyelashes and couldn't help but feel jitters flow through my body. He was so handsome. His dark hair was styled and spiked up in the *I woke up this way* look, but he probably spent at least fifteen minutes trying to make it look like that. Frankly, I was a fan of it. It was so different from Jason's messy look, but then again, I was pretty sure Jason didn't try to get his hair like that. It just happened naturally.

"What, is there something on my face?" He brushed at his cheeks rapidly.

"No, I just..." What was I supposed to say? I *was just admiring how sexy you are and comparing you to my old crush?*

"It's okay. I know I'm good looking. Take in your fill." Kingsley chuckled and made a ridiculous pose. He flexed his muscles and grunted a little at the effort.

I shook my head and laughed. "I guess you caught me."

"That's all right. I guess I'm just more observant than you are. After all, you haven't caught me staring at you." He lifted my chin slightly and looked deep into my eyes. "There, now we're really even."

I smiled brightly as he finally looked away toward the castle. "What class do you have first?" I was a little desperate to talk about something lighter. I didn't really know how to have these heart to heart conversations. They made me a little nervous.

"It's one of my emergency management classes. It's in the C wing on the third floor."

"Oh, my class is in D wing on the third floor."

"Great, I won't have to walk far after I take you to class." He wrapped his arm around my shoulders. The jitters faded and I was shocked at how comfortable I was starting to feel with him. Maybe it was because he didn't play games. He just said things how they were. I didn't have to wonder what he was thinking. It was a nice change.

We talked about our families for a little while as we made our way to class. As it turned out, Kingsley's family had old money. Like, a stupid amount of old money. His father was a successful divorce attorney and his mother was a top tier realtor. They were both trying to force him into law, but all Kingsley wanted to do was protect people.

"Money is nice. I mean, I've always had it, so I don't really know life without it, but I don't want to be stuck behind a desk. I just want to help people, but that's not good enough for them. So, I'm gonna finish this degree and when I'm hired as a full-time firefighter, hopefully seeing me happy will be enough to get them off my back."

"That's so honorable."

"That, and chicks really dig firefighters. Wait until you see me in my uniform. It will definitely impress you." Kingsley pulled his phone out and showed me a couple pictures. He was right, he looked amazing.

I didn't know what to say at first. He was clearly waiting for some kind of reaction from me but I wasn't sure what to do. I could be brave and say something about how the picture made me feel. But that wasn't really me. He needed to get to know me. Then it hit me. I could change. I could be flirty and suggestive. I could be a bit more like Violet. She got the guy she wanted, after all. But he liked his women more subdued. Maybe I just needed to be more honest about my feelings but do it my way. I needed to be open like Violet, but with my thoughts.

"I like the uniform. I'd like to see it in person." I placed my hand on his arm, feeling his bicep, and looked up at him. "Maybe you could show it to me sometime."

Kingsley's mouth fell open just for a second and then he flashed me a cocky smile. "I'll let you know the next time I get called in for a shift. Maybe you can meet me after."

My heart raced at the thought of rushing to a firehouse to meet up with my sexy…oh crap. I was about to say boyfriend. He wasn't my boyfriend. It seemed like we were on the verge of that, but I didn't want to scare him off.

"I think I could make something like that work." There was a bit of a shake in my voice, but I was glad I said it.

"You're going to be a lot of fun. I can tell."

***

I met up with Violet for lunch after my class and told her about Kingsley.

"Who the hell are you and what did you do to Annabelle?" She clapped her hands for a second and laughed. "That's going to be so much fun. I've never been with a firefighter, or really anyone in uniform. It's like you have your own personal porn star. Maybe you could ask him to do a private dance for you."

"Oh my god, I couldn't do that. I was barely able to agree to see him in his uniform. Let's not push it."

"Well, I'm surprised you did too. I know we kinda already talked about it but are you sure you're over your obsession with Jason?"

"I was never obsessed with Jason. Kingsley just kind of came out of nowhere, but I feel good when he looks at me."

"Just be careful. Everything is still new, but I'm still excited for you."

"Thanks, I'll let you know what happens. So, Berneli is back today. Are you excited for that?"

"Yes! It's only been a couple days but I still miss him."

"Annabelle! Violet!" Kyle screamed our names from the entrance to the cafeteria. We turned around

41

and saw him walking in with Jason.

"Hey, Kyle, how was your break?" I asked him, and we all sat down.

"It was great. I went on this cross country trip and we camped under the stars. We did some amazing experiments and I saw the most incredible sights. You guys should really think about joining geology club."

"Kyle, you told me you hooked up with almost all of the girls on the trip and you smoked pot with your professor," Jason said.

"Man, why would you say that in front of the girls?" He turned to look at Violet and me. "Obviously, I wouldn't tell you guys that part. I have more tact than that."

Jason rolled his eyes and mumbled, "Whatever," under his breath. We all laughed a little and my phone went off. It was a text from Kingsley again.

"Oh my god, Violet, look." I showed her my phone. "Kingsley invited me out to dinner tonight."

"Wait, you're going out with Kingsley?" Kyle asked. "Jason, isn't that the new guy who lives on our floor?"

Jason sort of nodded and shrugged his shoulders.

"Uh, yeah. Jason introduced us. Why?"

"Nothing, I just thought you'd have a problem going out with a guy who does drugs."

"What? He doesn't do drugs." There was no way. He didn't look like a druggie. He didn't hang out in dark alleys or have the addiction scratch. It wasn't like we met in a park. His family was loaded. Why would he need to do drugs?

"That's not what I heard. Some of the guys I

hang out with said he's usually trying to find some pills," Kyle said, and went to grab some lunch.

I turned to look at Jason. "Have you heard that?"

He shook his head. "No, but I don't really know anything about him. It's not like we hang out all the time. We were the only people on our dorm floor, so I asked if he wanted to get lunch with us. You know, to be polite."

"I'm sure it's just a rumor. He doesn't strike me as a druggie. I'm still going."

"You don't want to start something and then end up getting sucked in. I don't think you should go," Jason warned.

"It'll be fine. It's one date. It's not like they're going to get engaged or anything. Have fun and tell me all about it," Violet ordered.

"Yeah, will you come over after your class and help me get ready?" I asked Violet, turning away from Jason.

"Of course. Do you know where you're going?"

"No, he said it was a surprise."

"So cheesy," Jason murmured, then got up and left the cafeteria.

I turned to Violet, who was avoiding my gaze.

"I don't want to fight with him," I told her, and raced after him. "Jason," I shouted to his back.

He spun around and smiled, but then the smile faded and he looked annoyed again. "What's up?"

"Do you really have a problem with me going out with Kingsley?"

"I just don't trust the guy. He seems a little obnoxious, like chucking the putter, running off 'cause he lost a game of mini golf. Seriously, who

43

does that? You don't want to be with someone like that, right? Besides, what if he's using?"

He stared at me expectantly but I didn't know what to say. I didn't think the thing with the putter was a big deal. So he got competitive? It wasn't like Jason was much better when we went bowling. But at the same time, I didn't want Jason upset with me. I hated confrontation and I didn't want any problems in our group.

"Then I won't go out with him. I trust your opinion."

He smiled and nodded. "Good. Listen, I gotta run to class, but I'll talk to you later? Maybe we can hang out?"

"Uh, no. I'm just going to go to the EET office and get everything ready for our first meeting." We said goodbye and I walked back to Violet.

She folded her arms and pursed her lips at me. "What did you just do?"

I sat next to her but couldn't meet her eyes. "Listen, Jason and I are best friends and I don't want to screw that up over a guy when I don't even know if it's gonna work out. What's the harm in telling Jason that we aren't going out and then actually doing it?"

"Well, there's the whole lying thing. That's usually frowned upon when it comes to friends."

"It's a lie for his best interest. Jason and I can talk if things end up working out with Kingsley. Jason's big concern is that he doesn't trust Kingsley, there's a rumor he does drugs, and he thinks he's a little obnoxious. If I get to know Kingsley a little better, then I can tell Jason he has nothing to worry about. I would know if he was high. Besides, we hang out with Kyle and he does a lot of pot. Jason lives with the guy, I think he's being a hypocrite."

"There's a huge difference between doing pot sometimes and taking pills."

"Well, we were with him all night and he didn't take anything."

"Can I just say that I object to this plan?"

"Yes, but I'm going to do it anyway."

"Got it."

Kyle joined us then and we all finished our lunch.

***

Kingsley said he would pick me up around seven, and at six fifty I was sitting in my room with Violet, trying to keep my pulse under control.

"He's going to bail. There's no way he's coming," I whined.

"Relax, he has ten minutes before he's supposed to be here. He's not even late."

"But I feel like my date would be here early. I'm always fifteen minutes ahead."

"Yeah, but a lot of guys aren't like that," Violet reminded me. "You don't want to be in a relationship with a guy who is just like you."

I rushed over to the window in a huff to check again if he was there. This time, I wasn't disappointed. Standing in front of our building was a sexy man holding a giant bouquet of flowers.

"You're never going to believe this! Come

look," I shouted at Violet.

"Aww, that's so cute. Forget what Kyle and Jason said. Have fun and text me when you're done. I'll be at David's, but I don't care."

"Okay, uh, wait. Shouldn't I wait for him to tell me he's here? Don't I sound like a creeper if I go down before he texts me?" I looked back out the window and saw some girl walk up to him. She had long brown hair and gave him a giant hug. "Why is some hussy hugging on him?"

Violet looked down and swore under her breath. "No, I mean, he could just be friends with her. You hugged Kyle earlier."

"Good call. Okay. I'm gonna wait and see what happens, and hopefully it's just innocent, and he'll text me, and it'll be a fun night, and I'll have my first boyfriend."

"Okay, let's drop the expectations just a little bit. Let's just hope you have a fun night with a guy you like. See how it goes and then we can talk about putting a label on it. You're supposed to be getting to know him, not planning the wedding."

"Yeah, I know. I just have a really good feeling." I looked down at my phone and almost willed it to go off. It, of course, didn't make a sound. "I need to do something. I'm going to run to the bathroom and touch up my make-up, maybe run the straightener through my hair again."

Violet grabbed my arm and whirled me around. "Oh, no, missy! You look great and you're only going to mess it up. Sit down and just wait a minute."

My phone went off almost as if she planned it

that way.

"See, he's here," she said with a smug look on her face.

"Okay, I'll talk to you later!"

I walked down the stairs and toward Kingsley. He was wearing a blue button-down shirt with a thick black jacket over it and dark jeans. His hair was brushed down and spiked slightly in the front and his eyes were shining. He must have been excited because he was practically bouncing up and down. I fed off his enthusiasm and walked quickly toward him.

When I opened the door, Kingsley walked up to me and gave me a light kiss on the cheek. "You look even more beautiful than the last time I saw you."

"Thanks." I took the flowers he offered me and realized I had no idea what to do with them. Did I take them with me? I didn't have a vase or anything to put them in. I was going to kill the first set of flowers a boy had ever given me. As my mind started to swim, Kingsley held up his backpack.

"I thought you might need this."

I reached out to take his bag and he quickly pulled it away.

"Uh, sorry. I don't like people touching my bag. Just hold on a second." He unzipped the main pocket. Inside was a beautiful glass vase. "I didn't think you would have brought one of these to your dorm, so I went out and got one."

"You're right, I didn't have one. Let me take these upstairs and put the flowers in some water."

"Great, I'll come with you." He took my hand

and opened the door for me. We walked hand in hand to the bathroom to fill the vase with water, and then to my room. Geez, was I grateful I had nervously cleaned earlier, or this would have been really embarrassing.

"It's nice that you have a single. You don't have to worry about a nosey roommate or anything like that."

"I like that I can set everything up the way I like. For example," I said, and placed the flowers in the middle of my desk, "I like the flowers there and I don't need anyone else's opinion, well, except yours. Do you think they look good there?"

He laughed lightly and ran his hand down my cheek. "Yes, they look perfect. I'm glad you like them."

I smiled up at him as my pulse raced. He was standing very close to me and I could feel his breath on me. He was going to kiss me. I held my breath and closed my eyes, willing myself not to panic. His lips brushed mine gently and the butterflies in my stomach settled. It felt right kissing him.

Kingsley pulled away before the kiss could heat up and smiled at me. "I didn't want to wait until the night was over to kiss you. To tell you the truth, I've wanted to kiss you since I helped you get a hole in one last night. It was such a turn-on knowing I'd helped you do that."

I forced a smile. This was definitely not the time to remind him that I actually already knew how to play. Instead, I did the one thing I could think of to change the subject. I placed my hand on the back of his neck and pulled him in for another kiss.

His hands snaked around my waist and he pulled me closer to him. He licked my lip a little and begged me to open to him. As soon as I did, I practically melted in his arms. Kingsley took control of the kiss and taught me a thing or two. I fought desperately to keep up with him as the kiss became intense. It wasn't long before I caught up, realizing how easy it was to kiss him.

Suddenly, Kingsley pulled away but hugged me tightly. "If we continue this, I can promise you we will miss our reservation, and that green dress looks too good on you to stay in. I want to show you off."

I gave him a light kiss on the lips and sighed. "Okay, I guess we can leave." As we headed back out, I realized the truth. The thought of being with him in my room any longer was actually a little terrifying. Kissing was the furthest I'd ever gone, and I didn't want to move too fast. Hopefully, Kingsley didn't mind.

He offered me his hand as I climbed into his black Range Rover and we drove to the restaurant.

Chapter 4

Dinner was amazing. Kingsley had insisted I order the most expensive thing the menu and practically balked when I tried to pay. He told me that his father held meetings there all the time and we put dinner on his tab.

We were about to pull up to the dorms when Kingsley spoke up. "So, do you want to come back to my room? We can watch some TV or just talk."

My face flushed because I knew what he was asking. He wanted to have sex. My heart raced and I thought of something to say that didn't sound like a brush off. But before I had a chance to get any words out, he took my hand. Then he leaned forward and kissed my knuckles softly.

"I see the hamster wheel turning in your head. I really just want to spend some more time with you. No pressure. As much as I want to be with you in that way, I can wait until you're ready."

And just like that, my heart soared. He got me. I leaned forward, placed my hand gently on the side of his face, and kissed him. "I'd love to go to your room."

Kingsley smiled brightly and then pulled into a parking spot. As we were going up to his dorm, Kingsley was rubbing circles on the back of my hand with his thumb. It was actually really comforting. I bit my lip and looked up at him. I wasn't ready to go all the way, but I wanted to kiss him again and I couldn't wait.

"I think I need a pit stop," I said, leaning against the wall.

He looked at me, confused, until I grabbed his jacket, pulling him into me. Kingsley grinned and pressed against me hard. It was a passionate kiss as he slid his hand up my side and stopped at my breast. He lightly stroked my nipple with his thumb and I shivered with anticipation. It felt so good and I wasn't ready for him to stop. I didn't even care that we were in the middle of a hallway. Who would have thought I'd be all right with exhibitionism?

A soft moan escaped my lips as he groped my breast. I pulled him tighter against me as if the slight space between us was too much. Then we heard it.

"Damn, Kingsley, at least wait until you get her back to your room!"

I froze because I knew that voice. My eyes closed and I prayed this was a sick dream, because if that voice was there, then it was an almost guarantee that a certain someone was standing there too.

"Kyle, you know how it is. Sometimes you can't wait, and with this one, I sure as hell don't want to."

Kingsley had stepped away from me and turned to look at the guys.

Against my better judgment, I looked and saw Kyle and Jason standing in the hallway. Embarrassment flowed through me as if my dad had just walked in on us. "I'd better go," I murmured, and turned on my heel to head to the door leading out into the courtyard between dorm buildings.

"I'll walk you," Kingsley told me, and draped his arm around me.

"No, it's okay. You're already here. I'm just gonna go. Text me later?" I asked—almost begged—him.

"Of course." He gave me a light kiss and then turned around.

I practically ran out into the courtyard and refused to stop when I heard Jason calling my name.

Finally, he grabbed my arm and turned me around. "Annabelle, what are you doing with that guy? You told me you weren't going out with him."

"I just wanted to see if there was anything between us before I rejected him."

"Well, a few minutes ago, there wasn't anything between you two since he was all over you."

"We were kissing. Since when is that a crime?"

"You may have been just kissing, but he was doing a lot whole more than that."

My face flushed bright red and embarrassment flowed through me. "You weren't meant to see that."

"Then maybe you shouldn't have been doing it in the hallway. It's like you were trying to piss me off or something." He threw his arms in the air and took a few steps away from me.

"What? Why are you making this about you? I went out with Kingsley because I like him. He makes me feel good, and pretty, and appreciated. Why is that such a bad thing?"

"Because you lied to me about it."

"And I'm sorry. I was just—"

"I know, you were just trying to hook up with a hot guy."

I jammed my finger into his chest. "You listen here, I am not with him just to hook up, and how dare you say that. I'm not the kind of girl to do that."

"From what I saw in the hallway, you could have fooled me."

"You know what, Jason, you don't get a say in who I date. You know why? Because you have a girlfriend. I'm sorry she doesn't have time for you anymore, but that's not my fault."

His face changed and he nodded slightly. "So that's what you think. Thanks for making it so clear to me. As your friend, because that's what I thought we were, I was just trying to look out for you. Next time, I'll know better than to get involved. In fact, I'll just stay out of your way." He turned around and headed back to his dorm.

I collapsed on the closest bench and tried to calm down. That was harsh. I really didn't mean to say that, but it just came out. Why couldn't Jason see that Kingsley was actually interested in me? Was it such a strange idea for a guy to want to spend time with me? I was the one who had pushed things to get physical. He had no right to get involved in any of this. Yet, there he was, just assuming the worst of me.

After I took a few deep breaths, I took my phone out and called Violet.

"Oh my god! It's about time. The date must have been great."

"It was until we got back. He invited me back to his room, and while we were heading there, we kissed and Kyle and Jason saw it. Then Jason and I got in a huge fight and he said some awful things to me and then I said some even worse things back. It was just a mess."

"Right, hold on a second." Violet was whispering with Berneli but I really couldn't hear what she said.

"How do you feel about a sleepover?"

"No. Berneli just came back and I don't want you to come back."

"How about if you come here? You can take me back to school in the morning and we can talk about what happened and watch the dating show on David's flat screen."

I heard Berneli groan in the background and I had to laugh a little. Here was this serious literature professor about to have to watch reality television while his girlfriend's best friend cried on her shoulder. I doubted this was what he had in mind when he planned a quiet night in for the two of them.

"I really don't want to bother you guys. I'm sure there are several other things you'd rather be doing tonight." Violet was more or less a sex addict and I knew she needed her fix.

"Yeah, we already did that, twice, so you're good for another couple hours."

"Speak for yourself," Berneli quipped in the background.

"Annabelle, you were there for me last night, so let me be there for you now. Let's get you off campus and away from those awful boys and into a new carton of ice cream that David just volunteered to go pick up."

"By volunteered you mean that you just volunteered for him, right?"

"When you get in a relationship, you'll understand how volunteering your man for things is the right you get for giving blow jobs."

***

Fifteen minutes later, I was in the car on the way to Berneli's apartment. It felt really weird, and I was pretty sure there was no way it wasn't going to be unbelievably awkward. Even though he and Violet had been together for months, I'd still never really hung out with him. They only did things together and in closed off spaces, to minimize the chance of anyone finding out about them. It wasn't like they hosted game night every Thursday.

But if he was going to be in her life, I'd have to start looking at him in a different way. I knocked on the apartment door and Violet eagerly opened it.

"Hi, honey," she greeted, and handed me a drink.

"Um, what's in this?" I didn't like to drink alcohol and thought Violet knew that.

"It's either vodka, rum, tequila, and bourbon, or

a cup of ginger ale."

"Ha-ha," I said before smelling the drink. Realizing it was soda, I took a big a sip. She did know me. Ginger ale was my favorite.

"So, I called Jason," she started, and my face fell. Of course she called Jason. I felt a little betrayed but I knew why she did it.

"What? Is this going to be one of those awful intervention things where he comes out of the bedroom and you make us talk until we are friends again?"

"Um, no, but you need to stop watching so much TV. I just wanted to hear his side of the story. From what he says, you were practically having sex in the hallway," she relayed, giving me a judgmental look.

I rolled my eyes and put my drink down. "You do know that he's full of crap, right? That's not what happened."

"That's a shame. I kind of liked that part."

"Shut up," I said, trying not to smile. "No, he was just sort of feeling me up." I buried my head in my hands. This was so embarrassing to talk about.

"Under the shirt or over it?"

"Over it. My hands were around his neck and he had pressed me against the wall."

Violet nodded and a wide grin formed on her face. "Okay, Miss Thing."

"But that's not the point. I was embarrassed they caught us kissing, and of course he knew I was lying about the date and he got upset and then I got upset. It was a disaster."

"Well, I—"

"Don't you dare say you told me so," I

interjected.

"Well, what did you expect to happen? You did lie."

"I know, but he had no right to get involved in my relationship. I don't say anything to his face about how ridiculous his relationship with Janice is."

"No, you're right, you don't, and he shouldn't be butting in, but are you really surprised?"

"When you told him about Berneli, Jason didn't say anything negative, right?"

"He warned me to be careful. Wasn't that kinda what he was doing with you?"

"No, he flat out told me that it was a bad idea to date Kingsley. It's different."

"So, Annabelle, I hope you don't mind, but Violet told me what happened and I have an opinion," Berneli offered, walking in from the bedroom.

"Uh, sure, what do you think is going on?"

"Well, it's really both of our opinions, but David kind of confirmed it for me," Violet piped in.

"Well, yes, but I've thought it for a while now. Even before the fight," Berneli added. "I've seen you all around at EET for a semester and heard stories about you from Violet. It wasn't hard to deduce."

"Well, maybe one of you could share it with me and then we'd all know."

"Ah, yes," Berneli began. "So we think the reason Jason got so upset about you and Kingsley is because he's in love with you."

Chapter 5

"What?" I stared at the two of them in utter shock. "If he was in love with me, why would he be dating Janice? That doesn't even make sense. That can't be it." I shook my head, refusing to believe them. It was just Violet guessing again. She probably told him her point of view, which was wrong, and he'd obviously agreed.

"Okay, so I've been keeping this to myself for a while, but I feel like it's time I get it off my chest." Violet took a breath and then continued. "You and Jason are my best friends and I like to think I know you pretty well. The both of you have been in love with each other since you met. He's talked to me about how he feels. He's been with Janice for so long that he feels like he owes it to her to try to make it work. And you're comfortable with the friendship, but not happy. As soon as one of you bends, then you could really be something great, and I want that for you both."

"Listen, I'm with Jason all the time. He doesn't treat me any differently than he treats you. He hugs you, he buys your lunch when you're together, he helped buy you a present for Christmas, but I didn't get one."

"Okay, yes, Jason hugs me and buys me lunch, but that's because he's polite. You bought me a present and he was with you. But he stares at you longingly when you aren't looking, he pretty much always leaves a room when you do, and oh, oh, do you really think he likes decorating? He spent how many hours trying to help you with the homecoming decorations?"

I shook my head. "He only did that because he's my friend. If you remember correctly, you were there, and so was Kyle."

"Okay, you know what, you don't have to believe us, but you need to decide what you want to do about it. Jason is still one of your best friends and isn't going anywhere. From what I got from you, neither is Kingsley. But you may not be able to have them both."

"I don't know just yet."

"Well, you need to talk to Jason. That's the bottom line."

"I'll figure something out. Now, where is the ice cream?"

***

Berneli ran to the store to get the ice cream and Violet and I settled in on the couch.

"Did Jason say anything else?"

"Oh, no! I'm not getting in the middle of this with you two. I've said all I am going to say about

59

my conversation with him."

"What about girl code? Aren't you supposed to be on my side?"

"I'm Switzerland. You're my friend and he's my friend. I told him the same. You know my opinion and it's just a matter of what you want to do about it."

"Wait, what did you tell him about me? Did you say I had feelings for him?"

"No, but I told him he needs to figure out what he wants when it comes to you and Janice."

"What did he say? Did he say he had feelings for me?"

"No, he didn't. But I don't think that means he doesn't."

"It doesn't matter anyway. I have feelings for Kingsley. If what you say about Jason is true, then he waited too long." I was done with this conversation. I didn't want to talk about Jason anymore. I was frustrated that I'd lied to him in the first place because now everything was worse, but it was even more annoying that I felt like I had to lie him. I grabbed the remote for the TV and started flipping through the on demand shows to find the reality dating show we were obsessed with. "So, I think Louis should pick Courtney, don't you?"

***

Berneli only had one bedroom, so I spent the night on the couch. Frankly, I could fall asleep just about anywhere, so it wasn't long before I was passed out.

I awoke to Violet shaking me within an inch of my life.

"Come on, sleepy head, we need to get back to campus. I want to stop by my room for a minute. I left my schedule there." Violet looked bright and shiny and I wanted to strangle her.

"Why don't you just print another schedule?" I had put everything in my phone because I was afraid of losing mine.

"I have information about the books and where to find the rooms. Come on, I'll make you a cup of coffee if you sit up."

"If you don't make me a cup of coffee, I'll fall asleep driving you back to the dorm. I've never been in a car accident so I'd like to avoid that," I grumbled as I slowly rolled off the couch and managed to find my feet.

It wasn't long before a glorious scent filled the apartment and I started to see colors again. I grabbed my bag and shuffled to the bathroom to change while the nectar of the gods continued to brew. I had just put on my favorite sweater when Violet started yelling my name.

"Annabelle, come on. You're the one who is constantly on time but you're running late."

I rolled my eyes and headed to the kitchen. She handed me a thermos full of coffee and some milk to throw in it. Violet gave me a big smile and started to gather her things.

"Okay, it's not fair for you to give me so much crap right now. It's early and I didn't have any morning sex to improve my mood."

She shot me a sneaky grin. "Touché, but we

really need to move."

"I'm ready, let's go."

Violet said goodbye to Berneli and I downed most of the thermos before we even made it to my car. We had a pretty quiet ride back to campus. I didn't want to talk about Jason anymore and it was nice that Violet wasn't trying to push me.

As we parked the car and headed to our dorm, Violet spoke up. "So when are you seeing Kingsley again? Do you guys have plans?"

"Yeah, he said during our date that he has something big planned for this weekend, but I have no idea what is."

"Aww, that's exciting. I love that he's trying to plan things."

"You liked him, right?"

"Um, I didn't really get to know him. He was pretty focused on you and I love that. To be honest, he seemed a bit cocky, but he may have just been trying to show off for you. I'm also not a fan of the drugs thing."

"Well, no sign of drugs again last night. Besides, I think he was just a little nervous the other night. If he was showing off to impress me, is that such a bad thing? He was really sweet during our date."

"All that matters to me is that he treats you well and you're happy," she assured me as she opened the door to our building.

"I know, but I want you to like him." I was about to tell her more about him when we both stopped dead in our tracks. There was something sitting on the floor in front of Violet's door, and it was only too familiar.

"Annabelle, is that what I think it is?" She grabbed my arm for support and looked like she was going to faint.

"Let me grab it." I shook her grip off and walked to the door, but there was no mistaking the violet waiting for her. "There's a note." I handed the sealed envelope and flower to Violet.

She quickly shoved it back into my hands. "I can't. You read it."

I took the note and slowly opened the envelope. A photograph of Violet and Berneli kissing was the first thing I noticed. It looked like the picture was taken outside his apartment after one of their sleepovers. The sky was a little dark and Violet's overnight bag was on the ground next to her. I slipped the picture back in the envelope and pulled out the letter.

My beautiful Violet,

The last time I set eyes on you was in the courtroom, and that was far too long ago. I think of you daily and of the life we will have when I am released in a few years. However, I'm devastated to hear that you haven't been as faithful to me as I have been to you. I think it's time I remind you of the consequences of your so-called relationship. Come and visit me in jail or I'll be sending a copy of this picture to the dean.

Yours forever,

Samuel Finn

After I finished reading the note, I looked at Violet. "I think we should go in my room before you read this. I also think we should call Berneli."

"Is it that bad?"

"Yeah, it is."

I opened my door and Violet rushed to my bed. She took her phone out and texted Berneli. "Okay, I'm ready to see the letter."

I gave it to her and braced myself for the breakdown that was sure to follow. Her hands shook as she read line after line. She was already looking pale, but she turned an even lighter shade of white and the slight tears turned to heaving sobs.

"Annabelle, I can't see him. It was hard enough in court when there were tons of people able to keep him off me."

"I know. We'll think of something." I hugged her as I desperately grasped at straws. If she did go see him, he could mess with her head or she could play into his hands, creating more drama. He would know exactly what to do to play her like a fiddle. But at the same time, there was no mistaking who was kissing in the picture. It was obviously Violet and Berneli.

Her phone rang and she answered it almost immediately. "Honey, I don't know what to do.

Someone is working with him and they're threatening us again if I don't go see him in jail."

I could only hear her side of the conversation, but it wasn't hard to figure out what he was saying. There was no way he was going to allow her to visit Finn. Personally, I agreed with him, but I didn't know any alternative. If they went to the police, they'd find out about the picture.

"Okay, I'll talk to you later." She hung up the phone and looked at me.

Then it hit me like a brick wall. "Go with Berneli."

"What?" She stared at me with a confused gleam in her eyes.

"Finn already knows about your relationship with Berneli. So go see him with Berneli and make it clear the two of you have broken up. Explain to him that you broke up over break and you're single. Between the guards and Berneli, Finn won't be able to touch you."

She pursed her lips and looked at me. "That could work. If he thinks we aren't together anymore, maybe he'll stop with this crap. Most guys like this just want the chase."

"Right, take the chase away and make it clear you want nothing to do with Berneli. You don't want Finn thinking you broke up with Berneli so you could be with him, though, so come up with another reason."

"Yes, I can do that. Okay. Um, I could face him if David was there." She nodded and looked down at the ground. It was almost as if she was trying to convince herself. Then she slipped the letter and the picture in her overnight bag.

"I can come too. I'll stay in the car and wait for you guys to come back. I'll be like extra moral support."

"No, I'll just meet up with you after. I don't want you to sit in the parking lot of a jail. That doesn't seem safe."

"You do realize that the criminals can't actually get out, right? They aren't going to escape into the parking lot to kill me."

"Right, but still, you don't need to be there. I don't know how long it will take. But I appreciate the offer."

"All right, well, we need to get to class or decide to skip. Which do you want to do?"

"We're going to class. That jerk has disrupted my life enough. I'm not going to let him screw with my classes. Let's go. Besides, I'm not letting you get out of stats that easily."

She took her bag to her room and grabbed her schedule. I waited in the hall. When she came out, I noticed she was standing tall with her chin high in the air. It broke my heart to watch her put on this front. Her hands shook a little and I noticed a quiver in her lip. But other than that, she looked like regular Violet. I kind of envied her strength.

I walked her to her class and promised to meet her back in her room when she got out. I rushed to my class, a little panicked because I wouldn't be there early and might have to sit in the front. Obviously, that was minor when compared to what Violet was going through so I put it into perspective and moved on. I checked my phone and realized I had about three minutes before statistics.

As I picked up the pace, I realized I was going to just make it. This was going to be a terrible first impression on my professor, but I could always make it up to him later. I was a good student, after all. I kept focusing on this new perspective I'd found but the nervous person I was couldn't quite keep it together.

My heart was racing and I was embarrassed that I was beginning to sweat. I managed to slip into the classroom with a minute to spare. The only desk open was the front middle. I silently groaned, but took my seat before the professor began to lecture.

I liked to sit in the back of the class and hide a bit. I definitely wasn't one for class participation and hated being picked on. I usually knew the answer, but I tended to freeze up and panic. The last class where I was called on suddenly, I broke out in hiccups and had to leave the room.

This professor didn't plan on keeping us the whole time. He went over the syllabus, our big project, and our exams. Then he gave us a pretest. He said he wanted to see what level of basic math we had before walking into his class. Once we finished the test, we could leave. It was only thirty questions, and I had a pretty good understanding that I knew nothing.

After I turned the answer sheet in, I ran to Violet's class and waited for her. Her teacher didn't go the full length of the class either, and she quickly ran over to me. She grabbed my arm to steady herself but was still almost violently shaking.

"I don't know if I can see him. He already haunts

my nightmares, and now I'll have to see that monster in person again. No, we are going to have to think of a new plan."

"Right, okay. So, we didn't have breakfast this morning. Let's go get some food and we can revisit this when you've got something in your system. I bet that's just making things worse."

"Yeah, I could eat. That's probably why I'm shaking so hard." We headed to the cafeteria in silence. She wasn't holding onto me anymore but I kept my hand free just in case something happened. I was worried she was going to pass out at any moment.

Violet had left her student ID with her meal plans on it in her room, so I swiped her in and we got some breakfast. Then we headed to our favorite table by the windows.

"There is nothing better than cinnamon buns," I said, trying to start a little conversation.

"I know. They are definitely one of my favorite breakfast foods." She took her phone out of her bag and tapped it. "I told David that I was out of class and we're supposed to be meeting up to talk about all this."

"Okay, do you want me to come with you?"

"Yes, I don't want to be alone right now. It's so dumb. He isn't here, but I feel like he could pop out at any moment."

I nodded, unsure what to say, and silently thought about my schedule. I had another class at 11:30 and then we had an EET meeting. Except for that class, I could spend the rest of the day with her until Berneli took over. I was processing this when I noticed Jason walking into the cafeteria. He was alone and made a beeline to our table when he noticed the look on Violet's face.

"Vi, what's wrong? Is it Berneli?" he asked as he slid into the seat next to her.

"I left the note in my room and the flower in Annabelle's, but Finn left me a violet and a note. He wants me to go see him in jail or he's going to send a picture of Berneli and me together to the dean."

"There's no way in hell you can go see him."

"Annabelle suggested I bring David. Maybe try to convince Finn that he and I aren't together and we can end this game. If he thinks there's no more competition, maybe he'll leave me alone."

"Are you crazy?" Jason asked. "You need to take the letter to the police."

"I can't. If they see the picture, I could get kicked out of school and David could end up getting fired. I don't want that to happen. But at the same time, I'm not sure I can see him."

He kept quiet for a second and looked at Violet with true pain in his eyes. "Didn't you learn anything last semester? You need to get the police involved before it gets worse. I wish there was something I could do but this isn't something you can handle on your own."

She laughed a little manically. "I know. I just don't know how this happened. I was so clear to him that I wanted nothing to do with him and yet he's still obsessed."

"Okay, let's just take a page out of the criminal analyst book. Finn is going to do whatever he can to see you and he wants nothing more than to screw things up with Berneli so he can have you. Will seeing him really ruin your life? I think that you just go in there and deny the relationship. You could end this whole thing," I said, hoping I was right.

"Annabelle, don't underestimate the impact that this guy has had on her. She can't simply walk in there," Jason said.

"I'm not saying that. I'm just saying that it's not like he's asking for a conjugal visit. He just wants to see her. Maybe if she goes, she can determine what he wants."

"Don't be naïve, we know what he wants. He wants to screw with her head."

"Enough, you two," Violet cut in. "Look, I'm meeting with David in ten minutes, so I'm going to his office now and I'd like you two to come with me and retract your claws. The fighting is just screwing with my nerves."

***

The three of us walked into Berneli's office and as soon as the door was closed, Violet flew into his arms and broke down in tears again.

"How did he get a letter to me? Who the hell would be working with him? It's not like it came through the university's mail system." She was sobbing into his chest and he was stroking her back gently.

"I don't know, but I've spent the morning on the phone. I have a contact who's a private investigator. He's going to start looking into it. I'm going to do all I can to stop this wanker before he threatens you

70

again, love."

My heart smiled a little for Violet. Berneli really did care for her. They weren't just in this for sex, fun, or even the excitement. At first, I wasn't a big fan of the relationship because I was worried about them throwing their futures away. But in reality, they were perfect for each other. How could anyone want to break this up? It just didn't make any sense.

Berneli looked at Jason and me and nodded at the two chairs in front of his desk. "Please, take a seat."

We did as he asked and waited for Violet to calm down a little. As her sobs subsided a little, he sat her down in his chair. "So, I think we just need to let the investigator work. He can find out who this sidekick is and then supply the evidence to the police. There's no reason we need to go to the jail. We can discuss that later this week if nothing has been determined. Annabelle, I need you and Jason to watch out for her. As much as I'd like to, I can't be with her all the time. Now, we have no reason to believe that this yank's sidekick wants to hurt Violet, but I'm not willing to risk it."

"Professor, you don't need to worry about that. I'm not going to let her out of my sight," Jason assured. "I know Professor Berneli said it's not in the plan, but shouldn't you at least consider a plan if you do end up going to the jail?"

"Okay, on the off chance I go, I'd go Saturday. I don't want to go before any of my classes. Plus, we can give the investigator time. Maybe I won't even have to go see him. I should really focus on trusting the investigator. I don't even want to think about the possibility of seeing him."

"Yeah," I chimed in. "Positive thinking. Violet, whoever this partner is, they're probably watching you. You're going to have to be really careful when you're with Berneli. But more than that, I think you should act like nothing is wrong. You don't want whoever is watching you to know this is affecting you. They probably want to get in your head." I was trying to be strong for her but I was actually freaked out. I just didn't know what to do. This was way above my paygrade.

"I can do that." She took his hand and they looked at each other. "Yeah, I need to pull it together and be strong. This guy will not rule my future."

"That's my girl," I said, and smiled at her, hoping it felt real. I couldn't help but think we should go to the police again. Last time, I practically dragged her to the station, but that didn't go well, and it kind of soured Violet's opinion of them.

"Professor, are you sure we shouldn't contact the police?" Jason asked as if he was reading my mind. I was glad he said it.

"We are not going to the police," Violet insisted. "David, I can't have you losing your job over this. It's just a note. I won't go anywhere alone and we will let the investigator do his work."

Berneli started to object but she put her hand on his and smiled lightly. "I tried to report him last time and it did no good. They only did something after I was attacked. He didn't threaten my life, he didn't promise bodily harm to you. He just

72

threatened to tattle on us. It's not worth it to get the police involved. They may not do anything and then we will have outted our relationship for nothing. That's not what I want."

"But the chief told you to talk to him. I bet if you tried—" I started, trying to remind her of what he said, but she cut me off.

"No. He didn't break any laws since he didn't send the letter to me directly. We don't even know if he wrote the note."

We all reluctantly agreed. I couldn't help but see the similarities to the last time. I didn't want her to get hurt but she was right, she wasn't being physically threatened and the stalking laws were severely minimal.

Jason and Violet were going to hang out until the EET meeting. Both of them had a night class, so they'd be free for a while. I had about a half hour before my class so I decided to stop by the coffee cart. My system was begging for some comfort in the form of coffee and a chocolate scone. I needed to come down from this emotional rollercoaster before my class. It was all too much and I had a really bad feeling. Add to that the fact that I really couldn't do anything to help, the pit in my stomach was growing by the second. As I stood in line, someone stepped up behind me and covered my eyes. It terrified me and I jumped about three feet in the air.

"Hey, relax, it's just me." Kingsley laughed.

"Oh, sorry, I guess I'm a little jumpy if I don't have my coffee." I turned to look at him and smiled. It was perfect timing. With everything going on

73

with Violet, my nerves were a mess. He smiled down at me and gave me a light kiss on the lips.

"I'll keep that in mind. You look upset, is everything all right?"

I lost myself in his eyes. The incident with Violet was public knowledge. I closed my eyes for a second. He was a big firefighter who just wanted to help people. It definitely wouldn't hurt to have him around in case something happened. What could Jason do? It wasn't like he was buff or really had any muscles the way Kingsley did.

"You remember my friend, Violet? She was the one that officer attacked last October. He recently sent her a letter through this mysterious partner demanding to see her."

Kingsley eyes bulged out of his head and his hands balled up into fists. "If there's one thing I can't stand, it's someone messing with women. Is there anything I can do to help?"

"Yeah. We don't want to leave her alone, she's with Jason now, so maybe you could hang around some? I know I'd feel a lot safer with you around. She hasn't been threatened or anything but she's still a little jumpy around campus."

A smile broke out on his face and he leaned in and gave me a soft kiss. "Of course. Just call me, and as long as I'm not at a fire, I'll be there. Frankly, I'd feel better if I knew you were safe. I don't like the thought of you being that close to her if she's in danger. Maybe you shouldn't see her as much."

He cared. He barely knew me and he cared. "That's sweet of you to try to look out for me, but I don't think I'm in any danger. Besides, she's my best friend. I can't just stop seeing her."

"I just don't want anything to happen to you. If you're only with me, I know nothing will."

"You're amazing. Thank you so much. I promise I'll be careful when we're together." We got to the front of the line and he bought my coffee and scone. Then we went to a nearby table.

"So, this weekend, I know there is stuff going on with Violet, but I was still hoping to see you. Is there a time when you're free? Maybe we can take a risk and leave her with Jason for a few hours."

"Actually, I know she is going to be busy most of Saturday. We could do something in the late morning and afternoon. What did you have in mind?"

"It's still a secret, babe."

"I hate secrets," I complained, and pouted at him.

"I promise it'll be worth it."

I bit my lip and tried to contain my excitement. It was wrong for me to be this happy when Violet was so miserable, but I just couldn't control it. Plus, she'd want me to be happy. I couldn't wait to tell her about it.

Kingsley walked me to class and gave me a quick kiss before heading out. He said he had a class later that night, so I wouldn't be able to see him.

My class dragged on as I waited for the EET meeting. It would be nice to see Nat and Clarissa again. I'd texted with Clarissa a little bit during break, but we couldn't find time to meet up. Plus, Violet would be at the meeting and I was anxious to see her again. I wanted to make sure she didn't mind if I went out with Kingsley on Saturday. Obviously, if she needed me, I'd cancel, but I was really hoping we could work something out.

As soon as class was over, I all but ran to the room where the EET meetings were held. Jason and Violet were sitting on the couches outside.

I slowed down and waved at them. Violet smiled, but it didn't quite reach her eyes. Her color had come back a bit, but she still looked upset. I was used to seeing the light practically burst out of her eyes now that Berneli was keeping her happy.

"Hey, how was your class?"

"Good, pretty boring. I actually ran into Kingsley before it. He recognized I was upset and asked what was wrong. Basically, I know I should have asked you, but I was really concerned about your safety and Kingsley is the tough firefighter, so I told him that you were a little jumpy on campus but I didn't go into, like, any super-secret details." Okay, I kind of did. I should probably talk to Violet about that privately. I needed to watch what I said. I was so comfortable with Kingsley and I just felt I could tell him anything.

"What the hell were you doing? How could you tell him? You just met him," Jason chastised. "What, so some guy gives you a little attention and you spill all your secrets?"

"No, he is a firefighter and wants to help people. His muscles have muscles and he can help protect Violet in case anything gets violent."

"And what, you think I can't help her? You think I wouldn't do anything to protect her? She's my best friend." I thought I saw a tear in his eye, but it was quickly blinked away.

"That's it. I cannot handle the two of you fighting like this." Violet turned to look at Jason and pointed her finger at him. "Listen, Annabelle is dating Kingsley for now and you need to get over that. She decides who is best for her and we need to trust her."

I nodded my head at him but Violet then quickly turned to point at me. "And *you*, Jason is a good guy who was trying to look out for you. Yeah, he said it in the wrong way, but that's not what matters. What matters is his motivation, which was pure."

Then she stood up and faced the two of us. "This is not a good time for me, and you guys fighting like children is only making it worse. I agree, Annabelle, you should have checked with me before you talked to Kingsley. But at the same time, it won't hurt to have another set of eyes looking out for me."

"I'm sorry, you're right. Jason and I will quit the fighting and we'll definitely look out for you."

Jason agreed and we headed into the executive board meeting. Since Jason was elected head of marketing, he was now joining us in the meetings. I needed to play nice with him.

Chapter 6

After the meeting, I pulled Violet aside before we headed to the regular EET meeting. "Okay, so when I brought up Kingsley, there was another reason and I didn't want to mention it in front of Jason. He asked me to go out Saturday afternoon. I know you said you may be visiting Finn then, so I thought it would be the perfect time for us to spend some time together. But if you want me there, or readily available when you leave, or whatever, I'm there. No worries. Kingsley will still be there on Sunday or whenever. Hoes before bros, right?"

"No, no. Go out with him. I told you that I didn't want you to come to the visit, so by all means, have a good time. We can text afterward. If I'm with David, then I'll be okay. Besides, I have a lot of faith in this investigator."

"I mean it, call me and I'll drop everything and show up."

"I will. No worries." She took my hand and smiled at me. "What are you guys doing?" The light was back in her eyes. I guessed Kingsley was a good distraction for her.

"I don't know. He wants to surprise me," I replied, trying not to blush.

"Aww, that's so cute. I can't wait to hear all about it and live through you. I could definitely use something to boost morale around here."

I smiled and gave her a quick little side hug. "I guess I could go above and beyond to have an amazing date. Just looking out for you."

We headed to the EET meeting and got situated. Violet and Berneli pretended they didn't know each other, and so did Jason and I. To be honest, I was a little embarrassed by the way we were acting. Violet didn't need to deal with our crap right now, so I made a conscious decision to try to tolerate Jason and all of his nonsense. I looked at him and attempted to give him a genuine smile. He looked back at me and winked like nothing was wrong. Hopefully, we could put this behind us and be good friends for Violet, and just maybe, he could approve of Kingsley. I made a mental note to bring up the date this time. I didn't want to get busted for lying again.

I sat down at a desk near the door and began getting my notes out to take attendance. I was in the process of creating a sign-up sheet for the new members when a pretty bleach blonde walked up to me. Her big blue eyes looked a little scared, but she had a smile on her face as bright as her red lipstick.

She extended her hand to me and I shook it. "Hi, my name is Christie, I'm a commuter. I really enjoyed the comedy show last semester so I thought it might be fun to join."

"I'm Annabelle. I'm glad you liked the comedienne. I thought she was hysterical. We kind of got a little backstage show after her performance. It was really cool."

"Yes! That was one of the reasons I wanted to join. The backstage stuff sounds awesome, but to be honest, I've always kinda been interested in marketing."

"Great. Why don't you fill out the sign-in sheet, so we can contact you, and have a seat? We definitely have a lot of marketing opportunities."

"Sounds good." She completed the form and then went to sit by herself. I looked at her and noticed she wasn't making eye contact and didn't seem to know anyone. It must have been the commuter thing. I knew it was hard for students who commuted to make friends since most college kids became friends with the people who lived in the same dorm building. If you didn't live across the hall from an overly outgoing person who practically forced you out of your room on the first day of school, that could create problems.

I waved at Violet and she looked up at me. I nodded my head in Christie's direction and Violet's gaze turned toward her. She looked back at me and smiled a little mischievously. Violet, in her extroverted way, walked over and introduced herself. She said she wanted a distraction, and making a new friend would certainly fill her time. I just hoped Christie was ready for how pushy Violet could be. It had taken me a minute to get used to.

Nat was just starting the meeting when Kingsley waltzed into the room. He saw me in the corner and slid into the desk next to me.

"Hey, what are you doing here?" I asked as he placed his hand on my knee.

"You mentioned this was important to you the other night at dinner so I wanted to check it out." He brushed the tip of my nose with his finger and I smiled up at him.

He took my hand and we turned our attention to the front of the classroom. Clarissa had started talking about some of the smaller events that were going to be put on in the next month. They were planning a murder mystery party, some little game shows, and a few hallway fundraisers for various causes. She wanted us to break up and pick an event.

Kingsley and I stood up, still hand in hand, and headed to where Violet and Christie were sitting. I looked at Jason, trying to get his attention. Maybe if he spent some more time with Kingsley, he wouldn't despise him so much. But he wouldn't make eye contact and looked super into his own group.

"So, what do we want to be in charge of?" Violet asked, bringing my attention back to the group, and, of course, Kingsley.

"Well, I know I'm new here, but we should do a bake sale on a Friday. Everyone goes out to the bar or drinks on Thursday, you know, for Thirsty Thursday, and I'll bet they want something to munch on as they try to get through their classes," Christie suggested.

I looked at Violet and we both shared the same giant smile. This was a great idea. Then the problems began to pop up. "While I love the idea, we can't bake on campus. None of us have an oven," I pointed out, trying to hide my disappointment.

"Annabelle, I told you earlier that I'm a commuter. I live fifteen minutes away. Some of you can come over and we can bake in my kitchen," Christie offered.

"That's really nice. Are you sure? We don't want to put you out," Violet assured her.

"No, it's totally fine. I'm actually a big baker, so I can help all the beginners."

"Well, I'll let you ladies sort that out. I don't bake, but I'll definitely be there to eat. One of my boys is over there so I'm gonna change groups," Kingsley said. I was a little sad to watch him go, since it would have been a lot of fun to do something else together, but I could understand that he didn't want to bake.

Christie gave Violet and me her address and we planned to meet up Thursday afternoon.

The meeting was coming to a close and dinner was definitely calling my name. I watched Christie grab her things, and asked Violet if we should invite her to eat with us.

"Yeah, she seems nice. Besides, it would make Thursday significantly less awkward if we got to know her a little better."

"Good call." I walked over to Christie and she gave me another big smile as she brushed her hair out of her face. "Hey, do you want to come have dinner with us? A few of us get together after the meetings and go to the cafeteria. I know it's not a home cooked meal, but it's edible."

"Yeah, sounds great. Let me just shoot my mom a text so she isn't expecting me. She gets a little crazy if she doesn't know where I am at, like, all times."

"Awesome, we'll meet you outside." I grabbed my bag and headed to the hallway. I wanted to see where Kingsley went to. When the meeting ended, he practically ran outside. It was weird that he'd leave without saying goodbye, so I was eager to find out what happened. Maybe he just needed to run to the bathroom.

As I left the classroom, my heart sank a little. Kingsley was with the girl with the long brown hair again. I couldn't hear what they were talking about but they were sitting really close to each other on the couch and their heads were bent so only the other could hear their whispers. It looked heartbreakingly intimate.

I watched for a second longer as she handed him something but I couldn't see what it was. He quickly took it and shoved it in his bag. Had she just given him her phone number? No, that was dumb. Why wouldn't she just text him or something? It had to be something else. He gave her a nod and then he looked over at me. Kingsley forced a smile and rushed over to where I was standing.

"Hey, babe, what's up?" His shoulders were slouched and his hands were shoved in his pockets. I looked him over and couldn't adjust the frown on my face. He looked like he was up to no good and something in my gut was screaming out, desperate to be heard.

"Um, so, it's not a big deal, but who's that girl? I've seen you guys together a few times." I pulled him to the side, hoping Violet and Christie would stay in the classroom a little longer. But if they didn't, I was sure they'd realize I needed a minute. Or at least I hoped they would.

"Oh, her? Babe, you have nothing to worry about. She's just an old high school friend. I had a headache earlier and she offered to give me a pain reliever."

I remembered what Kyle had told me about pills and red flags started flying. "She just gave you one?"

"Well, no, I have another class later, so she gave me a couple extra in case it comes back. She's studying to be a nurse so she keeps stuff like that on her all the time in case someone needs something. Really, it's not a big deal."

"If it's not a big deal, why did you hide it? You two looked all secretive."

He reached out and touched my forehead. "Do you feel that worry line? That's why I was being secretive. I didn't want to worry you. I know you have enough going on with Violet and I didn't want you to worry about a little sinus headache. I have bad allergies, so it's just because of that. They happen all the time. Besides, I'd hate for someone to get the wrong idea."

"Okay," I said, suddenly feeling guilty for questioning him. I was practically accusing him of flirting with another girl, and here he was, feeling sick. "I'm sorry you don't feel good." I reached out and took his arm, giving him a mini hug.

"You're sweet." Kingsley leaned down and gave me a light kiss on the lips. "Come on, your friends are hiding in the classroom while we talk this over. I'm sure they're hungry."

"What? Oh." I turned around and saw Violet, Christie, and Jason hanging out in the doorway, pretending not to watch us. "Ready to get some food?" I reached up and started to fix my hair a little. I figured they'd give us a minute but I never thought they'd be watching. That was poor planning. Violet was nosey as hell. I should have expected her to be eavesdropping.

"I'll meet you down there. I'm just gonna run to the bathroom and take that pain pill before my headache gets worse.

***

"So, tell us a little about yourself, Christie," Violet suggested as we made our way to the cafeteria.

"Uh, I'm studying business with a concentration in marketing right now but my real goal is to be a top notch trophy wife."

"I like that plan," Violet managed between chuckles. "Have you found your sugar daddy yet? Does he look like Fabio?"

"Not so much. He has a military crew cut. My boyfriend's name is Rob. He is actually in an officer program at a college down south. He'll be graduating in a year and then he'll be a commissioned officer. So we want to get married shortly after that and I'll follow him to whatever base he is assigned to."

"Oh, that must suck. Long distance relationships are the worst. How do you do it?" I asked her.

"Sexting, of course," Christie said with a stone cold serious face. This time, Violet couldn't control herself and actually shot soda out of her nose. Of course, this just caused everyone to laugh harder. Violet had found someone just as brazen as her.

"No, in all seriousness," Christie said while Violet cleaned up her spittle, "we try to talk on the phone every night and he visits almost once a month, so that helps. My parents are crazy protective, so they didn't want me to go to school out of state, and forget about me traveling down to see him alone."

"My parents wouldn't let me bring my car on campus, so I understand crazy parents," Violet reminded us. It certainly would have been a lot easier for her to drive off and see her lover if she had a car. But then again, maybe her parents had a point. I didn't think their main goal was to ensure Violet had an easier way to get to the professor she was banging on the weekends.

Christie took her phone out and showed us a photo of Rob. He was the picture perfect military man. His brown hair was cropped short, his blue eyes shown brightly, and his muscles appeared to be bursting out of his shirt. He looked even more jacked than Kingsley, but he had a light and carefree smile on his face and looked at Christie like she was the most important person in the world.

"Good for you, girl," Violet cheered, whistling.

"The two of you together look like Barbie and

Ken," I said, handing her back the phone. "He is gorgeous."

"Thanks, he's definitely a good-looking guy," she responded, and put the phone away. "What about you guys?"

Jason practically threw his phone at her. "I'll have to introduce you to Janice. She's my girlfriend."

"Aww, she's pretty. You guys look good together."

"Thanks, we've been together forever."

I tried not to roll my eyes but clearly I was making a face. Violet kicked me under the table and I turned to look at Kingsley and smiled at him. Christie picked up on it and pointed at us. "So, are you two a couple as well?"

My eyes shot open and my mouth gaped a little. I wasn't ready for that, and frankly, I didn't know how to answer it. Kingsley wrapped his arm around me protectively and smiled. I placed a hand on his knee and realized it was bouncing up and down. Was he nervous too? There was a little sweat on his brow so maybe he was. Taking a page out of Violet's book, I spoke up.

"We're not dating, just trying to get to know each other a bit more." I smiled back at him and he gave me a kiss on the cheek.

"And, Violet, where's your boyfriend?"

I froze and waited to see what Violet would say. Maybe meeting a new friend was a little dangerous in our group.

"My boyfriend is studying abroad in England right now, but I say boyfriend loosely. I don't really like the idea of being tied down."

"Hey, live it up. I'm all for playing the field," Christie cheered.

***

When we finished eating, we all went back to Jason's room and had a movie night. But, man, Christie was not kidding about her parents. They actually called her three times during the course of one movie to find out what her plan was, when she'd be home, and who she was with.

Kingsley, on the other hand, could not take his eyes off the movie. I thought he was beginning to annoy everyone because he kept pointing out little things in the background, weird things about the cast, and tiny plot holes that were bothering him. It was like he was hyper focused. I kept whispering for him to keep it together, but it was like something was forcing the information out of his mouth. His knee was still going and I was desperate to know how he had all this energy. But then I remembered I'd been up almost all night with Violet. It suddenly made a lot of sense as to why I was exhausted.

I started fighting to keep my eyes open and leaned against him, stroking his chest gently. This seemed to finally calm him down as he wrapped an arm around me. Now he just spoke to me in a whisper. I didn't mind listening to him jammer on. It was soothing and I might have even dozed off a bit.

The movie ended too soon and we all started to

head out. Kingsley offered to walk Violet and me back to our dorm. I looked over at Violet, trying to have one of those best friend telepathic conversations that movies and books talked about. I wanted a few moments alone with Kingsley.

Either Violet and I were now psychically connected, or she was able to pick up on my meaning on her own. Honestly, with Violet, it could have gone either way. She insisted on walking with Christie back to her car, maintaining she was terrified Christie's mom would hunt us down if she didn't make it home safely. Jason went with them since we didn't want Violet walking back to the dorm alone either.

"Alone at last," Kingsley said as we walked outside. It was cold, but the night was perfect. The moon was full and there were a million stars out. Since the school was in a small town, about a half hour away from a major city, on clear nights, it wasn't unheard of to see a sky full of stars. I looked up at them and then smiled at Kingsley.

"I know. But I'm glad you were willing to hang out with my friends all night. It means a lot to me."

"Anything for you, babe. Besides, I needed to make sure you and Violet were safe." He pulled me against him and gave me a kiss. Not the light kisses from earlier today. This kiss had a force behind it and it made my knees weak. It was a good thing he was holding onto me, or I didn't know if I could have stayed upright. His touch sent a fire through my body and I no longer felt the wind's chill.

Then, as he nibbled a little on my lip, it happened before I could keep it together. I shivered hard, but it wasn't from the cold.

"Geez, I'm such an idiot. Let me take you back to your room before you freeze."

"I have some hot chocolate in my room, want to come up?" I asked, knowing the double meaning behind my words.

Kingsley looked me deep in the eyes for a moment, as if he were trying to decipher if I really meant what he hoped I did. He leaned down and gave me another deep kiss. "I'd love to come up."

Hand in hand, we walked up to my dorm room and I paused a second before opening the door. "Would it be terrible if I asked you to wait outside for a minute? I wasn't expecting this, so my room is a little messy."

"Sure, I'll just run to the bathroom real quick and then knock on the door. How's that?"

"Do you want me to take your bag with me? You don't need to take it with you to the bathroom."

He pulled the bag a little higher on his shoulder and gripped the handle tighter. "Not that I don't trust you, because I do, but..." He stopped for a minute and looked up at the ceiling, shifting his weight back and forth. "I don't know. It's this weird thing. I just like having my bag with me."

"That's fine," I said, and pulled him to me, placing a big kiss on his lips.

When I let go, Kingsley walked off to the bathroom and I rushed into my room. Truth be told, I wasn't a messy person. I had some dirty clothes next to the hamper that I quickly tossed away, and I made the bed. Yeah, it was probably going to get all mussed in a minute but it would look nice when he walked in.

As I took my coat off and hung it up on the back of the door, I quickly scanned the room for any embarrassing items. My eyes quickly fell on my duck collection. I liked to buy little duck statues whenever I went to a new city or state. I had quite the collection. Basically, I kept mom-and-pop tourist and knickknack shops in business.

Unfortunately, my mother had taken the duck collection to a whole new level. Whenever she went to a new city or state, she bought me a stuffed duck. I grabbed the stuffed animals and tossed them in the closet, cursing myself for not tossing them in my trunk. I was eighteen, why were there stuffed animals in my room? Probably because there was no man taking up that side of the bed, I thought to myself.

Then I checked my panties. No, I wasn't planning to have sex but I wanted to see which ones I was wearing. Just because I wasn't ready to go all the way didn't mean there wasn't a chance he'd see them. Besides, Violet always told me to work my best asset, and she definitely meant *ass*et.

The yellow and black polka dot hipsters were cute but definitely not sexy. I almost changed, but then decided to keep them on. It wasn't like I had any sexy lingerie. They would have to do. Then I checked what bra I had on. It was just a plain black one. He was almost definitely going to see that, and when I thought about it, I didn't mind. Black was supposed to be a sexy color, right?

I decided to stop second guessing everything before Kingsley came back and I was doing something embarrassing like falling over as I tried to pull my skinny jeans back up.

Instead, I turned to start mixing the hot chocolate when I heard a knock on the door. With my heart trying to pound out of my chest, I opened the door to see the best-looking man I had ever laid eyes on giving me bedroom eyes. "Can I come in?"

Chapter 7

I thought for a second. Did I really want him to come in? There was no telling what would happen if he did, and I wasn't sure what that would mean for me or for us. Ignoring the bad feeling he'd given me earlier, I nodded and he walked in.

"I can't believe how much stuff you managed to fit in this room. It all looks great," Kingsley complimented as he looked around.

"Thanks, I had to take a bunch of it to my car because I was out of floor space."

"Well, if you ever need to move anything, I'd be happy to help. I've got the muscle you need." He flexed and I realized his coat was still on.

"Oh, can I take you coat?" I asked, sticking my hand out.

"Sure. I'm glad you decided to let me stay. I saw the wheels turning in your head when you opened the door. You have this adorable look on your face whenever you seem to be considering something." He handed his coat to me and I quickly hung it up next to mine.

But now I had to turn around and face him. I looked down, embarrassed that he seemed to be able to read me so easily and I still questioned him. "I'm sorry, I just—"

"No." He put a finger on my lips to silence me. "Don't apologize. I'm glad you're taking this seriously. It's not just hooking up for me. If I wanted that, it would only be too easy, and I definitely wouldn't have to wine and dine her. I save that for girls I could be serious about."

I smiled up at him and bit my lip slightly.

"You look so sexy when you do that," he whispered as he placed a hand gently on my cheek. "That insecure lip biting thing. It drives me crazy." He placed his thumb on my bottom lip and grazed it softly. "It reminds me of when you nibbled on my lip last night."

I took a deep breath and stepped forward, meeting him the rest of the way. I remembered my plan to be a bit bolder and looked up at him. "I feel like you need another memory."

We kissed, and Kingsley ran his fingers through my hair and massaged my scalp. I melted into him as I wrapped my arms around his neck. The kiss deepened as I opened my mouth and he dove in. He placed his hand on my lower back and pushed me closer to him, eliminating any remaining space between us.

He broke the kiss and pulled my hair, forcing my head up so I was now looking at the ceiling and he had full access to my neck. Kingsley placed a trail of kisses from my earlobe down to my neck. He shifted the hand on my back to my side and slowly started inching it up toward my breasts. But he was moving painfully slow.

I pushed my chest out, hoping he'd take the hint, I needed to have him feel me. However, he didn't touch me where I was begging him to. Instead, he leaned down slightly and picked me up. In three short steps, he was at the bed and placing me down gently.

"I think we'll be more comfortable here, don't you? I plan on doing this for a lot longer and I'd hate for you to get tired." He nuzzled my neck and I tried to remember how to talk.

My pulse was racing and my hands were shaking a little as I reached out to hold the back of his neck. I pulled him into a kiss before I could change my mind. Following my lead, Kingsley kissed me hard and brought his hand, almost immediately, to my breast. He groped lightly and then reached for my nipple.

His fingers squeezed gently and I broke the kiss to let out a moan.

"If you like that, I think you'll like this even better." He slid his hand under my shirt, but still over my bra, and lightly traced the skin right above the lace fabric.

His fingers were warm and their heat, like earlier, seemed to flow through me, heating up body parts I didn't know were cold in the first place. I broke the kiss and tried to breathe as he slightly tugged on my nipple. But my breaths came out ragged and quickly turned to a moan as Kingsley took this opportunity to suckle at my collarbone. My head fell back and a loud purr came out before I could stop it. I shut my mouth quickly, embarrassed at the sounds coming out of me.

But then Kingsley looked at me and the fire in his eyes was real. He sat up, quickly yanking his sweater and then t-shirt off, giving me the perfect view of his six-pack abs, broad shoulders, muscular pecs, and the light trail of hair that went down to the band of his jeans.

I reached up and felt his taut muscles. Before I realized what was happening, I leaned forward and licked between his pecs. Then I reached out and traced the ripples of muscles roughly with my nails. They felt amazing and I was even more turned on. The skin to skin contact wasn't enough. I sat up on my knees and slowly eased my shirt off. However, I left my camisole on. I didn't feel confident enough for him to see me shirtless. Earlier, I thought I'd be okay with it, but in the moment, it was intimidating.

"Don't feel you need to cover up for me. I already think you're the sexiest girl I've ever kissed." He reached out and slowly touched the bottom of my shirt.

I stopped him. It was a reflex, and he jerked his hand away. "Relax, Annabelle," he murmured in my ear before kissing just below my earlobe.

I closed my eyes tight and took a deep breath, waiting for him to try again. I felt a chill as he raised the hem over my stomach and then my chest.

"Put your hands up, babe," he whispered eagerly.

I squeezed my eyes even tighter but did as he asked. The shirt gradually slid up my arms until I felt it pass over my fingertips. I hadn't opened my eyes, so it was a surprise when Kingsley kissed my lips.

"See? You're even more beautiful now."

I bit my lip again, knowing he liked it, and slid my hands up his torso and around his neck. "I feel the same way about you."

We kissed and he pushed me forward lightly so that he was laying on top of me. It was exhilarating as his hands slid up my naked torso and onto my breasts again. He kissed my neck, but this time he didn't stop at my collarbone. Kingsley continued kissing down my chest and stopped at the top of my bra, where he placed soft kisses along the curve.

I ran my fingers through his hair and pulled gently. Kingsley froze and then looked up at me. "Careful with the hair pulling, it turns me into a beast and I can't control what happens. Are you prepared for that?"

My eyes grew wide and my mouth went completely dry. I was kind of intrigued to see what he meant by a beast. For a second, I listened to his warning. Kingsley resumed kissing my breast. It felt amazing and empowered me. I tugged on his hair again, harder this time.

"You asked for it." He grabbed me, pulling me into a seated position. Then he reached behind my back and unhooked the bra on his first try. I was impressed—I couldn't even do that. But then all breath left my body as he grabbed one boob and began sucking on the nipple of the other one.

I forced my breathing to come in short bursts as I was growing lightheaded. Though it didn't seem to get any better as he started to twist my nipple slightly between two fingers. I grew more and more aroused, loving this side of him.

"Kingsley," I whimpered as I lifted my hips up to meet his.

He reached his free hand down to the one spot that, so far, I was the only one to explore. He began to rub the inside of my thigh and progressively inched higher. Suddenly, he was rubbing at my center and I was trying to shift my legs to get some kind of release but it wasn't coming.

Kinsley moved to unbutton my pants and I instinctively swatted his hand away. I smiled meekly up at him and tried not to let my embarrassment show. But I felt the blush creep up my neck and settle into my cheeks. I hid my face behind my hands, completely humiliated at my reaction.

"I'm just not ready for that quite yet," I replied meekly, hoping he wouldn't be upset. He was probably used to a whole lot more with a girl. After all, I had invited him up to my room. What girl brought a guy to her room and then swatted his hand away when he tried to please her?

But Kingsley didn't jump off the bed in a huff. He reached for my chin and tilted my head up so I was looking in his eyes. "I'll be here when you're ready. I'm in no rush."

I grinned at him and gave him a light kiss. "Thanks for understanding."

"Of course, but I'm not quite ready to leave yet. Can I just stay here and hold you for a bit? Maybe we can watch a movie or something?

"Yes, I'd really like that. Um, do you still want that hot chocolate? I actually made some that I can put back in my microwave." I pointed to my desk where the mugs were sitting.

"Sounds good. Why don't you handle the drinks, and I'll find a movie. There's gotta be something on that I like."

We fell asleep not long into the action movie Kingsley swore I'd love. I didn't really like it, but it was worth it to be lying in his arms. Kingsley had fallen asleep first and I thought about waking him. But it was so warm and cozy lying against him that I couldn't bring myself to do it. Instead, I skipped my nightly skin care routine and closed my eyes. The rhythm of his breathing soon lulled me into a deep sleep.

It was a good thing my alarm was programmed to wake me up at seven every day, because I would have completely forgotten to set it. As the annoying blaring woke the two of us up, I reached over Kingsley to my nightstand and quickly turned it off.

I looked at him and smiled. "Good morning, sunshine," I whispered, and gave him a kiss.

"Mhmm, that's a nice way to wake up." He brushed his fingers against my face and then kissed the tip of my nose. "All right, I have to head back to my dorm to get ready for my first class, but will I see you later?"

"Of course."

Kingsley put his shirt back on and I walked him to the door. "Bye, babe," he said, and gave me another kiss.

"Bye." I waved as he walked down the hall.

"You little hussy."

I whipped around and saw Violet walking out of

the bathroom. "Oh my god! You had to be coming back from Berneli's now?" I groaned and gave her a big embarrassed smile. "Come in, I'll let you know what happened. I know you're dying to know."

She nodded and followed me in. I started to pick my clothes out and she sat at the desk chair. "So, what happened?"

"Okay, he kissed me goodbye and it was cold. So I just invited him up to my room for hot chocolate. But that got cold when we were making out on my bed."

"Good thing I sat in the chair and not your bed."

"Oh, stop, nothing happened. I did take my shirt off, but that's it."

"How was Kingsley with going slow? He kind of strikes me as someone who likes to get a little action."

"That's what I thought too, but he was great. He said he'd be ready whenever I was. Then he asked if we could watch a movie and cuddle."

"Seriously? He did not strike me as a cuddler." She chuckled.

"Well, he is a great cuddler. I think it's the muscles." I posed like he had earlier, making her laugh.

"Yeah, he is pretty jacked. I'm happy for you. I'll leave you alone so you can get ready for class," she said, standing up and heading to the door.

***

I walked around on a cloud the rest of that day. It didn't matter that my face was a little dried out since I missed my moisturizing routine, or that I was a few minutes late to class. Nothing could take the smile off my face, especially when Kingsley showed up at my door that night with Chinese food and another movie.

He stayed the night again, and I slept soundly. We kissed but it didn't go any further than that. Kingsley insisted he just wanted to be with me at whatever level I was comfortable with. And as he fell asleep, Kingsley pulled me against his chest and didn't let me go until we woke up the next morning. That was definitely something I wanted to get used to.

"Good morning, beautiful," Kingsley whispered, nuzzling against my hair. He gave me a little kiss and then crawled out of bed.

"I need to run and get ready for class. Maybe next time I'll pack a bag so we can spend a little more time together in the morning." He tossed his shirt back on and then his coat.

"Yeah, I'd like that."

"Great. Will I see you later?"

"No, I'm going over to Christie's tonight to bake for the fundraiser."

"That's all right. I'll probably check and see if the station needs me to pick up another shift. Are you sure we can't hang out before you go? I'd love to have dinner or something." He sat back down on the bed and gave me a kiss.

"I want to, but I just don't think I have time today. My last class is at four, but they're calling for snow, so I want to try to leave as early as possible. I can drive in snow but I'd prefer not to."

He quickly got up, grabbed his jacket, and walked to the door. Before leaving, he turned to look at me. "Don't worry about it. I probably have things I need to do too. Talk to you later."

I swallowed hard, feeling guilty. I didn't mean to reject him. Throwing my robe on, I ran after him, just catching him before he went outside. "Kingsley, maybe if you aren't at a fire, you could come over when we get back?" I looked at him hopefully, placing a hand on his chest.

His heart rate slowed as he looked down at me. "Actually, that sounds great. Let me know when you guys get back to campus and I'll make sure I'm here." Then he grabbed my ass through my robe, pulling me toward him. "I definitely want to see you in these little shorts again."

I pushed at his chest, trying to get out of his grasp, but he held me tight. Kingsley raised his eyebrows at me suggestively and kissed me. I held onto his jacket, using it to keep me upright as his hand slid under my robe and connected with the bare cheek hanging out of my short shorts.

"All right," Kingsley said, finally pulling away from me. "Another minute and I won't leave. I'll see you later." He tapped my nose and headed out the door.

Grinning from ear to ear, I walked to Violet's door. Since she'd been threatened, she hadn't been staying with Berneli. At first, I was a little worried I'd hear her screaming, but so far, it all seemed good. Lola and her boyfriend were apparently on the outs again so she'd been spending most nights in her bed

"Why are you looking so chipper?" She rubbed her eyes when she opened her door.

"It's a nice day out, why not enjoy it?"

"Kingsley stayed over last night, right?"

"Obviously. So when do you want to head over to Christie's? I want to try to go right after class."

"Yeah, yeah, works for me. I'll see you later."

"Sounds good. I'll meet you at my car at around four fifteen."

I beelined it to the bathroom for a shower, a little sad I wouldn't smell like Kingsley anymore.

***

My last class ended early so I texted Violet and Christie to see if they were both ready. Christie said she had just gotten back from the store with the baking supplies so she was free whenever. Violet said she would be at my car in a few.

I headed to the parking lot and gave Kingsley a call.

"Hey, babe," he answered.

"I've been thinking about you."

"Oh yeah? Can you hold on a second?"

He must have pulled the phone away from his face, or covered it, because his voice was muffled. However, it wasn't muffled enough, and I could just make out what he was saying.

"Yeah, Karen, hold on. No, I need it now. Last night I needed it and I didn't get it. Now I've been feeling off all day today. I promise I'll get you what you need if you just help me out."

My heart was breaking. What the hell was he

asking Karen for? Was she more willing to hook up than me? What if she and Kinsley used to hook up back in the day? Seriously, who talked to the girl he was banging while on the phone with the girl he was seeing? Maybe Violet was right. He was a man of action.

"Sorry about that. Um, this is not the best time. Maybe we can talk later?"

"Kingsley, I really think we should—"

"I can't right now, babe," he said, cutting me off. "I'll call you later." Then he hung up.

I climbed into my car and tried not to cry. He and I weren't together. It was kind of like what happened with Violet and Trent. They weren't a couple and he was hooking up with his ex-girlfriend. Now, Kingsley was trying to do the same thing. My only hope was that Karen turned him down. I wouldn't be with a guy who couldn't keep it in his pants.

I jumped, like, five feet in the air when someone knocked on my window. I turned and saw Violet. She had two cups in her hand and a smile on her face. I unlocked the door and she climbed in.

"Hey, girl, I brought you some coffee." She handed me the cup and took a big sip of her own.

"I thought you didn't drink coffee," I said.

"It's hot chocolate. I don't like cold." She started talking about random things, her mood cheerful as ever.

I responded in short sentences and nodded when it seemed appropriate.

"So, things seem to be heating up with Kingsley. How's that going?"

I looked forward and ground my teeth a little. It was crazy how happy I'd been with Kinsley last night and how upset I was now.

"You going to tell me why you just tensed up at the mention of last night? Earlier, you were practically glowing."

"I don't want to talk about it now. Let's just go to Christie's. I could use some comfort food at the moment, and brownies definitely sound good."

Violet didn't ask why I was upset again. Instead, she talked about her classes, EET, and some things she and Berneli planned to do. I could tell she was trying to distract me, well, at least I thought she was. This girl would talk to a wall. Either way, I appreciated that all I needed to do was nod and focus on the GPS.

In about ten minutes, we pulled into Christie's driveway. It was a beautiful Cape Cod style home painted a bright yellow. There were flowerbeds all around the front of the house and a giant tree with a tire swing hanging from one of the branches. It looked homey and welcoming. Christie was standing at the door, waving as we walked up the front path.

"Hey, come in quick. It's freezing out there."

"I know. It smells like snow," I said as I walked in.

"What did you just say?" Violet asked, a little exasperated. "How can you smell snow?"

"I don't know, it's a thing. Google it. Don't you get a lot of snow in Maryland?"

"Yeah, tons of snow. I think last year we got, like, six inches. My high school was closed for two days. It was awesome."

Christie and I looked at her for a second and then back at each other before breaking out into giggles.

"What? You guys don't like snow days?"

"Oh, no, we love snow days," Christie assured her. "But six inches of snow is nothing. We'll probably still have class on days when it snows that much. At least that's how it was when I was in high school around this area."

"Really? I don't think I even have snow boots," Violet grumbled.

"Yeah, we're gonna have to go shopping for that," I promised her. "Besides, I think we're overdue for a girls' shopping trip. Christie, you'll have to come with us."

"Definitely, I am actually quite the skilled shopper." She laughed a little and led us into her kitchen. "Okay, so I started a batch of cookies. They're in the oven now, and I figured you guys could make some brownies."

"So, just an FYI," Violet warned us, "I've never baked anything before."

"That's okay. I'll help you," I told her, but I was a little afraid to let her make anything. Berneli told me about the time she tried to make him dinner and the fire department had to come put the fire out. Though, if the fire department came, maybe it would ruin Kingsley's evening plans and he'd have to come rescue me.

"I bake constantly, so I can help too." Christie handed me a recipe for double chocolate devil's brownies. "All right, let's get to work."

We had been baking for about ten minutes when

Violet was forced into clean up and DJ duty. I was struggling to fish all the egg shells out of the batter. The sad part, it was the second time it had happened. She really was a disaster in the kitchen but she tried so hard. I had to give her an A for effort.

Christie, however, was like Housewife Barbie and I was crazy impressed. Her long hair was pulled up into an elegant bun on the top of her head with a ribbon tied to it. Her makeup was flawless and her apron had a ruffled skirt. She expertly mixed, whipped, and decorated all different kinds of sweets without the slightest bit of flour on her face.

"So, how was your day?" Christie asked me.

Violet spun around and looked at me, concerned. There was an eagerness in her eyes, and I knew she wanted to hear what happened, but she was staying quiet. The more I thought about it, the more I realized thinking about Kingsley was eating me up inside. It was time to get it off my chest.

"All right, so here's what happened." I filled Christie in on Kingsley and Jason while Violet stayed quiet in the corner. She was giving me the reins to tell my own story. Normally, she would be cutting in and providing her two cents, but now she was silent. I began to wonder why she wasn't saying anything. Did she know something I didn't? Was there something she observed that I had missed?

"Well, I think it's obvious that Jason is in love with you," Christie stated.

"Thank you!" Violet shouted, and flung her arm up in the air.

"Whatever, I don't believe you guys. But that's not what this is about." I told them about the phone call and both of their mouths fell open.

"Shut up," Violet finally managed to utter. "Are you sure he said that?"

"Yeah, I heard it. His voice was a little muffled, but I still could make out the words."

"Okay, I think we're getting a little ahead of ourselves," Christie cut in. "He didn't say he was looking for sex. Besides, maybe he needed notes, or he lent her money. There could be tons of reasons he needs to see Karen immediately."

"Maybe there's an explanation and I jumped to conclusions. Do you think there could be a reason that doesn't involve him cheating on me?" I asked, feeling hopeful. Maybe I'd misunderstood the conversation, but I couldn't imagine what else it could have been.

"Well, maybe he had her pick a present up for you or something. Didn't you say Kingsley had a surprise for you? Maybe he wanted advice from her. They're old friends so it makes sense," Christie suggested.

Violet tilted her head and squinted her eyes. "Um, I don't think that's it. But it makes me think about what Kyle said. What if he was buying drugs?"

I whipped around and glared at her. I couldn't believe she had the nerve to bring that up again. I had already told her that he wasn't a druggie. "Violet, he isn't on drugs. I spent the last two nights with him and he was fine. He didn't take anything and we were together pretty much the whole time."

"Are you sure about that? He didn't seem irritated, sweaty, or maybe a little hyper?" Christie asked me gently.

"Sometimes he's, like, bouncing up and down, but it always seems like it's because he's excited. Kingsley is unbelievably sweet with me. It can't be drugs. The only time he was sweaty was when we were hookin' up," I said, smiling a bit, thinking about his face when I touched him.

Christie shrugged. "Well, didn't he say he didn't get it last night? He may not have used when he was with you."

"I think I just need to talk to him about it. It's probably something silly and I'm making a big deal about it. Let's talk about something else," I insisted. I wanted to make it work with him but I just couldn't ignore the pit in my stomach.

Violet held her finger up to try to speak but I quickly cut her off. "No, Violet. I don't want to start this thing thinking the worst of him. I'm aware that something may be up, and my eyes are open to it. I'll talk to him about it, but until then, I'm gonna be mature and stop speculating."

She held both her hands up to indicate she was backing off. "Okay, whatever you say."

"So, Christie, where are your parents?" I asked her as she pulled another batch of perfect cookies out of the oven.

"They went to visit my aunt and uncle. I told them you guys were coming over and they wanted to give me some space."

"That was nice of them."

"Yeah. I'm trying to convince them to let me live

on campus next semester. I feel like I'm missing out on the real college experience."

"Well, you're welcome to crash on my floor any time," Violet offered.

"Sounds good."

We spent the next half hour cooking and talking about past EET events and who we hoped would perform for the concert later in April. We were having a good time until Violet came back from the bathroom.

"You guys gotta see this. It's snowing like crazy."

We all rushed to a window in the living room and jumped on the couch so we could see. Everything was covered in snow. There was at least four inches on the ground.

"Wait, hold on." Christie grabbed a remote off the coffee table and turned the television to the Weather Channel.

The reporter was just beginning to talk about this storm. We listened carefully and stared in disbelief as they called for another five or six inches in the next couple hours. The flakes were supposed to be coming down pretty heavy.

Christie paused the show and looked at the two of us. "That's crazy. I can't believe it's snowed this much already," she said in shock. The window in her kitchen was over her sink and was a little high for us shorties to see out of. We really hadn't noticed it was snowing.

"Still feel comfortable driving in the snow?" Violet asked me, and I frowned at her.

"No, you guys can sleep here. I don't want you

going out in that," Christie insisted.

"Are you sure that's okay?" Violet checked with her.

"Yeah," I added. "We don't want to put you out."

"Oh, stop. It's totally fine." Christie waved a hand. "I bet my parents aren't going to come home, so it'll be nice to have the company."

"Sounds good," Violet said. "We can have an old-school sleepover with some of the cookies, movies, pillow fights, boy talk, and…"

"Lots of alcohol," Christie finished. "I'm Irish, so my dad keeps the good stuff in the house. Since he won't be home, it sounds like a good time to get into it."

Violet nodded and I kind of grimaced. I'd never had alcohol before. I wasn't even sure I wanted to try it. People did stupid things when they drank, plus it was illegal for us. But then again, we were going to stay inside. Maybe it was time for me to branch out a little. I didn't need to get trashed but I could have a little bit.

"Okay, so what do you guys like to eat?" Christie asked, interrupting my thoughts.

I turned to look at her, confused. "What do you mean?"

"Dinner. It's getting late and you guys are probably hungry. I can make us some food before we get our drink on."

"Whatever you have," both Violet and I said at the same time.

"Uh," Christie mumbled, and opened her fridge. "I could make chicken parm. Do you ladies like pasta?"

I snorted a little as Violet practically screamed at her, "I love pasta!"

"Great, why don't you put the sweets into the decorative bags I got for the fundraiser and I'll get started."

When we finished eating, Violet carried her plate to the sink and turned to look at Christie. "All I gotta say, Christie, is that if you ever want to bat for the other team, I'd totally wife you up."

"While that's a great offer, I wouldn't say yes unless the carat size was equal to my shoe size," she responded, continuing to clear the table.

"I like that philosophy," Violet commented.

"I don't want a big rock. I'd be afraid to leave my house with it," I said. Fancy bling wasn't really my cup of tea. "I like the idea of a solitaire and a simple wedding band. I'd rather have the big wedding," I added, grabbing my plate and walking to the kitchen.

"You all can just leave the dishes in the sink, I'll get to them later. Why don't we head to my theater room and grab the booze?" Christie grabbed some Sprite, lemon and lime juice, and two other things I didn't recognize. "How do you all feel about an Irish Redhead?"

"Blondes are more my thing," I joked since they were both blonde.

"Well, I guess you're going to have to settle." Christie laughed.

We followed her to the basement where both Violet and I stood in awe for a moment. "This is one hell of a room," Violet gasped.

Elton Hall Chronicles: Second Snowfall

There was a giant sixty-inch television with massive surround sound speakers mounted on the walls and an elaborate lush leather sectional. It was better than a movie theater. There wouldn't be any small children kicking the back of my seat, that rude, self-centered jerk who answered the phone during the movie, or those ridiculous teenagers who thought it was okay to Snapchat during the show.

"All right, so my movie rack is over there." Christie pointed to a wall filled with DVDs. "You girls pick one, and I'll make the drinks."

Violet walked over to the DVD rack, but I looked at Christie. She had three glasses in her hand and I was a little nervous. I was willing to give it a try but I still wanted to take it easy. I went over to Christie as she was free handing the measurements.

"Uh, Christie, I don't really drink. Maybe you could go a little easy on mine."

"Yeah, no problem. I can make you a virgin, if you'd like."

"No, that's okay. I'm willing to try it, just maybe don't make it as strong as you make the others."

"You'll barely taste the alcohol. There is so much other stuff in it that it kind of tastes like punch mixed with Sprite, but be careful, they kinda sneak up on you." She handed me a glass with a silly twisty straw. "If you don't like it, I can make you something else."

I gingerly took a sip and was pleasantly surprised. It was delicious. I gave Christie a thumbs-up and headed over to the movie rack with Violet.

We ended up going with a romantic comedy all

three of us had seen close to fifty times. The drinks were flowing and we were constantly misquoting the best lines. It was a really good time. Well, it was until my phone rang. I checked the screen and it was Kingsley.

I rolled off the couch in about the most ungraceful manner possible. But when I stood up, the room spun a little bit. I stuck my hands out to try to balance myself, however, when I did this, I dropped the phone. Around Violet, that was a terrible idea. She grabbed the phone off the ground and answered it for me.

"Hey, you have some serious explaining to do, mister."

"Uh, Anabelle?"

"No, it's Violet. Annabelle is right here, hold on." She tried to hand me the phone but I kept shaking my head forcefully. I may have overdone it. Who would have thought redheads could be so feisty?

"Annabelle," I heard Kingsley calling through the phone.

Violet grabbed my hand and placed the phone in it.

"Hello."

"What the hell is going on, Annabelle?"

"Nothing. It snowed and I can't get back on campus but I get the feeling you won't be lonely tonight."

"Oh really, are you inviting me over?"

"No, I just heard you talking to Karen. It sounded like you guys were going to, I don't know, hook up or something tonight."

"What the hell are you talking about? I was called into the firehouse. I got a migraine and I got a pill. I had to get to the station. Did you expect me to go out and fight a fire when I couldn't concentrate?"

"But why does she have to give you the pills? Can't you just take something, like, I don't know, over the counter?"

"Normally, I do. It's not a big deal. I'm fine. Will you please look outside? I can explain everything."

"Outside? What?"

"I'm outside Christie's house right now."

I grabbed my boots, rushed to the window, and screamed for Violet and Christie. "Guys, Kingsley isn't with that girl, he's outside with a big ass plow."

"Shut up!" Violet rushed over to the window, drink in hand, twisty straw in her mouth.

"Did he plow my street?" Christie asked.

"Looks like it," I said, staring at in him shock. He definitely didn't have time to be with anyone. I stuffed my feet into my boots, rushed to the door, and flung it open. Kingsley jumped out of the SUV, and ran to me. "What are you doing here?" I asked him.

Kingsley reached out and grazed my cheek with his hand. "I got called into the station earlier and saw the impact the storm was making. So I texted Jason and got Violet's number, then I asked if you all were all right. When she said you were snowed in, I contacted a friend of mine, and, well, let's just say I owe him a favor."

"You didn't have to do that. We would have been fine here." I saw Violet on her phone earlier but I thought it was just Berneli. She was really just being sneaky. It felt good that she was looking out for me. I knew she had reservations about him but I liked that she was giving him a chance.

"I know, but with me, fine isn't good enough." He wrapped his hand around the back of my neck and pulled me into a kiss. At first it felt nice, but I couldn't help but notice how he was shaking a little. Kingsley was the one decked out in a coat, boots, and hat. There was no reason for him to be this jittery. Maybe he was just excited to see me. I kind of liked it.

"Hot mama!"

"Get it, girl!"

I turned around to see Violet and Christie shouting obnoxious things at us.

"Sorry, you must be cold," Kingsley said as if he just noticed I was standing in the snow in a pair of boots, jeans, and a t-shirt.

"I don't know. You're warming me up."

"Perfect," Kingsley whispered, and kissed me again. "I'll let you get back to your friends, but now you can get out tomorrow and head back to the dorms. Who knows how long it would have taken the plows to get to this side street."

"Well, aren't you the considerate one," I said in a singsong voice as I slowly unzipped his jacket.

"How much did you have to drink?"

"I have no idea. Violet and Christie are terrible influences. You should take me far away from them and teach me a lesson."

"As much fun as that sounds, I'm not sure if that's the best idea. You seem a little—"

I cut him off with a kiss. It was dangerous and filled with heat, passion, and a whole lot of lust. I was practically begging him to shove those pretty morals aside and have his way with me up against Christie's front gate.

Kinsley wrapped his arms around my waist and pulled me in tight. He was playing it safe, and I didn't want that. His hands were warm and I needed that heat. I grabbed one hand and slid it up my shirt and over my breast. He eagerly held on and groped me as I broke the kiss to moan.

He kissed my neck and started to suck at my collarbone as his other hand slid down my back and grabbed onto my butt. My head fell back and I basked in the wonder of his abilities. Until we were interrupted.

"Okay, guys," Violet said, grabbing me by the shoulders and pulling me out of his grip. "So, Kingsley, that was awful sweet of you, plowing the street and everything, but I think it's time to bring Annabelle inside before she catches pneumonia or an STD or something."

"Wait a minute, Violet, she came on to me. There is only so much I can resist. I'm just a lowly human."

"I know. Let's talk about it all later. It really was great that you did this for us," she said, and pulled me back into the house.

I waved at Kingsley from the window and watched as he climbed back in his SUV.

"That was fun," Christie said, and smiled at me.

"I can't believe I spent all that time doubting him when here he was, just trying to look out for us."

"Did he say what the phone call was about?" Violet asked me.

"He said she had his notes or something. I totally overreacted." I didn't want to mention the pills. I'd heard migraines got rough so he probably just wanted a clear head before going into a burning house. I couldn't blame him for that but I had a feeling they would.

Christie's mom called to let us know she was staying over at her sister's and she wanted to check on us. Christie assured her we were fine and told her the street was plowed but that we'd be fine for the night. They said good night and we all decided it was probably a good time to go to bed before we could get into any more trouble.

Christie gave us some blankets and we set up some makeshift beds on the sectional. She joined us there, insisting she'd miss out on the bonding if she slept in her own bed.

We all awoke the next morning when we were blinded by the sun streaming through the blinds. Groaning, the three of us shuffled upstairs and Christie grabbed us cups for very large glasses of water.

"Ugh, I need grease," Violet complained as she downed her glass in what seemed like a single gulp.

"Easy there. It's a shame your boyfriend is in England. You're a good swallower," Christie pointed out.

Violet and I looked at each other for a second and she subtly shook her head. "Trust me," she said

118

with a forced smile on her face. "I won't let my skills go to waste. But I may waste away if I don't get some food. I think I'm gonna go out and pick up a breakfast sandwich."

"Not in my car, crazy lady!"

"Please, you aren't going out there just for a sandwich. Sit your butt down and I'll make you one," Christie demanded.

While she cooked, Violet and I sat on the couch and got our phones out. We figured classes had been canceled but wanted to double check. Turned out the whole school was closed. We relaxed a bit and I turned to her.

"You didn't have a terror last night."

"I know. Maybe the key is to get liquored up before I go to sleep."

"Um, you didn't seem that drunk. I was a mess and you helped handle me."

"Maybe it was nice to fall asleep knowing you guys were next to me. I'm sure he'll lose interest. That's all I need to do, get him to lose interest."

"I don't think it's that simple."

"He will. Berneli's investigator said he was on to something. He thinks he knows who the connection outside the jail is but he is checking on a few more things." She sounded so sure, but I had a really bad feeling about it.

There was so much that could go wrong, and she was at risk the entire time. The only thing I could do was trust her, and it made me feel terrible. That or this awful hangover was affecting more than just my stomach.

"Breakfast is served, bitches," Christie called a

little later. She had a plate of bacon sandwiches for each of us, and a massive plate of pancakes. "I didn't cut up any fruit because I figured we weren't in the mood for healthy food, but we have some if you want."

"Screw that!" Violet grabbed a sandwich and took a monster bite.

I quickly followed her lead and got my own. I was a little concerned she would inhale hers and then go for another one, leaving me with the dreaded fruit.

As I bit into it, I knew this was exactly what I needed. I groaned as my eyes rolled back into my head. Violet and Christie burst into laughter and I stared at them, confused.

"I'm sorry, was that your O noise?" Christie managed to ask between giggles.

"My what?" I started to blush, a little embarrassed.

"The noise you make when you come," Violet clarified.

"Shut up. That wasn't what that was."

"No, but seriously, is that the sound you make? Mine is more like an, 'oh gawd.'" Christie started to fake an orgasm in a very *Harry Met Sally* kind of way. I tried to ignore her, but it was hysterical. Soon we were all faking it and it sounded a bit too much like a brothel.

We spent the rest of the morning hanging out and getting to know Christie a little better. But by lunch, we were definitely imposing. Christie had made us three meals and refused to let us contribute any money, or even help her cook.

"I have a crazy day tomorrow that I need to get ready for. We really have to go," Violet said finally.

"Yeah, and since Kingsley and I are going on that date tomorrow, I should probably work on my homework a bit."

"All right. I guess that's fair." Christie walked us to the door and handed us some of the cookies. "But text me when you get back so I know you're safe," she called after us.

"Don't worry," I shouted at her. "I'm gonna drive. Violet can barely drive in perfect weather conditions."

"Rude," she insisted, and tossed some snow at me.

I shoved her gently and then climbed in the car. I didn't have gloves and she'd definitely win in a snowball fight.

"Do you mind dropping me off at David's?"

"Don't you want to go home and get some clothes or toiletries? You don't want to show up tomorrow looking like you slept in your clothes or anything."

"I actually have some stuff there."

"Wait, like you forgot some things there or you have a permanent place for your deodorant and your clothes go in their own drawer?"

"I have my own *drawers*, as in two," she bragged.

"That's a big step. But it's so great. I'm happy for you guys." I wanted to ask her what was going to happen at the end of the semester when he went back to England. But every time I'd asked her before, she always said she was living for the moment. This made me anxious since their temporary situation was sounding a whole lot more like a permanent one. Guys in movies didn't give a girl a drawer until they meant business. But then again, what right did I have to say anything? Here I was, dating for the first time. At least they had some kind of plan, even if it was a day by day kind of thing.

I dropped Violet off and then headed back to school to get started on all of that homework.

***

It was around ten and I was climbing into bed to watch some TV when Kingsley called.

"Hey, babe, are you ready for tomorrow?"

"I would be more ready if you would tell me what we were doing."

"Well, I called to give you some hints."

"Oh, I like hints."

"But you have to earn the hints. For the first hint, tell me what color bra you're wearing."

I looked down at my ratty sports bra and did what any girl would do in my situation. "I'm wearing a red lace bra"

"I like the sound of that."

I hoped he never asked to see it since I didn't own anything close to that sexy. It was probably time to go lingerie shopping with Violet and Christie.

"All right, the first hint, wear comfy shoes. They won't get dirty, but we'll be doing some walking."

"But there's snow on the ground. Where are we

going to be walking?"

"You earn your hints, babe. What are your panties like?"

I wanted to be flirtatious and fun, but the truth was I didn't always sleep in panties. You had to let your hooha breathe sometimes. Then I realized that was probably an even better answer than anything I could have made up and I went for it. "Actually, Kingsley, I'm not wearing any panties. Just a pair of those short shorts you like so much. They are even smaller than the ones from the other night." I hoped this worked, but it sounded ridiculous to me.

Kingsley definitely didn't think that though. He groaned. "Aww, babe, you're killing me. All I want to do is come over and rip those shorts off."

"No, you're breaking the rules. Where's my hint?"

"Okay, fine, I just hope you still have some Christmas spirit in you."

"Wait. Why? I love Christmas."

"No, you don't get any more hints. I'll pick you up at ten."

We said good night and I sat with my phone in my hand for a few more minutes. I did want to see him. I was a bit eager to finish what we started the other night. The more he touched me, the more I wanted to do with him. Maybe he would be my first. He just made me feel so special. But I couldn't ruin his surprise. It sounded like he was going all out.

Chapter 8

I woke up early and rushed into the shower. I wanted to have plenty of time to get ready. On a good day, I changed my outfit twice so that didn't take too much time. On a day like today, without Violet's advice, there was no telling how long it was going to take.

After the shower, I stood in front of my closet and had no idea what to wear. After three outfit fails, I grabbed my phone and video called Christie.

"Everything okay?" she asked through a yawn, eyes not entirely focused yet.

"No." I told her about my hints but left out the dirty talk, though she probably would be pretty proud of my attempts. I'd tell her about it later when I wasn't in a time crunch.

"All right, so, black skinny jeans, a red blouse or sweater, and brown riding boots. The red will be Christmasy, the boots will be comfortable, and the skinny jeans will make your ass look great," she rattled off.

"Thanks. Hold on, I'm gonna put it on. I have

this pretty, off the shoulder red sweater with glittery silver thread throughout it. I have a black tank top I can put underneath it."

"Sounds perfect."

I grabbed my clothes and quickly got dressed. Then I took my phone and stood in front of the mirror. "What do you think?"

"Turn around so I can see that ass!"

I laughed and spun, bouncing my butt up and down her.

"You look great," she managed when she stopped laughing. "Don't forget to tell me all about it. I'm so excited for you."

"See you later!" I hung up and started on my hair. I liked it straight, like, really straight.

***

I was working on my make-up when he texted. Kingsley was going to drive in front of my dorm so I didn't have to walk in the snow. He said he'd let me know when he was here.

After taking a few deep breaths, I quickly finished with my make-up and sent Violet a text that I was thinking of her. They'd decided not to go to the jail. The snow seemed like a good excuse and it would give the investigator a little more time. Besides, I really didn't think Violet could handle it.

A few minutes later, Kingsley texted that he was waiting for me in the car. At first, I was a little flustered. Wasn't the guy supposed to pick the girl up at her door? When he said he was going to let me know he was here, I thought he meant in front of my door. He knew which one it was. Then I shook the idea from my head. It was so cold and snowy outside, he probably didn't want to deal with all that for, like, two seconds to come get me. Besides, I shouldn't be nitpicking at these little things. He did plan this big date for us. At least I hoped it would be a big date. Maybe it was a mistake to set my expectations so high. It would be better to be pleasantly surprised.

I took a second before opening the main dorm door and tried to calm down. I was going to be excited no matter what we were doing. Except hiking…I definitely would not go hiking in this weather…or in any weather really.

When I opened the door, I was immediately hit by a rush of cold air. It was awful. I hurried to his SUV and quickly opened the door.

"Thanks for picking me up. It's freezing."

"No problem. I'm just glad it stopped snowing. The sun has started melting the snow but it isn't going fast enough yet."

"Yeah, um, is it safe for us to be out today?" I'd be so pissed if the weather ruined our date. Then again, it wouldn't be the worst thing to spend the day curled up in bed with a movie. I'd lean against his warm, shirtless chest and he'd wrapped his strong arms against me as I breathed in the delicious scent of his cologne.

"Don't worry about that," he said, interrupting my thoughts. "I've got chains on the tires and I double checked the place. It's still open."

"What place?"

"You're going to have to wait."

"You're no fun." I pouted a little at him. I stuck my bottom lip out and fluttered my eyelashes. He started the engine and began to drive off.

"Oh, no, don't you try that with me."

"Try what? I'm not doing anything." I tried to sound both innocent and sexy at the same time.

"Just relax, it's about a half hour away so you should calm down a little."

"So, how was your night?" I asked him, deciding to move on.

Kingsley got excited and broke into a tale about how he singlehandedly saved a family when their car got in an accident. The more he told the story, the more I realized he may have been exaggerating a little bit. But I thought it was cute. It wasn't like he was lying. He was just embellishing the story to impress me. I was sure he really did help with the rescue, and to be honest, I was a little flattered that he wanted to astound me.

I continued to listen to his story, completely taken by how animatedly he talked. He just had this way about him that sucked me in. One day, he'd tell his kids the best bedtime stories.

My eyes grew wide as I panicked a little. Where had that thought come from? I couldn't believe I was thinking of him like that. Shaking my head, I pushed those thoughts away and let him finish his story. By the time he was done, we were pulling into the parking lot of a giant building. It looked like a bubble in the middle of a field. I had no idea what it was nor any idea what we were going to be doing there. But at least it didn't look like we would be braving the elements, so that was a plus.

"I still don't understand what we're doing here," I told him when he put the Range Rover in park.

"I know." Kingsley leaned over me to reach into the glove compartment. He pulled out a red blindfold and winked at me. "Do you trust me?"

"Um, why?"

"Because I want you to be really surprised. Now, turn your head so I can put the blindfold on you."

"We really don't have to. I can just close my eyes. I promise I won't peek," I insisted.

Kingsley raised his eyebrows at me and tilted his head in judgment. "We both know you'll cheat and ruin the surprise."

"Fine," I said, succumbing to him. I turned my head and he placed the blindfold over my eyes.

"Okay, turn back and let me know if you see anything."

"No, I can't—"

He quickly cut me off with a kiss. He held the back of my neck and pulled me closer to him. At first, I didn't like the sensation. I had no idea what was going to happen next and I was positive that I was going to fall off the seat and break the gear shift. But Kingsley held me down and slowly lowered the seat a few inches.

I was almost laying down while he was leaning on top of me. His hand started moving up my body and the anticipation made me squirm. Then he stopped kissing me and gently blew in my ear. His hands were now suddenly on my hips. Everything he did was slow and deliberate. Kingsley didn't slide his hands over me, but rather placed them as he felt my body. I didn't know where he was going to touch next, where he was going to kiss next, what he would do with his tongue, and I was even more aroused than normal.

The other times he had touched me were nothing like this. Before, my pulse was racing because I was nervous I'd do something wrong, but here, in the middle of a random parking lot, with a blindfold on, it felt like I could just let all of my inhibitions go. I couldn't do anything wrong, because Kingsley was in control. It was like my brain was shut off and it was the best feeling in the world. Nothing else mattered as it was just the two of us.

Then it stopped. "Whoa there. Sorry, seeing you in a blindfold distracted me for a second. This isn't our date."

"Well, what is?" I was a little disappointed, but I figured I could keep the blindfold for later.

"Come on, I'll help you out of the car."

"How about I take the blindfold off to get out of the car, and then you can put it back on?"

"Don't you trust me, Annabelle?"

I took a deep breath and nodded. "I trust you."

"Good," he whispered in my ear.

I heard his door slam and a minute or so later I heard my door open. He grabbed my hand and turned me slowly. Before I knew it, I was up in the air, Kingsley lifting me out of my seat. Frankly, I was way too clumsy to try to get out of the SUV blindfolded, so I was glad he was looking out for me. He was getting to know me pretty well.

Kingsley held my hand tight with one hand and had the other wrapped around my waist. I felt safe in his arms. After all, he was a firefighter.

"Okay, I'm gonna open the door," he instructed after a few minutes of walking. "When you step inside, you can take the blindfold off."

I nodded, almost too excited to speak. I felt a rush of warm air finally hit my face, and I assumed he opened the door. Then his hand returned to my waist as he led me inside.

"All right, take the blindfold off," he chanted as he pulled me to the right.

I yanked it off and my mouth fell open at what I saw.

We were in a massive room. It looked like a gymnasium without the basketball hoops or the stands. In their place was a winter wonderland. There were giant Santa statues everywhere and each one had a different type of suit, elaborate carvings, and bright colors. The Christmas tree in the center was massive and the ornaments were the size of my hand. Snowflakes about three feet tall hung on the walls and glistened in the sparkling lights that were draped over anything that stood still. But the best part was the carnival rides. I loved amusement parks and Kingsley had remembered I'd said that on our first date.

"This is the most amazing place I've ever seen," I whispered in awe as my head swiveled from side to side.

"There are no other amusement parks near here that are open in January. This place is actually open year round. They change the decorations for the season. We hit Carmine's Winter Wonderland's last week. They're about to turn it into a Valentine's Day festival." Kingsley took my hand and kissed my knuckles.

I looked down at our linked hands and then back up into those beautiful eyes. "It's perfect. Which ride should we go on first?" I asked as I zoned in on the Tilt-A-Whirl. It was my favorite.

"Why don't you look around and I'll go get the wristbands we need to go on the rides? I'll be right back."

"Thanks." I wondered off and headed to one of the display boards.

Santa Claus has been around for thousands of years. But it isn't his longevity that makes him so legendary. Nor is it the effect he has on children. We can all admit it is beautiful to see a child light up when they open up a gift marked "With Love, From Santa," but it is the effect he has on adults that is captivating. Santa has the ability to take an adult and remind them of beautiful memories from their past, instill them with hope, and reignite the child within so many of us forget about. As you walk around the festival, try to keep the spirit of Santa in your heart.

I smiled as memories of my childhood did flash through my mind. I remembered sneaking down the stairs to try to catch a glimpse of Santa. Instead, I saw my parents cuddled up on the couch. There was a roaring fire and their laughter filled the air. It was a beautiful moment, and even as a small child I recognized the love in their eyes. My dad traveled a lot for work and it was rough on my mom. However, it was the little moments like this that reminded me how much they cared for each other. The funny thing was they got married two months after they first met. My dad proposed three weeks in because he knew she was the one for him.

Kingsley and I had been seeing each other for a week. As he walked over to me, I couldn't help but wonder if he was the guy for me. He rushed the rest of the way to me, a smile plastered on his face and a glisten in his eye. I sighed as tingles spread through my system. I didn't know if we would be getting married anytime soon, but I did know he was beginning to matter to me. I just hoped he felt the same way. If I had to guess, I'd say that look in his eyes wasn't one he flashed at everyone.

"So, what first?" he asked.

"Tilt-A-Whirl, it's my favorite."

"Eh, I'm not a big fan of that. Why don't we head to the Ferris Wheel? We can look over everything and kind of take it in. Then we can plan out the rest of the day. Besides, I know how much you like to take pictures, you can probably get some good shots up there." Kingsley gave my hand a little kiss and pulled me over to the Ferris Wheel line.

I was a little sad because there wasn't a line for the Tilt-A-Whirl while the line for the Ferris Wheel was crazy, but this was Kingsley's show, so I wanted to please him. There would be time for the Tilt-A-Whirl later.

We got in line and began to wait our turn. "Are you a big Christmas fan?" I asked.

"Yeah, my parents always make a big deal about

it. They throw this massive party every year with, like, two hundred people in attendance. I've been going to that party since I was able to walk. It's a lot of fun and I usually invite a bunch of friends. We steal some booze, maybe something a little harder, and find a spot away from the parents."

My face fell a little. Did he say something harder? Maybe Kyle had a point. I forced a smile and leaned into him so that I could whisper in his ear. "So, you actually do use drugs?"

Kingsley gave me a little wink. "Well, sometimes we like to have a little fun, but nothing like what an addict would be in to."

I looked at him a little differently. Was he a user? Did I just get in the car with a drug abuser? This was freaking perfect. I finally found a guy I could really see myself with and who knew what he was in to.

"What do you do? Heroin or cocaine or something?"

He chuckled a second and shook his head. "No, sometimes I take some pills. It's not a big deal."

"Are you on them now?" My heart was racing. What if he had the pills with him? He'd mentioned needing them for his migraine but maybe that wasn't it. Could he have been lying to me? What if the cops found out? Would I go to jail too? I could definitely not go to jail. I wouldn't last a couple hours behind bars.

"No, relax. I did some pot in high school but I don't really do that anymore. Only when I'm crazy stressed, and I haven't needed to do that since I met you." He smiled, stroking my cheek lightly.

"Is that it?" I knew a lot of people did pot, and, yeah, it was wrong, but I could live with that, especially if he didn't do it while we were together. Maybe I could change him.

"Well, sometimes I take a Ritalin when I need a little extra energy. When I'm heading to a fire, I'll pop one to increase my focus. If I didn't take it, I could miss someone. Do you have any idea how dark it is in a fire? It's not like I can just turn my cell phone flashlight on. I'm just trying to be a better firefighter. Don't you want that?"

"Well, when you put it that way…" I was trying to be supportive, but I didn't think I sounded convincing.

"Exactly. I only want to be a better firefighter. Yeah, I made some mistakes when I was younger and I used stuff I shouldn't have, but I know better now. You know me, I'm not an addict." He sounded so self-assured and inspiring. I didn't like that he was using pills, but it was just Ritalin. It wasn't like he was using anything too rough. People used that on a regular basis when they needed to focus in school.

"Right, I didn't think you were but—"

"Next," the guy at the front of the line called to us.

I gave him a soft smile and Kingsley took my hand to help me into the car.

"Look, it kind of slipped out," Kingsley said, shrugging his shoulders. "I didn't want you to get upset. We're here and it would be a shame to waste all of this." He waved his arm in the air and sighed heavily. Then he leaned his forearms on his knees and looked up at me through his impossibly thick lashes. "Okay, the pills aren't a big deal to me. I'm already a pretty kick ass firefighter, so I can stop them if you want me to. I won't have the edge anymore, but I don't think it will have that much of an impact on me. If it matters to you, I'll stop, because that's how much I am beginning to care about you."

I took his hand and closed my eyes for a second. "Do you really think it helps you? Don't people use it to get high?"

"Is that what you think I'm doing? Do you think I would risk it if I didn't think it made me better? It's not about the way it makes me feel, it's about what it can make me do."

"Just please don't do it around me. I don't want to get caught with them and I really don't want to be around people when they're doing it."

"Done! Now, let's enjoy this." Kingsley quickly hopped from his seat across from me and moved to my side. He wrapped his arm around my neck and reached for my chin with his other hand. Gently, he pulled my face close to his and gave me a kiss. It was sweet, tender, and almost loving.

When he let go, my eyes stayed closed for a moment or two longer as I tried to settle the intense effect those lips had on me.

"You are so beautiful."

I looked down and blushed bright red. I still wasn't used to being called that, and definitely not while sitting this close to someone who really meant it.

"I've been trying to think of the best time to ask

this since that first night we hung out. Looking out at this festival, there is no one else I'd rather share it with than you. So, Annabelle, I think it's time we become official."

"Do you mean it?" I felt a warmth flow through me as I became unbelievably giddy. The frustration of the drug use quickly subsided at the thoughts of a future with him. I'd help him see he didn't need the drugs anymore and he'd be the man I wanted him to be.

"Yes, I want to be with you and only you. Hell, I don't even want you looking at another guy when I'm around. Golfing with Jason was killing me. I don't share with anyone."

"Well, you don't have to worry about Jason. He has a girlfriend, and I don't want you to share. I would love to be exclusive."

Kingsley grabbed the back of my neck with both hands and pulled me into a rough and passionate kiss. "Uh, I was so nervous."

"You don't have any reason to be nervous. Don't you see how happy you make me?"

"Yeah, and I also see how Jason's gaze lingers a little too long on you. He may have a girlfriend, but she isn't the only one he's thinking about." Kingsley slid away from me a few inches and dropped his hands in his lap. His brow was creased and I saw a slight tick in his jaw. He looked upset.

I slid over to him and placed a hand on the side of his face, moving it slightly so that he had to look at me. "Listen to me, you're not the first person to think he has feelings for me. But you're wrong. He is in love with his girlfriend. Besides that, I don't feel that way about him. You're the one I want to be with." I tried to sound as sure as possible. It was only a little lie. Obviously, I did have some feelings for Jason, but I almost never thought of him when I was with Kingsley. He really was the one I wanted to be with. I just hoped Kingsley believed me.

He leaned his face into my hand and nuzzled it lightly. "I believe you, but I'd still feel better if you two didn't spend any alone time together."

I laughed too loud and it was a little obnoxious. "You don't have to worry about that. Jason, Violet, and I get a lot of crap because the three of us rarely go anywhere apart. And lately, Jason and I haven't been seeing eye to eye on things so it won't be an issue."

"You have no idea how good that makes me feel. I'm glad you agree." Kingsley kissed me again but quickly let go. We had made the full circle and it was time to get off the Ferris Wheel. He quickly jumped out and then extended his hand. Thrilled at what a constant gentleman he was, I placed my hand in his and walked a little taller back into the festival.

"What now?" I asked as we started to walk around. But Kingsley didn't get a chance to answer. A band took the stage and we heard the sounds of "I'll Be Home for Christmas." "Aww, I love this song," I told Kingsley as I walked over to the stage. There were four people on the stage, a singer, a drummer, a guitarist, and a piano man. But only the singer and pianist were in the spotlight. She sounded so amazing and my hand flew to my mouth as I took it in.

137

Kingsley quickly spun me around so that I was facing him. "Dance with me."

I bit my lip as a giant smile spread across my face. This would be my first slow dance with a guy. Well, second if you counted homecoming with Kyle. I didn't, since we didn't have those feelings for each other. I nodded and Kingsley took me in his arms.

We twirled in a small circle with his hands on my lower back and my arms wrapped around his strong neck. Then, when I thought the moment couldn't get any more perfect, Kingsley pulled me closer and began to sing along softly in my ear. He had a rich baritone voice and was actually pretty good. I closed my eyes and leaned against his chest. This would rank as one of the best moments of my life.

As the song ended and we separated, I was actually really disappointed. Kingsley seemed to recognize it. He gave me another soft kiss and then whispered in my ear, "Don't worry, babe. This won't be our last dance."

"Good."

We spent the rest of the day going on the rides. However, the Tilt-A-Whirl had broken down, so we didn't get to go on it. Kingsley insisted this was a good thing and that I should definitely pick a new favorite ride. I was actually thinking the Ferris Wheel might be a good replacement.

Kingsley and I were heading to get a late lunch when his cell phone rang. He made a few grunting and agreement noises and then hung up. "Sorry, babe, I have to check out early. They need me to be on call for the night and I don't want to have to ditch you if I have to go in."

"No, that's totally okay. I have to get back and check on Violet anyway."

"Are you sure you want to be hanging out with her? I really am worried all of her drama is going to put you at risk."

"I appreciate your concern, but I have a feeling the drama is going to be ending soon. She has a private investigator working to resolve all of this." I tried to be hopeful but I was just as nervous as he seemed to be. But then again, I tended to worry a lot.

Kingsley dropped me off at the dorms and I rushed to Violet's room. I knew there was a chance she was with Berneli, but I figured it couldn't hurt to look.

As it turned out, she wasn't there. I grabbed my phone and gave her a call.

Violet answered but I could barely understand her through the tears.

"Just tell me where you are. I'm coming there."

She managed to say that she was with Berneli and begged me to bring Jason. I wanted to tell her that Kingsley would be pissed if I was in the car alone with him, but Violet needed us. Kingsley was becoming important to me, but Violet already was.

I took a deep breath and texted Jason. I told him Violet needed us and I'd be picking him up in five minutes. I quickly changed into leggings and a comfy sweater. Then it was off to break my promise to my boyfriend and to make my best friend feel better. After all, hoes before bros.

Jason had insisted on driving, something about doubting my abilities while the roads still had snow on them, so I grumbled as I climbed into the front seat of his car. I was not a fan of this cocky attitude.

"Do you have any idea what's going on? I thought she was seeing Finn." Jason asked me as he pointed the car toward Berneli's apartment. He had the address in his GPS. I realized he probably had never been there before, since the other day was my first time.

"No, she decided not to because of all the snow. Plus, she mentioned the investigator figured something out. When she called, she was too upset to speak. I was hoping Berneli would cut in, but nothing." I looked down at my fingernails and tried to busy myself with the chipped polish.

He pulled into a spot in front of the apartment complex. Someone must have just plowed because the spots were mostly free. Considering I didn't have a shovel, or even gloves, I was definitely glad for that. Then the thought of Kingsley plowing the street outside Christie's house crossed my mind. A rush of guilt washed over me and I quickly reached for the door handle to get out of the car. But Jason reached out and held my arm gently.

"Just wait a second, I want to talk to you about something." He loosened his grip on my arm and ran the back of his knuckles over his face.

I looked straight ahead at the windows to the lobby and tried not to meet his intense stare. Kingsley had been so good to me, and here I was going against his wishes. He deserved better than me. I really should get out of the car; it wasn't like

Jason and I were on the best terms anyway. Yet something had me pinned to my seat. I needed to know what he was going to say.

"Listen, I owe you an apology. I judged Kingsley too harshly and said some nasty things to you. It's not my place to say anything about your relationship."

We were silent for a few seconds and I turned to look at him. Jason gave me a weak smile and his dimples started to appear. My breath caught in my throat and I tried to contain the tears that were fighting to come out. Truth be told, I'd missed him and how easy it was for the three of us to be together.

"I also said some things I shouldn't have. I didn't mean to criticize you and Janice," I replied, trying to smile back at him.

"Thanks. I'm glad we can move past this. I think Vi will need us at our best." Jason opened his door and got out. He was right, we needed to get it together so we could be there for Violet. Her problems were much bigger than the petty crap Jason and I were fighting about.

As I exited the car, I started to slip. I tried to grab the door to keep myself upright but it was slick with snow and I couldn't get a grip. I closed my eyes tight and braced for impact. But it never came. Confused, I opened my eyes and looked up into the light blue eyes of Jason. He had walked around to my side of the car, apparently to help my clumsy ass. Now he was holding me in a dip with a playful look on his face.

He didn't pull me up straight away. Instead, I

hung there as we just looked at each other. It was different from when Kingsley looked at me. I felt adored and special whenever he stared deep into my eyes. But with Jason, I felt a little confused and maybe a little uncomfortable. Something in me stirred and I didn't know how I felt about it. Maybe it was like the feeling you got going up a giant hill on a rollercoaster. Some people really liked that feeling of anticipation while others dreaded it. The jury was currently out as to which group I was in.

"It's a good thing I didn't trust you to walk on your own. We might be on the way to the hospital," Jason teased as he finally pulled me to my feet.

"It's your parking job," I insisted, walking slowly on the sidewalk to the entrance of the apartment building. "You parked right next to a giant pile of snow. I bet you did it on purpose."

"Obviously, I really wanted to see you wipe out."

"Then why did you catch me?"

"I guess I don't like being the bad guy."

"I figured as much," I said, and took Jason's extended hand. He clearly didn't trust me to make it inside on my own. Frankly, he was probably right. These were new boots that I'd gotten for Christmas and I definitely should have scuffed up the soles a little before I wore them. I just wasn't getting any traction.

We walked the rest of the way in silence as I tried to ignore the return of the rollercoaster feeling in my stomach. His hand was warm and seemed to radiate heat up my arm and straight through my soul.

Elton Hall Chronicles: Second Snowfall

An attendant opened the lobby door for us and we walked in. It wasn't until we were entering the elevator that I realized we were still holding hands. I thought about letting go. It was on my mind the entire ride up to Berneli's floor. But for some reason, I couldn't get my hand to cooperate. I kept hoping Jason would let go on his own and I wouldn't have to worry about my decreased motor function.

Finally, as the elevator opened, Jason released my hand and let me exit before him. I walked quickly to the apartment, desperate to be in mixed company. I shouldn't be alone with him. I didn't even know where that came from. It wasn't something we'd done before…well, except at that hockey game.

I knocked on Berneli's door and he was quick to answer. "Hey, guys, come on in."

I almost ran in and saw Violet, a puffy mess of tissues and snot, balling her eyes out on the couch. "Oh, honey. What the hell is going on?" I asked, rushing to her side.

She tried to speak but was quickly taken over by a plague of hiccups. She grabbed a used tissue and tried to wipe her face. Jason grabbed some paper towels from the kitchen and handed them to Violet, sitting on her other side.

"Vi, take a deep breath. What's going on?"

She attempted to speak again but the hiccups worsened. Jason and Berneli both gave her a sympathetic look as Berneli leaned over the back of the couch and slowly massaged her shoulders.

I needed to break her out of this and get her to

talk, and it seemed there would only be one way to do it. I stood up and looked down at Violet. "Enough," I shouted at her. "Get it together. We can't help you if you don't calm down. All you're doing right now is getting snot all over this beautiful couch and Jason's shoulder. That's gross and really unnecessary."

"Annabelle," Jason scolded, trying to stop my outburst.

"No, Jason. This isn't helping anyone. Tell us what's going on so we can fix it. Once we know what's up, then you can go back to the blubbery mess, okay?" I said.

Violet looked up at me, a little shell-shocked. Her eyes were wide and her eyebrows were raised so high I could hardly tell the difference between them and her hairline. But she nodded and took a few deep breaths.

"Trent visited me with a message from Finn."

Chapter 9

"What the hell!" Berneli shouted. "Why didn't you tell me? Love, you should have mentioned that wanker stopped by. I would have—"

"You would have what? He already guessed I had a thing for you. We don't need to encourage that. Who would that help?"

Berneli nodded, but he didn't look all right. His jaw was clenched tight and he kept cracking his knuckles one at a time. Violet had mentioned to me that was a nervous habit of his and it drove her crazy.

"Okay, so what did he say?" I asked to break the spell.

"So. David dropped me off at my dorm for a few minutes. I needed to grab a few books so I could do some homework. He was waiting for me at the door." She looked over at Berneli and he brushed her cheek lightly.

Violet, empowered by her man, continued her story. "He didn't tell me how or why but he said Finn got in touch with him, told him he knew I

145

wasn't going to come. He's already mailed the picture." The tears started again and she reached for one of the paper towels Jason had waiting for her. After blowing her nose, she looked at Berneli and held his hand.

"I'm sorry about this," she managed to get out.

Berneli slammed his fist onto the couch and raked his fingers through his hair. Then he took a deep breath and looked back at Violet. "I don't regret a moment of this. You have been my sanctuary. I will resign on Monday. There is no way this will affect your future."

"It might be too late," I piped up, almost regretting interrupting their moment. Everyone looked at me and I spoke softly. "The affair happened while you were employed with the school. You quitting just confirms the rumor. Violet would still be at fault. I looked up the rules and some similar cases. I wanted to be prepared if something like this happened."

"Is there any way out?" Jason asked me.

"I'll keep looking, but I haven't found anything yet." I motioned to Jason, and pulled him to the side.

"What's up?"

"Let's just give them a moment to themselves. Berneli probably wants to talk to her."

"We'll be in the hall so you guys can talk for a second."

Jason and I went outside and I slumped against the wall.

"It will be fine. This is probably the best case scenario. Who knows what would have happened if she went to see him in jail. So it's a picture of them kissing. That doesn't prove an affair happened, and it certainly looks bad coming from the guy Vi put in jail. We don't know what's going to happen." Jason slid down the wall and sat next to me. "There's a chance it could work out. Worst case, she gets kicked out of school. At least she's not hurt."

I rubbed my face with my hands, ignoring my make-up. "I hope you're right. I didn't have a lot of friends in high school. If she gets kicked out of school, I—"

"You'll have me. I'm not going anywhere," he promised, draping an arm around my shoulder, and I leaned against him.

I didn't have the heart to say I might not have him either. I liked Kingsley, but I didn't want him to be the only person in my life. That was too much time together. I'd have to talk to Kingsley. I still needed Jason in my life.

"What were you up to today?"

"This is probably not the time to mention it but, uh, well, you wanted me to be honest, right?"

He nodded and I continued. "Well, I went on a date with Kingsley today and we decided to become official."

Jason's face fell and he pulled his arm from around me. "Good, that's good."

"If it were so good, then why do you look like I told you that your cat was run over?"

"Well, I've had that cat for many years, and if he were run over, I'd be devastated."

I hit his arm. "I'm serious. I don't want this creating any more problems between us. You're my

147

friend too."

He stood up and paced in the hallway. "I don't know. There is just something about him that sets me off. And he's such an ass around the dorms. Do you really think he's going to be cool with us hanging out all the time?"

"Kingsley might have mentioned that it bothers him when we're together, alone."

"See, that's what I mean. Why is he trying to control who you're with?"

"He's not. He's just threatened by you and our friendship."

"But why?" He knelt down in front of me, his face inches from mine. "Is there a reason for him to feel threatened?"

The door opened and Violet was standing there, mouth open, eyes wide.

"I'm sorry, I'll leave you two alone." She closed the door.

"We definitely can't do this now." I got up quickly, stumbling and tripping over Jason's shoelaces. I grumbled, frustrated, and turned to look at him. "Just tie your shoes and meet me inside."

Berneli walked around the couch and knelt in front of Violet. He put his hands on her knees and looked up at her. "Listen to me. I don't care what he says. I'm not leaving you. If Trent can just walk up to you, then I'm afraid for you. It's a nightmare to think those two might be teaming up."

Violet sighed and tears started to pour out of her eyes. "Do you think he's who left the flowers?"

Jason and I looked at each other and he had the same confused look on his face that I did. "It doesn't make sense. Why would Finn and Trent team up? How would they even know to do that?" I didn't think this was true. Someone must be pulling the strings. Neither one of those guys seemed that clever or manipulative. Yeah, they were jerks, but they weren't super sneaky.

"I don't know. But I'm just—"

"Violet, love, if these blokes are playing games, I think you need to spend a little more time at your place and less time here."

"What are you saying? Are you breaking up with me?" She grabbed his hands tighter, as if it was the only way to keep them together.

"No, I just think we need to keep apart until the investigator figures out what's going on. I don't think it should be much longer. If us being together is setting these wankers off, then I won't risk it. It's not about jobs or education, it's about your life. I'd hate to think that someone was following you."

"Someone has to be following you," I insisted. "Where do you think they got the picture?" I'd kept it in as long as I could. I was done trying to be strong for her. I needed to speak my mind.

"Not helping," Jason growled at me.

"What? We can't pretend like she isn't at risk."

"My love," Berneli interjected, and turned to look at Violet. "I'll call the investigator, and up my payment. We're going to get this sorted out soon. It won't be for long." Berneli reached out and gently wiped her tears away. "I'm going to end this. I'll tell them I caught you by surprise. Let me take the blame for this. I can get another job. They may even take me back in London. The dean of our program is one of my mates."

"Just promise me this isn't over," Violet begged him.

"Never." He leaned in and gave her a sweet kiss.

I stood up and tried to keep my own tears at bay. It was heart wrenching to watch the two of them together. Their love for each other was strong and I hated to think of this stalker playing with them. It wasn't fair and it was affecting me. To make matters worse, looking at how Berneli cared for Violet made me jealous. I hoped I would find someone who cared for me like that. Maybe I had. I couldn't help but think what Kingsley would do if he thought someone was trying to play the same games with me. All I could see was Kingsley going after Finn and Trent with a fire ax. I had to force back the smile as I pictured him standing up for me. I had no doubt he would. It probably wouldn't help, but it was nice to think I had someone willing to fight for me.

"Vi, why don't Annabelle and I leave you guys. I can pick you up tomorrow and we can grab some takeout and watch a couple movies. Annabelle and I will be there for you. It won't take forever for this to be dealt with. Have some faith in Berneli's investigator." Jason walked over to me and placed his hand on my lower back. "Come on. You said it yourself, they need to be together."

I made eye contact with Violet and she nodded her head, indicating it was all right for me to leave, so I let Jason lead me out of the apartment. We drove in silence and were in the parking lot of the dorms before it all overwhelmed me. I was scared.

Scared for what could happen to Violet, scared for Berneli, and scared for what their future could be. What if something else happened to her? After last semester, she didn't deserve it.

Jason looked at me and placed a hand on my knee. "Don't cry. You heard Berneli. The private investigator is going to handle it and they will be fine."

I turned to look at him but I barely saw his face through my own tears. I forced them away, disgusted at myself. I didn't do tears and here I was balling. "Jason, she barely got away last time. She's my best friend and she's in danger. Like, real danger, and I can't do anything. Finn is in jail, and that's awesome, but what about this sidekick? What if…" I managed before my body started shaking.

He got out of the car and opened my door for me. I climbed out and Jason pulled me into a hug. He started stroking my back and I crumbled into him. "Come on, let me get you back to your room. Those tears are going to freeze to you pretty face and then we're not going to be able to take you anywhere."

I started laughing and we walked up to my room. Earlier, I had been scared to have him in my car, and here he was coming up with me to my room. Kingsley was going to freak out if he found out, but I needed Jason. I didn't want to be alone just yet. I knew I couldn't tell Kingsley exactly what was going on with Violet, but maybe if I explained to him that things had gotten bad, he'd understand exactly why I needed Jason. He wasn't available to be there for me at the moment.

Jason followed me in and I walked over to my bed. "Hungry?" Jason asked as he sat down in the desk chair.

"Yeah, I think we definitely need some Chinese food."

Jason nodded and took his phone out. The two of us had spent enough time together that he knew my order by heart. I loved the sweet and sour chicken with steamed dumplings and egg rolls. Actually, I definitely needed more egg rolls. Tonight was going to be a comfort food extravaganza. I was about to tell Jason to get an extra order but he held a finger up at me.

"Yes, we're going to need four orders of egg rolls." He finished ordering and smiled at me. "Is that going to be enough? I can call back and add to it."

"No, that's plenty. How much do I owe?" I got up and grabbed my wallet out of my purse. It was sitting on the desk in front of Jason where I left it when we walked in.

He stopped my hand and shook his head at me. "I got it, don't insult me. Come on, we need a distraction." Jason led me over to my bed and turned the TV on. "If you beg enough, I might even watch that stupid dating show you and Vi love so much."

"I think you actually like it too. Let's not deny that the drama gets you all excited." I took my laptop out from under my bed and hooked it up to the TV so I could stream it.

"Yeah, I'm sure that's what gets me excited." He climbed on the bed and settled in.

The food came and we chowed down. "What are we going to do about Violet?" I asked him as I inhaled my third egg roll.

"I'm working on something but I don't want to say it yet in case it doesn't work out. Between my plan and Berneli, no one is going to lay a hand on her and Finn's fuckin' letter won't matter."

I nodded but I still couldn't suppress the thoughts. "I just wish we knew why Trent was working with Finn and if he is the only one helping him. Then we could shut this down. It's not like Finn can actively do anything."

"Annabelle, look at me." Jason placed his hands on my knees. "Listen, we aren't going to let anything happen to Vi. If I have to walk her to and from class every day, to her dorm, wherever. Hell, I'll drive her to Berneli's and pick her up. If I need to, I'll sleep on his couch. She's my best friend too."

"The couch is actually very comfortable."

It took a moment but then I remembered. He and Violet were almost as close as I was with her. I now saw the hurt in his eyes, the wrinkle in his forehead, and the jitter in his leg. I had been so self-centered that I didn't think to check on him. He wasn't just saying these things to make me feel better, he needed to feel better too.

I didn't know who moved first, but we were hugging on my bed. He gently tucked my head into his neck and I tried to even my breathing as Jason stroked my hair. It was so relaxing that I closed my eyes for a second.

***

I woke up cuddled up next to Jason. His arm was wrapped around my back and our legs were intertwined. My hand was up his shirt and resting on his pec and his hand was on my upper thigh, my upper, upper thigh. He was breathing heavily, and at first I didn't want to wake him. Then I realized just how ridiculous that was. I sat up quickly and jarred Jason.

"What's going on?" I exclaimed.

Jason's eyes shot open and he jumped out of the bed. "You fell asleep and I figured I'd sit with you for a few minutes. I guess I must have passed out too."

I grabbed the cover and brought it up to my chin, even though I was still fully clothed. Then the guilt hit me hard. Yesterday, I became official with Kingsley and he asked me to start limiting my alone time what Jason. What was the first thing I did? Climbed into bed with him.

"No, we shouldn't be doing this. I'm sorry, but you need to leave. Kingsley is gonna freak out if he finds out."

"So that's what this is about? Your precious boy? Where was he last night, huh? Who was there for you when you fell apart? It was me. He knew this was going on and he didn't even check on you. We fell asleep, it was innocent. If he doesn't understand that, then he's a tool."

"Oh yeah, are you going to tell Janice?"

"She already knows. I texted her that you and Violet needed me and she said to take all the time I needed." Jason grabbed his shoes and put them on.

"But did you tell her it was just me? You made it seem like it was the three of us. Did you tell her that you were just with me, in my bed?"

"No, but what does it matter? Kingsley is the guy you're thinking of."

"He is, and I need to go see him. You're right, he is the person I should be leaning on right now."

"Fine, I'm leaving. Text me if you hear anything from Vi." Jason walked out and slammed the door a bit too hard.

I sat in bed, lost and confused. I desperately wanted to talk to Violet, but she had enough going on. Instead, I called Christie.

"Hey, I really need to talk. Can I meet up with you somewhere?"

"Yeah, I'm craving a coffee. Why don't we go to that café across from campus? From the sound of your voice, I'm thinking we're going to need some pastries too."

"You are probably right about that." We agreed to meet up in an hour. I needed to hop in the shower to wash off Jason's essence from my body.

I rushed getting dressed and didn't even bother putting make-up on. I was going to be early, but I didn't want to be in my room any longer. It turned out that I was about fifteen minutes early. Christie had sent me a text that she was also running early, so I wasn't going to be sitting by myself for too long. I ordered a coffee and a big cinnamon roll, then found a little table near the window.

By the time the barista announced my coffee was done, Ski Patrol Barbie was walking into the café. I smiled at Christie and she gave me a big hug. "Look at you. Did you get all dressed up for me?" I asked her as we let go.

"Obviously," she teased, and went to order her own coffee. She was wearing a beautiful red coat with a feathered hood. Her bright blonde hair fell over it in loose curls and her black wedge boots hugged her faux leather leggings perfectly. As with every time I saw her, her make-up was perfectly applied, and I was pretty sure she was wearing false eyelashes. It must take so much work for her to look this good but she made it look flawless.

She came back to the table with her drink and sat down. "Okay, what's going on?"

"Kingsley and I went to this beautiful winter festival and he asked me to be exclusive. So that was great. But then I got a call from Violet. She was devastated so Jason and I went over to see her."

I thought about how I was going to talk about Violet. It wasn't my place to tell her the big secret, but it was obviously important to my story. There was probably a way I could talk around it.

"Violet does have a boyfriend and she'll introduce you when she's ready. They want to keep the relationship on the down low, but something happened last year. One of the security guards attacked her because he was jealous. Luckily, Violet got away and he was put in jail. Now he's causing trouble again."

"But what can he do? He's in jail, right?"

"He is. Uh, it's a long story. Finn, the guard, is working with someone on the outside. Anyway, so that happened and I was really upset because I can't

156

do anything. I felt so useless and helpless. Jason and I went back to my dorm and chowed down on some food. But he was upset and I just hugged him because he's my friend and I love him too, but then we fell asleep."

"Okay, and…"

"And I just became exclusive with Kingsley and I was cuddled up with Jason, like, twelve hours later. Plus, Kingsley told me that he isn't comfortable with me hanging out alone with Jason anymore. I'm, like, the worst girlfriend on the face of the planet and I feel crazy guilty and I don't even know how that happened."

Christie put her coffee down and took a deep breath. When she looked back up at me, it was with sympathy and pain at the same time. "Oh, honey, it is not good to start a relationship with rules like that. If Kingsley wants to be with you, then he should trust you."

"I want to tell him to trust me. But then, as soon as he was unavailable, I turned to Jason. I mean, he's my friend and that's it. But what if Kinsley takes it a different way?"

"Like what? You and your friends had a dramatic day and your guy friend was there for you. I think the question you should be asking is why you turned to Jason and not Kingsley."

I sat there and pondered this. I didn't even text Kingsley good night. Then again, he didn't text me either. "I think I turned to Jason because he was there. Besides, Kingsley was on call last night with the fire department. I knew he couldn't be there for me even if I wanted him to be."

"Did you text him or anything?"

"No, but I figured he was probably at a fire or something."

"So nothing happened with Jason besides sleeping and cuddling?"

"Right."

"Well, do you think there is a reason for Kingsley to be jealous of Jason?"

"No. I want to be with Kingsley. Jason is just my friend. Besides, Jason has Janice and he cares about her too much to consider something else."

"What would he be considering?"

"You know, possibly having something with me."

"And why would he think that was a possibility?"

"I don't know. I haven't led him on or anything so if he thinks something more could happen, then…"

"Then what? We talked about this. He has feelings for you and I don't think you're as innocent as you think in the feelings department."

"Fine, I had feelings for him. You're the first I've admitted this to. Hell, it's the first time I've even said it out loud. But it doesn't matter. He has Janice."

"What if there was no Janice?"

"It doesn't matter, there is. Kingsley is good to me and I want to be with him."

"There is something to be said for fighting for your man."

"I am, I'm fighting for Kingsley because *he* is my man and I want to make it work." I nodded and took my phone out to text him. "He doesn't need to know about Jason, but I do need to see him today."

"Good. I mean, if that's what you want to do."

"It is," I told her, but she didn't look convinced. Luckily, she let go of whatever was bothering her.

"Anyway, tell me something about you. What's going on with your boyfriend? When are you going to see him again?"

"Um, hopefully soon. He has a break from school coming up so he's going to be out to see me."

"It's nice that you're making this relationship work long distance."

"Our families have been friends for years so he's kinda always been around. But it's nice to have a little distance every now and then. That whole absence makes the heart grow fonder crap."

"So, is he the one? I know you kinda mentioned that before."

"I mean, it's still the plan. But I don't know. He is such a nice guy and very good looking. My parents would be so excited if we got married. I feel like my mom is planning the wedding in her head already. But sometimes I wonder if this is enough. You know?"

"I do, but if your parents like him, maybe there is a reason for it. I doubt they'd want you to be unhappy."

"Right, and I think my parents do know me pretty well, but I never really dated before this. They didn't let me. I mean, obviously, I had some boyfriends that I kept quiet, but nothing too serious. Frankly, I almost wish I could have some more time to play the field, or at least to pick my own man."

I was about to respond when Kingsley texted me. He was heading to the station because there was a fire and he was called in to help. He didn't know what time he would be done, but he guessed it would be a couple of hours.

"Well, I won't really be able to see him. He's at a fire."

"So? Stop by the firehouse in some sexy lingerie."

My mouth dropped open. There was no way I could do that. "Um, I don't even own a piece of lingerie. I have, like, a million pairs of underwear, but they're all…practical."

"All right, that's a problem. Let's go." Christie got up and motioned for me to join her.

"Wait, where are we going?" I asked as I chased after her.

"Shopping. It doesn't matter who you're doing, you need to look good doing it."

Chapter 10

I'd never been so embarrassed in my life. Christie shoved me into a dressing room and insisted on grabbing things for me to try on. They were skimpy, lacy, and I would never be caught dead in any of them.

"Christie, you need to go easy on me. This is too much," I begged when she handed me a black teddy with a matching thong and dark patches over the breasts. The rest was completely see-through. "I'm not on this level yet and my thighs will never be on this level. I think my ass would eat these panties."

"Okay, give me a second. I'll try again."

I sat down on the little seat in the room and anticipated the worst. Surprisingly, I was actually impressed with what Christie brought. She handed me a pair of grey boy shorts that had lace connecting the sides and a black lacy tie up the front. They were subtly sexy. There was a matching bra with lace all over it and a see-through band. Sending her out of the dressing room, I took my clothes off and slipped into it. As I looked at my

161

reflection, I instantly felt sexier. This was a new feeling and I kind of liked it, but more importantly, Kingsley was going to like it.

"How does it look?" Christie asked while shaking the curtain.

"Um, I actually think I'm gonna buy it."

"Really? I'm coming in."

"Wait, what?" I asked, but it was too late. Christie walked into my dressing room and took a good look at me.

"Dang, girl, Kingsley is one lucky man."

"Thanks. I feel good in it." I looked in the mirror again, turning around to stare at my butt, surprised that I actually liked how pronounced it looked in the boy shorts.

"Let's get it and get you all sexy so you can drop by the fire station. Maybe you can meet up with Kingsley and give him a little taste."

"I think I will." I changed and headed straight to the cash register.

As we headed back to the car, my secret weapon in hand, I had a little bit of a panic attack. I'd bought lingerie. There was only one reason for a girl to buy lingerie and I didn't know how I felt about that.

"What's wrong?" Christie asked, noticing my silence.

"Actually, I think we should return the lingerie."

"Why? You just said you loved it."

"I don't think I'm ready for what it means. I'm still a virgin," I told her as I turned around and started to walk to the store.

Christie grabbed my arm and stopped me.

"Okay, just because you bought it doesn't mean you have to have sex tonight or tomorrow. You can keep it until you're ready. It made you feel good, right?"

"Yeah, it did."

"Then keep it. Wear it under your clothes when you want to feel confident. Wear it to sleep to have sexy dreams. Who cares? Lingerie is supposed to make you feel even better than you look. Come on, I'm going to unlock the car. Climb in the back and put the underwear on."

"No, I'm not changing in a car. Anyone could be walking by."

"Oh, don't be so innocent. The windows are tinted so no one is gonna see you. Just put it back on and if you don't feel more confident, sexy, or even a bit more relaxed, then we'll return it."

"Fine," I grumbled, and slid into the back. I put on the bra and panties while covering myself the best I could. Once I pulled my clothes back on top of the lingerie, it was almost magical how I instantly sat up a little straighter. They were like magic lingerie. I climbed out of the car and smiled at Christie. "You're right, I love the way I feel. I think it's something to do with the lace. I've never worn it before."

"Work it, girl. Besides, you don't have to have sex if he sees you in it. You could just have some fun."

"Yeah, you're right. But then again, at the festival, I had this feeling when I was with him. What if he's the one? What if this is the guy I've been saving myself for? He really seems to care. If I want to make this work with Kingsley, maybe I need to give us a shot. Maybe this is what I need to do."

"As much as I'm all for sex, you don't want to just do it like that. Is that how you want your first time to be?"

"No, it's coming out wrong. I just mean that it might help our relationship move further and prove I'm serious."

"Are you sure about this?"

We got in the car and, as she turned the heat on, I smiled at her. "We've done a lot up to this point and it feels amazing. I think I'm ready. Besides, isn't this what you do in college? Try these things out?"

"Actually, this might be good for you. You can experience it, and hopefully it will bring you two closer." She nodded and sounded hopeful.

Christie drove me back to my dorm and helped me get ready to surprise Kingsley.

***

How did I get here? I was sitting in my car, wearing the new underwear and a sweater dress with leggings. Christie tried to get me to just wear a coat, but I wasn't at that level yet. So instead, my sweater had buttons down the front and Christie decided that the striptease I could give Kingsley with it was even better than the jacket.

Kingsley had said the fire was going to take a little while, so I took my time getting pretty. I let Christie put a bit more make-up on me than I normally allowed and we curled my hair. I felt a bit like Violet, and even sent her a picture. She was so angry that I let someone else do my make-up.

It had been about two and a half hours since Kingsley texted about the fire, so I was hoping he would be done soon. My nerves were not going to stay up for a whole lot longer. Thankfully, I didn't have to wait. The firetruck pulled in about fifteen minutes after I did. Kingsley, in all of his glory, climbed out of the truck in his uniform and I about had a panic attack. Some people made jokes about men in uniforms, but I understood it now. There was something about the fireman's jacket, hat, boots, and pants that had me practically panting. He had some ash on his face but a smile almost covered it. He was in his prime and practically shaking with exuberance. At that moment, he was the sexiest man I'd ever seen in person.

I opened the door and decided it was now or never. "Kingsley," I called out to him as he was taking his boots and pants off.

He looked over to me and gave me a big smile. "Hey, babe, you look amazing." He pulled me into a hug and gave me a little kiss on the lips.

"Thanks. I missed you," I gushed, placing my hands on his chest. "Aww, you looked so good in that uniform."

Kingsley bit his lip a little and his eyes seemed to darken. "Oh yeah? Is it working for you?"

"You could say that."

"How would you feel if I said I was a major part of saving someone's house?"

"I would feel…" I wanted to say something sexy so I quickly thought over my options. I could say I felt aroused and exhilarated or I felt like falling into his arms so he could ravish me. But I couldn't do it, and instead I said, "I feel like getting a tour from the sexiest man in the building." It was close enough.

"I could definitely do that." Kingsley reached out to take my hand and I noticed it was shaking like crazy. I fed off his energy but tried not to bounce as I followed him into the station.

***

Before we walked in, Kingsley grabbed a spare t-shirt from his Range Rover. He was pretty sweaty from the fire. I kind of found it hot, but I definitely appreciated it when he sprayed some cologne and covered the weird chemical smell coming off of him. In his fresh fire department t-shirt, smelling like a mix of ocean and fresh air, he looked like he could star in a calendar.

We walked into the station hand in hand to a loud group of cheers and jarring. Kingsley introduced me to some of the guys as we walked around. They teased him a bit for bringing a girl in, but Kingsley seemed to appreciate the attention. He didn't let me take more than one step away from him the entire time. We went through the station, stopping in almost every room for Kingsley to introduce me as his girlfriend. I loved hearing that word, but most importantly, I loved hearing the pride in his voice when he said it.

He was taking me out to show me the truck when I finally felt courage flow through me. It may have been the underwear, hearing Kingsley brag about me, or my hormones kicking into overdrive, but whatever it was, I took hold of it fiercely and tapped Kingsley on the shoulder. He turned to look at me and I motioned for him to come closer. I leaned in to whisper in his ear, trying desperately to sound sexy. "Hey, so this isn't exactly why I came here. I was hoping we could go somewhere a little more private." Then I nibbled on his ear.

"Oh, I know just where we should go." He kissed my hand and pulled me along with him.

"This is one of my favorite rooms," Kingsley told me as he closed the supply room closet.

"Why?" I asked, a little confused. It was pretty dark and definitely not as exciting as the firetruck.

"Because there is a lock on the door." Kinsley reached behind me and turned the lock on the knob. He leaned forward and gave me a kiss.

"Wait," I said, pulling away from her for a second.

"Um, okay." Kingsley took a step back, raising his arms in surrender.

"You said this was your favorite room because it has a lock. Does that mean you've been, uh, you've been in this situation before?"

"No, but the thought has crossed my mind. You're the only girl I've wanted to bring back here."

I smiled and pulled him back toward me. As he leaned into me, I tried to let go of all the fear and trepidations flowing through my mind. I wrapped my arms around his neck and Kingsley held me close to him.

I broke the kiss and pushed him away slightly. "Just wait a second. I have something to show you."

I slid my jacket off and let it fall to the floor, kicking it to the side.

"What are you doing?" he asked, and raised his eyebrows at me.

"Don't say anything or I'm going to lose my nerve."

He nodded and waited for me to continue. I gradually started to unbutton my sweater dress, sliding it off my shoulders after undoing the last button. Then I reached for my leggings and slid them off, throwing both of them on top of my jacket. I stood there in front of him in the sexy lingerie I'd bought earlier, nervously waiting for his response.

"You are the sexiest woman I've ever seen, and that includes the chicks in porn."

"I bought this with you in mind."

"And you actually just got sexier." Kingsley pushed me up against the door. He kissed me hard and delved into my mouth. His hand slid up my naked torso and caressed my breast. As he circled my nipple, I let out a moan. His hands felt amazing and I arched my back, pushing my chest into him, trying to give him better access.

He kissed down my neck, along my chest, but stopped at the top of my bra. Lightly kissing the sensitive skin that only he had touched, softly grazing the lace at the top of the cup. I ran my fingers down his chest and felt his definitive muscles, but his shirt was still on so I reached my hands under it, afraid to break the kiss and have him remove it. Kingsley growled a little and bit my lower lip. My head fell back and hit the door lightly as I basked in the feeling of anticipation flowing through me. I decided it was time to step it up a notch.

It must have been the lingerie, but I was completely comfortable with this decision and I actually wanted to push forward. I lifted my leg up and he grabbed ahold my upper thigh. Kingsley broke the kiss and took a deep, ragged breath.

"I don't know what's gotten into you, but I like this girl."

"It's the underwear," I insisted, and gave him what I thought was a seductive look.

He must have bought it because he cupped my butt and nibbled on my ear. "Then I'll buy you a set for every day of the week." Kinsley ran his hand from my butt to my knee and then back up, digging his fingers into me. I groaned and moved his other hand to my ass, encouraging him to grab ahold of it.

As he squeezed my ass, he lifted me up at the same time. I wrapped my legs around his waist, terrified I was going to fall. As if he could read my mind he said, "Don't worry, babe, I've got you. I lift hoses that weigh a lot more than you."

He kissed me hard, his tongue exploring my mouth, and I tried to take control. I thought maybe it would keep me from changing my mind. He quickly shut that down.

Breaking the kiss, he looked at me and gave me a sexy but sinister look. "Let me do this. Give me the control."

I bit my lip a second time and then nodded. I was willing to do this his way mostly because I didn't really know what he was doing. He dropped his head to kiss my breast. He reached for my shoulders and slid my bra straps down so that he could grab my bare breast. As he stroked one nipple with his hand, he teased the other through my bra with his tongue.

I started to shift a little as I was uncomfortable. The sensation between my legs was practically burning and I craved more. I needed to get closer to him but he seemed to want to go slowly. This was not going to work for me.

"Kingsley, I want more," I begged him as I grabbed his shirt and yanked him closer to me.

"Whatever you want." He reached down and brushed the panties to the side. I took a deep breath as I felt him slide his finger inside me. It was the first time I'd let a guy near me but I wanted this. Hell, it felt so good I didn't know why I'd waited so long.

He slipped in and out of me with one finger at first and I felt a tightening inside me. It was amazing and I moaned louder and gripped his shoulders tighter. It still wasn't enough. I dug my nails into Kingsley's back and he let out a gasp.

"I can do better," he assured me as he inserted a second finger. It was even better than before and I couldn't keep it in anymore. I cried out in pleasure as he started to circle around my small nub. I tried to shift a little, hoping to satisfy the urges that were begging for me to be handled.

"I love it, babe. But it's not enough." I clung to his shoulders as I felt my body start to shake.

He placed me on the ground and pulled his shirt off. I reached out and rushed to undo his pants. As they slid down, I took a deep breath. Was I ready to do this? Now that I was this close, nervousness hit me. My first time was going to be in a supply closet of a firehouse. But then again, it was going to be with someone I really cared about and who clearly cared about me. Yesterday, I thought he could have been the one. Who else would I want to share this with? It was time to get this out of the way. Everyone said the first time was awful. I was ready to move into that love making side everyone always raved about.

Before I could second guess myself, I grabbed his boxers and yanked them down. He was huge. I couldn't believe it and I panicked a little. Was that actually going to fit inside me? I was going to enjoy finding out.

"I'm ready," I told him as I tried to breathe normally. I locked eyes with him and then slid off my own panties and unhooked my bra. I stood in front of him, naked, and waited for him to respond.

"I got this," Kinsley said excitedly, and reached into his wallet to get a condom. As he slipped it on, I smiled and pulled him in for a kiss. He picked me up again and slid inside of me. I felt a bit of pressure at first and closed my eyes tight against the bit of pain that was trying to ruin my time. But Kinsley kept on and I soon forgot the pain. Instead, I felt something else. It was like a raw sensation that overwhelmed any other thought coming to mind. I bit my lip to keep from calling out and ran my fingers through his hair, pulling as I felt myself beginning to get excited.

Kingsley, up against the door in the supply

closet, was actually hitting that elusive spot. I'd always heard guys struggled with that, but there he was, and I was coming undone in his arms. I focused on the feeling resonating from inside me and held onto it as I went over the edge. I called out his name and shook violently as the aftershocks flowed through me.

"Yes, babe," he said, and sped up a little bit. He pushed me harder against the wall and I felt him explode inside me.

He gently placed me on the floor and kissed me hard. "Now, *that* was fun."

Chapter 11

Kingsley walked me back to my car and lightly pushed me against the driver side door.

"Do I have more of these surprises to look forward to?" He thumbed the side of my breast teasingly through my coat.

I swatted his hand a little and smiled. "I don't know. I guess you'll just have to wait and see what I have planned for you. It's like my own surprise. Consider it payback."

"I guess that means I'll have to keep planning fun things for us to do so the payback never ends."

He winked at me as I climbed in my car and sped off.

I used the little bit of a drive to try to figure out how I felt. Some people felt really empty after their first time and some people felt a sense of disappointment. They put their virginity on a pedestal and then when it was gone, they were left wondering what the big deal was in the first place.

As I contemplated what it meant for me, I realized all I could focus on was how much I

173

wanted to do it again. It was amazing to turn my brain off and just let my body take over. I spent so much time focusing on consequences, possibilities, and problems. But when Kingsley's hands were on me, it was like all of the stress from the day was gone and I could focus on the physical side of things.

I headed to my dorm room and sat down on my bed. Then I jumped up, as if it were made of fire. The sheets smelled of the cologne I'd bought for Jason. I didn't want to remember that because then guilt would start to build up inside. Keeping this secret from Kingsley was going to eat me up. I stripped the sheets and tossed them in the hamper. I quickly remade the bed and tossed my collection of pillows onto the comforter. But now I had a clean bed, so I had to go shower.

By the time I was done, it was after two in the morning. I kicked myself for not calling Christie and Violet earlier. They were going to freak when they heard all about what happened. I lay down to get some sleep in the hopes I'd be able to calm my racing heart.

***

I woke up early on Monday and started to get ready for class. My first one was at nine that morning and I didn't want to be late. I was leaving the bathroom when Violet walked in to get her make-up ready.

"How are you doing?" I asked her gently.

"Uh, I came back here last night and I barely

slept. I was afraid of the dreams I would have and all sorts of crap."

"I could have come and crashed in Lola's bed, or you could have snuggled with me. You don't have to do this alone."

"I know. But I feel like I have to. I don't want to still be afraid of Finn. I don't want to think that maybe someone is hiding in the shadows."

"Well, let's do something about it. Maybe we can take some self-defense classes or something like that. It might make you feel more empowered."

"Yeah, I like that. We should look into it. I feel like it would make me more confident." She nodded and gave me a huge smile. "Now hurry up and get ready, I want to hear all about your date."

I told her about the winter festival and how we were exclusive now. Then I finally dropped the bomb about the lingerie and my v-card.

"Holy crap, are you serious?"

"I still can't believe it happened, but it was great."

"What was great?" Jason asked, walking up to us in the hallway.

I whipped around and looked at him with wide eyes. I wasn't going to tell him, but Violet jumped in.

"Violet and Kingsley hooked up yesterday."

I glared at her and she shrugged her shoulders as if to say, "Oh well."

"Wait, what? Just like that? Didn't you just meet him?" Jason growled.

"Don't judge me. We just have this amazing connection and it seemed right. Besides, why should you guys get to be the only ones having sex? It's a lot of fun."

"Actually, Jason—" Violet started to say, but Jason quickly cut her off.

"No, she's right. You two have fun. Who am I to stop you?" He gave me a hard look that I didn't appreciate and then turned to Violet. "So, Vi, how's everything going?"

"Annabelle and I decided to take some self-defense classes. I just feel like I need something like that to help me feel more confident."

"If you guys want, I could take you to the gun range after classes. We don't have anything to do with EET, and it's not like we have a lot to do to prepare for the meeting tomorrow."

"That sounds great. I'd feel like a badass. Let's do it," Violet insisted, giving us a big smile. "Do you actually know anything about guns?"

"Yeah, my dad has had me at the range for years. Believe it or not, I'm pretty lethal," Jason informed us with a sinister look.

Violet and I cracked up and I gave him a little shove. Picturing Jason with a gun just didn't seem right.

"No, seriously, you will be impressed. Meet me outside the dorms at four. I'll make a reservation."

***

My classes went smoothly and I was heading back to my room to drop my stuff off when I ran into Christie.

"What's up, sexy mama?" she asked, greeting

me with a hug. "How was last night? I've been dying to know how it went but I've been doing that whole respecting boundaries shit."

"Yeah, how'd that work out for you?"

"I don't have the patience for it, so tell me!"

"We did it in the supply closet of the firehouse." I blushed bright red but Christie barely had time to register it as she pulled me into a hug.

"Ah, I'm so happy for you. Well, I think. Was it good?"

"I enjoyed it. Kingsley, obviously, has done it before so he knew what he was doing. All I had to do was strip and hold on."

"My kind of girl! Make him do all the work, I like it." She smiled, nodding her head at me. "So, what are you up to now, round two?"

"We're actually going to head over to a gun range. Violet is just feeling a little concerned about the incident last semester and Jason thought it would be a good way to help her."

"That sounds like such a good idea. Do you guys mind if I come too? I like to go to the range and blow off steam."

"Are you an expert gunslinger?" I asked as I opened the door to my dorm for her.

"Obviously. I'm right up there with Bonnie from Bonnie and Clyde."

I dropped my bag and changed my boots to sneakers and Christie walked up to my bulletin board of pictures.

"Well, Jason claims to be an expert, so it will be great to have another pro there. You could help me and he could help Violet."

177

"That sounds perfect. I'll get you bitches in shape."

"But there is something else I need to talk to you about," I said quietly. "Jason is going to be there today."

"Yeah, you said that already."

"What do I do? If Kingsley finds out, he's gonna be pissed."

"No, he said he didn't want you guys alone together. Violet and I will be there ready to cock block at any second."

"That helps. It's just, sometimes that guy makes me so angry, and then other times he can be the sweetest person. Like, he's giving me crap about hooking up with Kingsley and then suggests the gun range to help Violet feel better. It's hard to stay pissed off when he pulls it together. And I don't think it's an act either. You know how some guys know when to put on the charm, it just seems to be the way he is. He's almost like a girl with his emotions all out there."

"Well, I don't know him very well, so let me watch today and I'll see what I can pick up."

"I guess just let me know if it looks like I might be leading him on or something. I don't want there to be anything between us anymore."

"Then don't let there be. If you feel like he is crossing the line, then tell him that."

I nodded, but in reality, I wasn't a confrontational person. I didn't think I could just bring it up, but maybe I could be a bit more standoffish to him.

We headed outside. Jason and Violet were

already waiting there. Their last class of the day was together so I was sure they headed out together.

"Shotgun," Violet called as she saw us and opened the front door.

I rolled my eyes at her at her bad pun, but I was happy to see her goofing off again. Tomorrow was probably going to be a hard day when she saw Berneli at the EET meeting.

"I hope it's okay, but Christie wants to come. She is a gun person too."

"Yeah, sounds good," Jason said, and gave me a smile. "I'll just text the owner and let him know. He and my dad are friends, so he's hooking us up."

"Thanks," I responded.

Jason looked at me and held my eye contact. He smiled sweetly and opened the passenger door for me. Christie walked to the other side and climbed in behind Violet.

"Thanks," I repeated as our hands slightly grazed each other. I quickly snatched mine away and got in.

"So, thanks for letting me come, guys," Christie said as Jason started driving.

Christie and Jason spent most of the drive talking about the guns they liked to shoot and their past experiences. I was listening with half an ear and texting Kingsley.

He told me that he desperately wanted to come with us, but he had too much other stuff to deal with at the moment. I was a little bummed, but I couldn't expect him to be available constantly. And I hadn't actually invited him. I told him what we were doing and he sort of took that as an invitation. It was sweet that he wanted to hang out with me so much.

Then he asked if we could hang out this weekend. I blushed, thinking about our last night together, and told him that I would definitely like our date to be a private one. That got him excited and he moved it to Wednesday. I smiled, satisfied he wanted to see me, or at least wanted to be with me that badly, and focused on my friends.

We walked into the gun shop and I was completely overwhelmed. I walked straight to the counter and looked up at the guy behind the register as if he was my savior. Christie and Violet were in the corner looking at some pink weapons and chatting quietly. Part of me wanted to know what they were saying, but the other part figured Violet was filling Christie in on everything that happened. I'd let them have their moment.

Jason walked over to me and shook hands with my savior.

"How's it going, Jason? It must be good, bringing three beautiful ladies into my shop."

Jason laughed and smiled down at me. "The ladies want to feel a bit more comfortable with guys confronting them."

"We can definitely do that. What kind of guns do you want to look at?"

"Um, probably shot guns. Whatever you recommend. I was thinking a forty-five, maybe a twenty-two or a nine millimeter."

"Considering your dad isn't here and these lovely ladies don't appear to be over twenty-one, I'll get the shot guns. Nice try though."

Jason turned to look at me and the corner of his

mouth tuned up. "So, should I be scared? You with a weapon?"

I gave him a push. "Yeah, say the wrong thing and I'll end you." I formed my hands into a gun and acted like I was shooting him.

Jason's hands flew to his chest and he acted shot before falling dramatically to the floor.

I laughed and reached down to help him up. He wrapped his arm around my shoulder.

"I actually think I'm going to stay out here. I don't have a crazy stalker's assistant after me and I'm not the biggest fan of guns."

"Relax, guns aren't a bad thing if you know what you're doing."

"Well, that's the issue. I don't know what I'm doing."

"I'll stick by you. You're not going to shoot yourself in the foot or anything."

"Oh yeah, and what if I shoot you in the foot?"

He turned me around, placing his hands on my shoulders, and dropped his head to look me in the eyes. "Keep the gun pointed down range and you won't shoot me in the foot. However, even if you do, I won't die, but you'll have to take care of my every need for a few weeks."

I pushed his arms off my shoulder and rolled my eyes. "Well, there's the motivation I need to make sure I don't shoot you by mistake."

The owner came back and called us all over so he could take us to the range.

We walked into a very long room with what looked like a bunch of little cubicles. They were facing, what I guessed, was the actual range. It was

181

just like the movies. There were posters with silhouettes on them really far away from the cubicles. They were definitely too far. There was no way I was going to be able to hit any of them. Each little cubicle had a chest-high shelf on it and partitions that separated each spot from the rest.

"Ladies, this is Mike, he's the owner of this range. He's going to give you some instructions so that you don't kill anyone," Jason told us as we all walked to our own cubicle.

"All right, ladies, I'm going to show you how to load them, but before you even touch a gun, there are some things that you need to know. Always point the gun down range. Never point it at someone, even if you're joking. Always think of the gun as loaded. It could be empty, but you should treat it like it isn't. Fire at your own target, or at least aim in that direction. When you're done shooting, place the gun back in the case you got it out of."

He gave us some more instructions and I felt my heart pounding. I was nervous about this. People died from guns. I really didn't want to screw anything up. These partitions kept me from shooting someone else, but not myself.

When it was our turn to load the weapons, I was barely able to open the case. My hands were shaking and I dropped it to the counter. Jason laughed and came to my cubicle.

"Here, watch me before you kill yourself." He took my gun out of the case and showed me slowly how to load it.

"Stop, it's not funny. I'm actually really afraid of

that. This is not my cup of tea."

"No, you can do this. I'll help you."

Jason stood behind me and handed me the gun. "Okay, grab the gun but keep your finger away from the trigger. I'm going to hold your hands and adjust your grip."

He smelled amazing and was still wearing the cologne I'd bought him. At this rate, I'd have to buy him a new one for his birthday in March. Then I shook my head and realized what was going on. This was not what Jason and I should have been doing. I tried to move, but he wasn't letting me out.

"Annabelle, I don't want you to be afraid of this. Just trust me, I'm not going to let anything happen to you. Don't you believe me?"

I took a deep breath. I did trust him. There was nothing that could happen here at the gun range. Besides, I wouldn't let it happen. Today was about Violet, and I also didn't want to fight with Jason. If he thought I didn't trust him or believe in him, then we would definitely be fighting.

"Yeah, of course I believe you. Let's just get this over with." I put the gun down so I could secure my earplugs in place. Then I picked up the gun again and Jason wrapped his hands around mine. He lifted the gun up and tried to adjust my aim.

"Okay," Jason yelled, and moved my finger to the trigger. "So the gun still has the safety on. You won't be able to fire. Try it."

I did and nothing happened. I couldn't pull the trigger all the way.

"While the safety is on, aim. See the little notch at the top? That's what you use to aim. Match that

183

up with where you want to hit. But keep both eyes open."

Nodding, I moved the gun slightly and aimed so that I'd get the poster guy straight in the nose.

"Great. Now I'm gonna drop my hands and hold your hips. This gun has a bit of a kick and I don't want you falling on top of me." His hands slid down my arms and rested on my hips. My shirt had slid up a little and I felt Jason's fingers on my bare skin. It was like a blast of heat radiating through me. "Take the safety off, like Mike told you, then fire whenever you're ready."

"Okay, I'm ready." I squeezed the trigger and was slammed back into Jason's chest.

"Easy there, slugger. Plant your feet and try again," he shouted in my ear.

I placed the gun on the counter in front of me and kind of shook all over. Jason lifted his hands off me for a second but as soon as I stood still, he was there again. My shake had raised my shirt up even higher and now most of his hand was on my bare stomach. I took a deep breath and tried to ignore the feeling.

It wasn't him I wanted, but I was just too sexually energized. Holding the gun was filling me with adrenaline and it had nothing to do with being this close to him or smelling the cologne I bought him. I needed to see Kingsley and get that dealt with. I nodded with that thought and aimed at the target again. I fired a couple more rounds, and this time, I didn't fall into Jason.

***

184

"Not gonna lie, I'm a little afraid of you," Violet warned as she examined my target. "Are you sure you haven't done this before? Because I'm thinking you might need to be my new body guard."

"Right, maybe she's a super spy," Christie suggested. "Though, if you were a super spy and didn't tell me, I'd be disappointed."

"No, I was just excited. This…I don't know…it all got me amped up." My pulse was pounding and I felt a little winded.

Violet and Christie looked at each other and tried to control their giggles.

"What?" I asked, feeling self-conscious.

"You're a little horny now, aren't you?" Christie asked me.

I blushed and shook my head vehemently. "No, it's just…" I was at a loss for words, because as soon as Christie said it, I realized it was true. I was practically shaking with it.

"It's the adrenaline. It goes straight to your hooha," Christie assured me.

"Why are you all talking about hoohas?" Jason had just walked up and it was probably the worst time. I ducked my head and tried to ignore the pounding of my heart in my ears.

Violet, as per usual, stepped in, but she didn't have my back. "Well, Annabelle was just telling us how turned on she felt when she was shooting with you."

My head flew up and I gave her the death stare. I couldn't believe she said that. Jason also appeared to be shocked, as he didn't say anything. But she and Christie were snickering behind their hands.

I quickly responded, "Well, no. It wasn't you behind me. I barely noticed you there, actually. I was just thrilled to control that kind of power. Pulling the trigger was the best feeling ever," I rambled, turning to look at Jason and forcing a smile. "It wasn't you, promise."

"And you'd never break a promise, right?" Jason asked me. He looked at me as if I was the only one in the room and it made me very nervous.

There was only one thing to say. "I'd never break a promise to you," I insisted.

Jason nodded lightly and headed to the register to talk to Mike. As soon as he was out of earshot, I slapped Violet on the arm.

"What the hell is wrong with you?"

"What?" Violet asked, lifting her hands in the air, clearly pretending she was innocent.

"Why would you say that? I'm with Kingsley. I don't need Jason thinking he turns me on. That's not what happened." I shrugged and ran my fingers through my hair. This was ridiculous.

Christie and Violet looked at each other again and seemed to have a telepathic conversation that I was not included in. Those bitches.

"Okay," Violet started, and then turned around to make sure Jason wasn't watching. "The other day, David and I told you about how we think Jason is in love with you."

"Right, and I told you that's nuts. He has feelings for Janice."

"Yeah, and he also has feelings for you. Even Christie figured it out by watching you two today. Anyone can see the sparks that are flying off the two of you, because guess what, honey, I know." She nodded and paused for dramatic effect or whatever crap she was trying to pull.

"What do you know?"

"I know that you care about him too."

"Wrong. He's my friend and that's where it ends. I don't have feelings for him or anything."

"Lie to me, but I hope you're being honest with yourself. I know you like Kingsley and I know you want it to work, but that's because it's neat and tidy. Jason comes with messiness and risk but he could—"

"Don't even say it. He isn't the one. He is the one I'm friends with, just like I'm friends with the two of you. That's where it ends. It wouldn't work with Jason anyway. He is a slob, he dresses like a thirteen-year-old boy, he laughs too loudly, and he has a girlfriend. I'm not a homewrecker. What do you want me to do, walk straight up to Jason and say, 'Hi, so, I might be in love with you, but I'm not one hundred percent sure. Leave your girlfriend of almost three years and be with me. By the way, we could possibly ruin our friendship. I also have feelings for Kingsley, so that could complicate things.'"

Christie probed me, joining the conversation. "You told me yesterday you had feelings for him. Are those feelings actually love?"

I felt slightly defeated. "Kind of. Okay, I was at one time. But then I realized there was no point. Kingsley came into my life and he's good to me. He listens when I speak and looks out for me. I want to be happy with him."

187

"Well, what's stopping you?" Violet whispered.

My smile wavered for a second as I thought about this. I was happy, right? I wanted to be with him. I didn't have doubts when we were together. Hell, I just gave him my virginity. No, nothing was stopping me. Actually, there was one thing. "You hoes are stopping me! Let's get out of here so I can meet up with Kingsley." I started walking to the door, ignoring the feeling in the pit of my stomach, refusing to label it. I turned around. Jason was still talking with Mike but Violet and Christie had started walking toward the exit with me.

"Jason, we're gonna leave you," I called to him, and then walked to the door, my jacket in hand.

Chapter 12

I wanted to surprise Kingsley, so I was going to head over to his dorm to see him. We could give the bed a good try. That was probably where we should be hooking up anyway. I had Jason drop me off in front of my door, then turned to look at Violet before getting out of the car. "As much as I wanted to see Kingsley, I don't want to leave you if you need me. We can get some Chinese food or—"

"Why do you girls only ever eat Chinese food? You know that there are other types of food, right?" Jason asked. It was nice that he seemed to have forgotten our original conversation.

"Chinese food has the right amount of grease to fill our souls," Violet told him, and then smiled at me. "No, babe, go see your man. I'm gonna take these two to get Indian, or something that appeases this man."

"Okay, but do you feel like today helped?"

"Yep, it opened my eyes and I'm looking at things a whole new way now."

I stared at her for a second, a little confused by

what she meant, but I nodded anyway. "Call me if you need me and I'll come straight over."

She agreed, I said goodbye to them, and Jason drove off. I thought about texting Kingsley and letting him know that I was coming, but then changed my mind. I wanted to keep being spontaneous. I kind of liked this version of myself. Besides, the look on his face when I stripped down to the lingerie was perfect. He liked being surprised almost as much as I hated it.

I walked down the path to the other dorm building and took a big breath outside the door. I was almost even more nervous than the first time. What if I did something wrong? What if he realized I was still bad at it? It had only been one time, what if he expected me to have, like, learned from it? Maybe I should have paid more attention. I made a mental note to focus on what he was doing and what made him feel good instead of how he made me feel.

I had a plan and red underwear on. It wasn't the sexy kind, but it would do until I could get to the store. I rushed into his building and almost ran to his door, hoping I wouldn't lose my nerve. I was about to knock when someone exited. It was the girl I had seen him with. His family friend, Karen, was leaving his dorm and her pupils were overly dilated. She looked crazy relaxed and there was a goofy smile on her face. It was similar to the face Violet walked around with after she and Berneli spent a particularly long weekend reacquainting with each other.

My breath caught in my throat. What was going

on? "Kingsley?" I called, still standing in the hallway. For some reason, I was afraid to go in.

"Hey, babe, what's up?" He leaned in to give me a kiss, but I dodged it and gave him the cheek. He had the same peaceful and relaxed expression Karen had.

"What's going on?"

"No, no. Babe, just come inside. We'll talk in here." Kingsley draped his arm around my shoulder and half guided, half pulled me into the room. "How was your day? Did you have fun with Violet and Christie?"

"Yeah, uh, we knew the owner so he really helped us out." I sat down at his desk, letting him quickly rush around and pick things up. But I didn't want to continue the conversation since I didn't tell him Jason was the one who took us to the range.

"Oh cool. Did Christie know him? That's a good friend to have."

I nodded, but he didn't see it.

"Hmm, did they teach you to shoot? I mean, I could probably show you a thing or two. My dad's had guns in the house since I could remember. I'm a great shot." He smiled at me and I tried to smile back, but his eyes were distracting me.

"Listen, Kingsley, sit down. Please don't change the subject. What's going on?"

"What're you talking about?"

I didn't know what to say. I wasn't an expert or anything but I sat through health class when they went over the basics of drug abuse. His eyes were glassy and he seemed to be sweating. He told me he wasn't going to be using anymore and he definitely wasn't trying to fight a fire. So what was he doing?

"Annabelle, what's going on?"

"Kingsley, you said Karen was giving you pills for your headache. Does she give you the Ritalin too?"

"What? I'm not using anymore."

"Then why…" I started but I was having a hard time keeping my nerve. He was looking at me but I hardly recognized him. It was like he was possessed or something, but this was something I needed to know. "Then why does it look like you're high?"

Kingsley jerked around, rubbing at his eyes, but it didn't seem to help the glaze blocking the eyes I'd grown accustomed to staring into.

"I told you I wasn't using anymore. Are you calling me a liar?"

"No, but I know things like that are hard to quit. I mean, you mentioned you tried some harder stuff back when you were in high school. Did you, um, did you fall back into your old ways?"

"Listen," Kingsley said fiercely. He stuck a finger in my face for a second and then jerked it back. He started pacing, raking his fingers through his hair. The sweat on his brow increased and his shoulders seemed to shake with the effort to stay calm.

"Babe," he begged, standing in front of me again. "Listen, you're kinda right. Something is wrong and Karen offered me an extra something. I didn't take it and I'm just trying to fight the urge, for you. I want to be a better man, for you."

"What happened? You said something was wrong."

"So, I told you Karen and I are from the same town, right?"

"Yeah."

Kingsley sat down on the bed. I kneeled in front of him, waiting for him to open up. Whatever was wrong must have been serious. He looked devastated.

"Karen's cousin died and she was really upset. I knew him pretty well, so when she told me, I got a bit emotional." He dropped his head in his hands and let out a sob.

"Oh, I'm so sorry. I didn't realize…"

"No, you didn't. And that's why I was hesitant to tell you about my past with drugs. People just assume the worst, right? Like I used once so I must be a user. Well, that's not the case. I just…" He covered his face again and took a couple deep breaths. "It just scared me that I wanted to use. If I didn't hear your voice in the hall, I don't know what would have happened."

"Why didn't you just tell me this?"

"I don't want you to think I'm weak or soft. Karen and I just decided to put on a brave face so no one would know something was wrong."

"No, I'm so sorry." I started stroking his back as he pulled himself together.

"I don't know what to do." He slurred his words a little and tried to brush at the tears. He was really upset about all of this. I quickly pulled him into a tight hug and tried to absorb all of his pain. I couldn't believe I was just accusing him of using when he was actually this crushed.

Then a memory flashed in my head. Violet had

told me that after she was attacked, she wanted to be with Berneli because she needed a distraction. Maybe this would help him too. I nudged his chin up so that he was looking at me. Giving him a weak smile, I bent down and kissed him slightly. At the carnival, I decided I'd prove to him he didn't need drugs to feel better or worthy. It was time to make good on that.

Needing no further invitation, he took control of the kiss and laid me down on the bed. I threw my arms around his neck and pulled him close to me, deepening the kiss. Kingsley slid his hand up my shirt and started to slowly stroke my chest. I purred as he grazed my nipple and relaxed into him. Then my eyes shot open.

I couldn't help but think something felt different than before. He was a little sloppier with his kisses, and his hands didn't feel as steady as before. I quickly brushed the thoughts aside and closed my eyes again. Kingsley needed me and I needed to take control from him. With a little force, I pushed him off me and then straddled him, just below his hips. I wanted access to him.

"I like where this is going," Kingsley kind of slurred again.

I winked at him and reached for his belt buckle. Slowly, I undid it and slid it out of the belt loops, making sure he was watching. Then I worked on his button and zipper, until I could reach into his boxers and feel just how firm he was.

Well, how firm he should have been. Kingsley wasn't that hard yet. But then again, it was still really early into hooking up. Maybe he needed a little more attention or something. So I stroked him from shaft to tip. Tenderly at first, taking my time while keeping eye contact with Kingsley. When he didn't get harder, I sped up a little bit, hoping that might be the solution. As I got faster, Kingsley closed his eyes and made a face. It was kind of forced and looked like he was in a lot of pain.

I stopped. "I'm sorry," I said, terrified I'd hurt him.

"Why are you sorry? Keep going. Pay attention to the tip," he suggested.

I grasped him again and started to run my fingers over the tip as I slid up and down, but nothing was happening. I felt tears starting to build up. It was me.

"Suck it, just suck it. I haven't gotten a hand job in forever. I'm just not used to them. Typically, girls move a lot faster."

I licked my lips and pushed back my fear. I needed to make him happy. He was dealing with a death *and* my inability to please him. So, I slid his jeans off and then his boxers, hoping to get at more of him. I bent down and took him in my mouth. As I slid up and down, sucking as I reached the tip, I realized that I actually liked this. This act I thought would freak me out was actually turning me on. I liked the idea of the power I had and I started to really get into it. Until I recognized he was still pretty soft. How could I still be doing this wrong?

I stopped for a second and looked up at him, refusing to allow myself to cry. "What am I doing wrong?"

"Everything. You need to go watch some porn or

talk to one of your slutty friends. I'm sure Violet could give you some tips." He pushed me off him and quickly grasped himself, forcing his hand up and down his shaft as fast as he could. "Look, I can't even get myself there, I'm so turned off. Just, please leave. I don't want to deal with this crap while trying to deal with all the other shit in my life."

Kingsley jumped off the bed and grabbed something out of the top drawer of his dresser, tossing it into his backpack. Then he shoved his bag over his shoulder and turned to look at me. "Please be gone by the time I get back." He walked out and slammed the door as he left.

I waited a few minutes, in case he came back, but after six minutes, he was still gone so I decided it was time to leave.

After I left Kingsley's room, I debated going to see Violet or Christie, but they were with Jason and I didn't want to deal with him. He'd probably blame Kingsley or talk about how I didn't do anything wrong. How could I not have done anything wrong? My boyfriend was grieving and I only made it worse. It was time to lick my wounds and consider doing a little research. Though, to be honest, I didn't know if I could. I had enough of a hard time saying the word out loud, let alone actually typing it into the computer and hitting play.

***

I awoke the next morning frustrated in more ways than one. As hard as I tried, I couldn't get any real research done. Every time I went to type something in the search bar, I panicked. What if someone was monitoring the internet? What if they saw what I was watching and kicked me out of school? Couldn't it be some kind of honor code violation or something?

I went to class and just tried to focus on what my professors were saying. It was as if I was in hyper focus mode. I took intense notes, actually participated when the professors asked a question, and fake laughed when the girl next to me made a cheesy joke. But as soon as class was over and I was walking down the hall to the EET office, it all came back to me. I was out of things to distract me and the cloud of sorrow returned quickly. Then I bumped into someone.

"Annabelle!" Kyle screamed as he turned around and pulled me into a hug.

I tried to smile at him, but my heart wasn't in it and he seemed to notice.

"What's wrong? You look like someone beat you with a stick."

"Not exactly. I just had a bad night, that's all."

"Was it Kingsley? I hoped he wouldn't be doing drugs around you. I told him it'd upset you," Kyle said as if he was doing me a huge favor.

I stared at him, shocked, trying to even formulate words. Shaking my head, I stammered, "No, he wasn't doing drugs. One of his childhood friends died and he was really upset. Besides, I talked to him about that. He told me that he only sometimes takes Ritalin when he needs to focus. He isn't using to get high." I stormed off and tried to bite the tears back. Why was I such a mess? I never cried. I hated tears, they showed you were weak and emotional.

No, I wouldn't cry over this. I squared my shoulders and walked straight to the EET office. We had a bunch of new members and I needed to input their information into our database.

I was about halfway into the list when the door flew open. I whipped around and saw two very angry girls who looked very dangerous. "What's wrong?" I asked my two friends. I was instantly on guard, ready to go after whoever upset them.

"You tell us," Violet said, giving me quite the judgmental look with pursed lips, creased brow, and hand on the hip. Christie had almost an identical look on her face.

"What?" I stammered, the wind kind of knocked out of me.

"We ran into Kyle and he told us something happened with Kingsley last night," Violet informed me. "So, let's have it. What happened?"

"His childhood friend died. He was just really upset." I turned back to the computer, hoping they would accept the excuse and let me get back to work. The database needed to be completed before the meeting today.

"Right, but why would that affect you to the point that you cried?" Christie asked.

"I wanted to help him feel better, but it didn't work. But let me deal with this, we can talk later," I said, hoping to finalize the issue.

Violet walked over to me and pulled me into a hug. "It's okay, honey." She drew me into a standing position and I closed my eyes for a second.

Big mistake. "Grab the keyboard, Christie," she yelled, and dragged me toward the door, away from the computer.

Christie quickly unplugged the keyboard, holding it behind her back.

"Listen, honey," Violet ordered. "You may think you're hiding your pain, but you aren't. Kyle saw it and he is high half the time. How obvious do you think it is for me? I know you."

"Fine, but don't laugh."

They nodded and I took a deep breath.

"Last night, I saw this girl leaving Kingsley's room and I instantly got upset. You know those stupid health videos where they show you people who are high. Kingsley looked like he was auditioning for the Blu-ray version. His eyes were like glazed over and he was sweaty, and he couldn't sit still. I don't know. Karen had just left his room and I remembered she'd given him some headache pills before so I asked if he was using."

"You did what?" Violet asked, mouth open, eyes wide.

"He told me he wasn't going to use anymore and—"

"You told us he wasn't using in the first place," Christie reminded me.

"I know. It's not something I'm proud of. He takes Ritalin when he's on call at the station 'cause it helps him focus. He used to do some harder stuff in high school, but he's been clean since we've started dating."

"What, a whole couple weeks?" Violet murmured.

I ignored her and continued. "Anyway, he said, well, that girl he's always with, Karen, they were friends from home and that her cousin had just died. Kingsley and Karen's cousin were good friends so they were devastated. She offered him some drugs but he turned her down and it was hard for him, but this wasn't the problem."

"Seriously? This isn't the problem?" Violet asked, getting more judgmental by the second.

"Listen, I didn't judge you when you started dating a professor. Back off, please."

Violet lifted her hands in the air and took a couple steps back.

"What happened?" Christie asked, bringing us back to the issue.

"Well, I was trying to make him feel better. You know, like..." God, I couldn't even say it. How could I try to do those things when I couldn't even say them. I took a deep breath and looked at my friends. If I was going to talk about it with anyone, it'd be these two. They liked sex more than breathing. "Okay, I was trying to give him a blow job but he couldn't get it up."

"He stayed soft?" Christie asked.

"Yeah. Kingsley was upset because I couldn't, well, I couldn't get him hard. What kind of girlfriend can't cheer up her man? He told me I needed to go watch some porn, but I couldn't even do that. What if I get kicked out of school?"

Christie scoffed. "You won't get kicked out of school for watching porn. Do you have any idea how many guys would be kicked out if they did that? We'd be going to an all-girls school. Well, maybe. Some girls watch porn too."

"Well, I couldn't do it. That's not me. I just don't really know what to do. If I can't make him happy, what if he leaves me?" I sat down in the computer chair, utterly defeated. This thought had been bouncing around in my head all day, but I kept pushing it away before it could cause any real harm. Now that I said it out loud, I didn't know what to think.

This was stupid. He and I had only been together for about two weeks, and only official for a few days. But at the same time, we just seemed to have such a connection that I thought maybe we could really be something. I needed this to work.

"Okay, this is the first penis you've ever touched. Relax. You two had a good time the other night and he didn't have a problem getting excited, right?" Violet pointed out.

"Right, but I was in the lingerie Christie helped me buy. Maybe that was the issue. Maybe I had too many clothes on," I suggested weakly.

"Yeah," Violet said, nodding slightly. "He could have an underwear thing—some guys do have things."

"Hopefully all guys have a thing," Christie teased, pushing me gently.

Violet laughed a little and rolled her eyes. "I swear, Christie, you're the equivalent of a thirteen-year-old boy."

"That's why you guys love me. Anyway, listen, if you want to watch porn, we can all grab the popcorn and watch some pool boy entertain the bored housewife at my place. Then the administration won't kick you out of school. But I think we're forgetting one thing. It might not have been your fault."

"He tried to deal with the problem himself but that didn't help. He said I was such a turn-off to him and told me to leave and do some research."

"Under no circumstances should he be treating you like that. That's crazy disrespectful," she insisted. Violet nodded in agreement.

"It was my fault. Don't blame him for the whole thing."

"No," Violet yelled, balling her hands into fists. "It isn't your fault. This is bad behavior on his part. I don't like the way this is going."

"Me too. I wish it hadn't happened, but—"

"Stop," she screamed again. "I can't stand by and let you blame yourself for something like this. You sound like a battered wife. Have some respect for yourself. Did you ever stop to think that there may have been another reason he couldn't get it up? Kyle told us that Kingsley is a druggie. You said you thought he was using when you saw him. Sometimes it doesn't work when you're high. Maybe he did use and lied to you. I wouldn't be surprised if that's what happened."

I looked at her as if she'd slapped me. "So you're saying he lied to my face? Your suggestion is that he looked me in the eyes and lied? Why would you say that?"

"Annabelle, I'm just looking at the facts as you told them. I—"

"No. We all can't have someone like Berneli. Kingsley is good to me and, so far, he's been honest with me."

"But you just met him!"

"So what? Why can't—"

"Annabelle, you're being naïve. You want this to work so badly that you're willing to listen to whatever crap this guy feeds you and it's ridiculous."

"Is that what you think of me?"

I stood up and left the room. I was upset enough as it was. She was supposed to be making me feel better or giving advice, but instead she was bashing him. I never spoke to her about Berneli like this. I never told her she probably screwed up her future by dating Berneli. I supported her. Why couldn't she do the same for me? It was just all too much. I didn't need to be yelled at like this. Friends didn't do that to each other.

I left the room, done with the conversation but still too ashamed I'd broken down in front of them. I ran into the bathroom, locking myself inside with my guilt and misery.

"Annabelle," Christie called from outside the stall I was hiding out in.

"Not now, Christie. I don't want to talk about this anymore. I just need to pull myself together and get to the meeting." I ripped up some toilet paper and forcefully wiped my tears away.

"Let me help. Come on, open the door." She knocked on the door and I slumped my shoulders. But I didn't open the door. This didn't seem to faze Christie, as she climbed under the door and stood up in the stall with me. "It's cozy in here."

"What are you doing?"

"Things got a little intense in there. Violet means well, but she just got too emotional. It's obvious she loves you."

"I know, but she has this relationship with a man who truly cares for her. He would do anything for her so it's easy for her to say that's not right. Kingsley had a bad night. I really think he could be the one for me. Even if he was using tonight, he'd stopped. He just had this big crisis. I want to be there for him if he needs me. What's wrong with that? I want him to be the one. Normally, he is so sweet and considerate when he is with me. People deal with grief differently. Isn't it possible he didn't handle it well but is still a good guy?"

"Yes, it's very possible. Now that you've seen that bad behavior, you just need to watch out for it. I'm not saying that's how he's going to treat you for the rest of your life, but you need to be aware that he gets like this. Maybe you can help him handle it in a different way, maybe that's not going to change. Sometimes, girls think they can change a guy, but usually they can't. Just be careful. Did he get physical with you?" Christie asked gently.

"No, he just grabbed his backpack and left me in his room. He really isn't like that." I practically begged her to believe me.

"Okay. Just be vigilant. Now, about the drugs..." Christie started.

"Stop, I won't get into the drugs conversation again. He promised he wouldn't do it around me and I surprised him. If he was using, then it's my fault I didn't let him know I was coming over. Maybe if I did, it wouldn't have happened."

"You do know Ritalin isn't something he'd take if he were upset like that, right?"

"What?"

"Yeah, he probably wasn't taking Ritalin when you saw him. He was probably—"

"Stop. He already told me he used to use some harder stuff. He was honest with me about his old drug use. If that was what he was doing, then I'm sure it was just a slip up. That happens, right?"

"Yeah, I mean, a lot of people use recreationally, but I think it's when people use while they're depressed that it becomes an issue."

"I don't think it's an issue."

"You don't think, or you don't want it to be?"

I looked up at her, a little crushed. I didn't want it to be an issue. Obviously, that was my answer, but I didn't want to say it out loud. He told me he was stopping. Maybe he just needed someone to help him quit.

Christie looked at me and tucked a stray hair behind my ear. "Look, I don't want to be the bad guy here. I dated a guy, before my main squeeze, and he was a user. I went to narcotics anonymous with him, I held his hand while I walked with him to rehab, and I cried when he relapsed. Being with a user is a big deal and it's not something that can—"

"Kingsley isn't an addict. He has a job, he gets good grades. He wouldn't let something like that affect his life. So he had a bad day and may have used something. We don't even know if he did. I think I may be making a bigger deal about this than I need to."

"Are you sure?"

"Yeah, besides, people use Ritalin like candy around here. It can't be that serious."

"Well, good." She stroked my hair a little and sighed heavily. "All right, let's go to this meeting, and afterward, the three of us can get some food and you two can work this little fight out."

"Yeah, I'll talk to her after the meeting. I'll let her calm down a little bit first. I don't want a repeat of that fight because we're both still emotional," I said, and smiled at Christie. I knew Violet got over the top, and usually I loved that about her, but she crossed the line. I was sure she realized it and we both just needed a few minutes to calm down. No way was some guy getting between our friendship for good.

Christie and I left the stall and went straight to the mirror. Luckily, I had grabbed my bag before storming out of the office. I had a powder compact in there so I quickly fixed my make-up a little bit. Then my eyes bulged as a realization hit me. I never finished the database.

We were going to be sending out important information for the concert and giving people access to club events after the meeting. There was a minor event this weekend and members were going to need early access to the auditorium to help set up.

"Crap, I didn't finish the database," I told her.

"Yeah, I know. Violet is dealing with that now."

"Nice," I said, and smiled.

Chapter 13

After the meeting, Kingsley called me, but I wasn't quite ready to talk to him. I was still embarrassed and didn't know what to say to him. Instead, I spent most of the night curled up in my bed with a king-size chocolate bar and a reality show. Violet and Christie watched with me for a few hours, but then left.

Eventually, I had to dislodge myself from the bed because my bladder got the best of me. As I was walking back from my room, I heard Violet scream. The terrors were back. Lola must have been with her boyfriend and Violet didn't want to tell me. I rushed to my room and grabbed my phone. She promised to keep her phone on loud in case something happened.

I called again and rushed out to pound on her door. After two additional calls, she finally came to the door. Violet took one look at me and burst into tears. I walked into her room and we climbed on the bed.

"What I'm going to do? I can't sleep here

anymore. It's ridiculous. He's in jail, so why am I still scared?"

"I don't know. I've only had one semester of psych. Maybe it's time for you to talk to someone. Speak to a therapist outside the school."

"I think I might look into that at some point. I want to be strong, but he broke into my room, and every time I fall asleep, I see him coming in here again." The tears continued to fall and I grabbed the tissue box next to her and handed them off.

"All right, let's get it together for a moment. He is in jail. He can't come touch you. If you see him this weekend, it could be over. Hold out until then."

She turned and looked at me and I saw the sadness in her face. "I don't think that plan is going to work. I think I was just being naïve. David said his investigator is working on something, but we haven't heard any updates since Sunday. I know things take time, but I just don't have the patience for that. And who left that note? Who took the pictures? Was it Trent the whole time or did he also have help? But why was he even involved in the first place?"

"I'm not sure, but that's what the professionals are for. Let the investigator handle it. Berneli would only hire the best, so I'm sure he is going to find a way to fix all this."

"Yeah, I'm sure Berneli did hire the best."

"Leave it to them and you'll be back with your man doing dirty, dirty things to each other."

"Uh, I hope the universe hears that! I'm hornier than I think I've ever been."

"On that note, I'll leave you be. Just make sure

you keep your phone on," I insisted, and headed to the door. As I was about to walk out, Violet stopped me.

"I'm sorry I yelled at you earlier."

"It's okay. I know you were just trying to show you care. Your little body can't handle too much emotion," I teased, and winked at her.

"Obviously! But in all seriousness, why are you trying so hard to make this work? You really just met the guy." She spoke in such a soft voice and I saw pain and hurt in her eyes. Something about the way she was looking at me made me think.

I twisted my hands together, trying to find the words. I climbed back on the bed and just started talking. "So, my parents had this super fast relationship and married quickly. They just knew they were right for each other. My mom says it felt right in her gut. When Kingsley smiles at me, I feel that. I don't know, it's hard for me to explain. He seems to just know me and he's always trying to do these elaborate things because he wants to impress me. But the truth is, I'm just impressed he wants to be with me. He's ready to fight Jason he wants to be with me so bad. It's a good feeling."

"But…"

"I know. We're having some problems. But you and Berneli did too. You thought he was seeing other girls."

"And he wasn't."

"Well, Kingsley may use occasionally but so does Kyle and we still love him. Give me the chance to help him realize there are better ways to cope with issues. I really think I can help him. I want to help him."

"I don't feel good about it."

"I didn't feel good about Berneli, but I trusted you. Don't you trust me?"

"I do."

"Good, I decided you weren't a crazy lunatic and became your friend so my judgment can't be completely off."

"Well, there are some who may argue with that," she said with a smile. There was still tension in her jaw and her eyes still looked sad, but at least she seemed to want to give me a chance.

"Exactly. That's all I was trying to get out."

"But it couldn't hurt to learn a few things," I said, looking down at the floor.

"Well, just make sure you do it to yourself, I mean make sure you learn it for yourself."

I nodded, feeling a bit better.

"Do you want me to stay in here tonight? Is Lola not coming back?"

"In all honesty, I don't actually think Lola is going to be coming back to school. A lot of her stuff is gone."

I looked around the room and noticed her closet was half empty and her dresser, usually filled with make-up and hair stuff, was now pretty bare.

"Did something happen with Tyler?"

"I don't know. I saw her yesterday and she wouldn't talk about it."

"I hope she's all right."

"Me too. I'll ty to talk to her again, but I don't think it will do any good."

"Well, my offer to stay here still stands."

"No, I'm just gonna turn the TV on and try to fall asleep to an old show or something. Lola likes to fall asleep to *Happy Days* and I think I could use something like that right now."

"All right, well, let me know if you change your mind. I'll turn my phone on loud."

***

As I was getting ready for my morning class, Kingsley called again. Part of me wanted to pick up, but I didn't want to get distracted. I did need to get to class and I didn't want to fight with him anymore. I let it go to voice mail, tossed the phone in my tote bag, and headed out the door.

Thankfully, I had managed to pass my math class last semester, but I had a new problem. Statistics. It was a completely different language and I was actually worse at it than pre-calculus.

In other words, I needed to focus. As I left the dorm building, a feeling of déjà vu came over me. Kingsley was standing there with coffee. But this time, I wasn't happy to see him.

"Babe, please, let's talk."

"Kingsley, I don't want to talk to you right now. I have class in ten minutes and I don't want to be distracted." I kept walking, hoping he'd let me be, but knew he wouldn't.

"Come on, just give me a minute. I thought about what happened and I shouldn't have gotten mad at you. I know it's not your fault that you didn't know what to do and I just let my emotions take over." He was walking fast to keep beside me and talking way too loudly.

I stopped and pulled him aside. "Listen, things got heated and I get that. I really do need to get to class right now, but maybe we can talk later?" I hoped he'd agree. I really did want to talk to him but I was kind of scared of what he might say. He didn't sound like he was going to blame me, but what if he did? I already blamed myself enough, if he said it too, well, I wasn't sure what I'd think.

"You're right, babe. I wasn't thinking, but I feel awful and I want to fix things with you. I shouldn't have kicked you out of my room," he said, dropping his voice. "I need you in my life."

I smiled, blushing as he said the words I needed him to say. I didn't even have to ask. He just got me. "Really?"

He smiled and kissed me gently. "Girls like you don't come around every day, and if I thought I'd screwed it up, I couldn't live with myself. I get it. I don't want to disrupt your studies. Can we meet up after your class? Please? I have a gift to give you, but I think we should be in private when I give it to you." He reached his hand out and stroked my arm gently. I felt a warmth flow through me again and when I looked up at his eyes, they were completely clear.

"Meet me at the coffee stand after class. We can talk then, but you didn't have to get me anything."

"I wanted to." He kissed my cheek and then backed away slowly, still grinning big at me.

Then I looked at my phone and panicked. My class was set to start in six minutes and I was definitely going to be cutting it close.

Much to my dismay, I had to sit in the front row. Didn't these people know the rules? True, we didn't have assigned seats, but technically, we had assigned seats.

The class was a disaster, as always. I had no idea what was going on nor any idea how to figure it out. But I was super visible in the front and the professor called on me. Of course, my answer was wrong and I was unbelievably humiliated. This was going to be a long semester. In a worse mood than before, I walked to the coffee stand and ordered a large french vanilla latte. As I was waiting for my coffee, I heard my name.

"Hey, Christie," I said, giving her a weak smile.

"What's up? How are you doing?" she asked, and then placed her order.

"Not much. Kingsley is coming and we're going to try to talk things out. He was waiting outside my room with coffee, but I needed to get to class."

"Well, that's good. He definitely needs to do some sucking up."

The barista called my name and I grabbed my cup.

I wasn't exactly comfortable with the idea that he had to suck up after doing something wrong. I didn't want to talk about it anymore. I'd see what happened when Kingsley got here. "So, what else is going on?"

"Not much. Go grab a table so you have one when Kingsley gets here. I'll wait with you." She waved me off and I picked one of the tables off to the side. As long as he didn't speak too loudly, no one would hear us. I was a little nervous.

I took my phone out of my bag and double checked my messages. Maybe his class went late or something. Letting out a sigh, I put the phone away and turned to look at Christie. She was smiling at a guy who seemed to be holding her coffee hostage.

Frankly, I'd kill someone if they tried to take my coffee. She wasn't as crazy as I was.

This guy stood a little over a head taller than Christie, but then again, she was wearing tall, chunky leather boots. Though his height was helped by his hair. It was black, brushed out of his dark almond-shaped eyes, and gelled straight up. There was a good chance he used more hair gel than Violet but it looked good. He looked good and I definitely thought Christie noticed.

I heard her giggle loudly and couldn't help but watch more intently. She was flirting. I'd never seen her in action, but I always thought she'd be this sex kitten. As it turned out, in front of a hot guy, she turned into a giggly school girl just like the rest of us. I felt a little bit like I'd found out there was no Santa Claus.

She started to walk toward my table and I gave her a skeptical look.

"Well, who was that?"

"Um, his name is Shane. He grabbed my coffee by mistake. We ordered the same thing, and the barista placed it on the counter and said Frappuccino instead of my name. So he grabbed it and I stopped him, you know, because I wasn't gonna let him take my nectar of the gods."

"That's my girl."

"Anyway, he tried to pull the whole, 'oh, I'll

give you your coffee if you give me your number' thing. But I have a boyfriend, so I don't want to just give out my number."

"Right. But then why were you giggling?"

"I don't know. Maybe it was the leather jacket or the muscles underneath it. I mean, did you get a look at him? Geez, I could do some real damage to a body like that."

"Oh really?"

"Hey, just because Rob is down south doesn't mean I can't appreciate a good-looking man when I see one."

"Yeah, he was pretty fine. Are you into that bad boy thing?"

"Who isn't? I don't know. Rob is basically the polar opposite of a bad boy. He is just your typical altar boy."

"Is that a problem?"

"No, it's great. It means I trust him." She smiled at me but it looked forced and she looked a little scary. Her eyes were too wide and her eyebrows went up too high. Whatever was going on with her damn sure didn't look great.

She looked down at her perfect manicure and searched for what were clearly made up flaws.

"Annabelle?" Kingsley asked. He had walked up to the table while we were talking.

I looked at Christie and the forced but scary smile was back. "Hi, Kingsley. I just stopped by for a coffee and saw Annabelle. I'll see you guys later."

Kingsley gave her a smirk. "Thanks, we have some things to talk about."

"I'll call you later?" I asked her. I didn't want to

leave her when she was opening up to me, but I did need to deal with Kingsley.

"You'd better, bitch." She slipped her sunglasses on and headed out the door.

"She's pretty vulgar," Kingsley pointed out, and made a face. "I don't like women who swear like that. I hope she doesn't rub off on you."

"Kingsley, she's one of my friends…" I started, trying to defend her.

"You're right. I'm sorry. I'm supposed to be groveling, not insulting your friends." Kingsley reached out and took my hand.

I looked down at our hands together and tried not to smile. They fit perfectly. "Kingsley, I'm so sorry for the loss of your friend. I really feel for you, but—"

"You don't even need to say it, babe."

"You were nervous, I was upset. Everything was just a mess. I accept your apology. Do you accept mine?"

I couldn't help but notice he didn't actually say sorry. But I quickly dismissed the thought. Some people just had an issue apologizing. I knew he meant it and that counted for me.

"I just need to know if you were using that night." I looked down at the table, unable to look back up at him. As soon as I said it, I realized I really did need to know this. To me, if he admitted it, we could make something work. If he didn't, well, I wouldn't worry about that just yet.

Kingsley reached out and gently pushed my chin up. "Yeah, I did. I'm sorry I lied to you. I was embarrassed that I'd sunk to that level. I was just devastated and didn't handle it right. That's why I yelled at you. Under normal circumstances, I'd never speak to you that way. I want you to know that."

"Are you intending to use again?"

"I can promise you that it won't happen again. I'll even go see the school therapist about my issues if that will make you feel better. If I get their help, I won't need to use. I just, I don't always know how to handle all the thoughts in my head. But I'm done with that life. Will that work for you?"

"Actually, I think seeing the therapist would be a good idea." I really liked this plan. It was the perfect solution. I could tell Violet and Christie he was going to do something about the drugs and then they could see the amazing guy I normally saw.

"Then I'll make an appointment and get that sorted out. Please say you forgive me."

I looked at him and felt that tingly sensation in my stomach again. It was his eyes. They were clear and bright and obviously full of love. They completely took me over and I couldn't stay angry with him if I tried.

"All right, go see the therapist and I'll forgive you."

Kingsley smiled big, practically showing me his wisdom teeth, and pulled my chair close to him. I laughed as he pulled me in for a kiss. "I don't actually have your gift on me, but I promise it will be worth it."

"Kingsley, you didn't need to get me a gift."

"Uh, don't say that. I want to spoil my girl and make up for my actions. Let me make it up to you."

I nodded and kissed him. The terrible feeling in my gut seemed to melt away as I felt a whole different emotion flowing through me. I definitely needed to get a handle on it. I should not have been that horny while sitting in the middle of the school building.

***

Kingsley and I separated and went to our next classes. He was on call that night so he said he couldn't meet up, but he'd be planning something fun for Saturday night and I'd get my gift then. I spent most of the night with Violet trying to figure out my statistics. She had taken it last semester and passed with a B. Berneli had helped her out and, eventually, she grasped the concepts. When that failed, we also got together on Thursday with Berneli in the EET office for another lesson.

Violet was desperate to see him and I was desperate to pass my class. They figured I'd be a good buffer and no one would assume they were up to no good if I was in the room. I was happy to help if it meant I could pass my class.

Even though Violet mooned over him and there were some stolen kisses when I was trying to apply the notes Berneli gave me, he really was a great help. I generally had an idea of what was going on, or at least I thought I did. We left the office and I felt a lot better. However, Violet did not.

"I'm just not sure what I'm going to do about Saturday. In reality, I don't know what to say to him and I really don't want to see him anyway. It's not going to help the terrors. I just hoped the investigator would have more information for us by now. Maybe I need to transfer schools before they find out."

My heart sank. How could she leave me here? Okay, that was selfish. Would changing schools actually help her? No, it couldn't. "Stop, I don't think that's the solution in the middle of a semester. School just started, so you're not going to be able to get accepted in another school this semester and you can't drop out. Then he wins. I know you hate waiting, but you need to let the investigator do his job."

"Right, I keep trying to remind myself that. I just miss him. I'm scared to sleep alone so I've just stopped sleeping, but then I'm exhausted all day, so I fall asleep the next night and the dreams come. This just needs to be over."

"No, we just need to look into the legality of things. If you spoke to a therapist outside the school, I don't think they are allowed to tell anyone about your relationship with Berneli. I'll look into all this and then maybe we can get you some help. Until then, I think maybe you should look into a sexual assault support group. Someone there could have a way to help you."

"After this weekend is over, I will definitely find one. Let me deal with this one problem first, and then we can tackle the sleeping. Maybe I'll look so awful on Saturday that Finn won't want me anymore." She smiled and gently shoved me.

"Well, who could blame him, with bags under your eyes are the size of my tote bag?" I pushed her back and we went back to my room.

"Shut up," she said, laughing. "I just need more make-up."

"Yes, that's the answer to everything."

Violet tried to leave, but I insisted she sleep in my bed with me. If she was going to have terrors, I'd wake her up immediately. If she changed locations, there was a chance the terrors wouldn't come, after all, they didn't happen at Christie's. Maybe she needed to change rooms since her scared her so much. Sure, she'd had some terrors in London, but she said they didn't happen every night.

We awoke to the sound of the alarm screaming and not Violet. She made it through the night without a terror and looked better than ever now that the bags under her eyes were the size of a small clutch.

She left to get ready and that was when I heard her scream. I ran out the door and stopped short when I saw what was waiting for her.

"Is that what I think it is?" I asked as she fell to her knees.

There was a vase of wilted violets in front of her door with a card taped to it. I reached down and opened it.

My Vivacious Violet,

I assume the snow delayed your visit so I checked the weather for this weekend. What do you know, it's going to be forty degrees and sunny. I will see you then. Remember, I have spies everywhere. Don't think I don't know about your study session last night.

Ever yours,

Finn

"What does it say?" she asked in a monotone voice. She sounded defeated and crushed and it pulled at my heart.

"It just says he knows about the snow and it will be forty and sunny this weekend, so he's excited to see you," I said, sticking the note in my pocket before she could read the whole thing.

"Thanks for not telling me the rest. I don't want to know." She nodded and then walked into her room. I followed quickly, leaving the flowers in the hallway.

"Okay, can we go to the police station now and report this? It looks like a threat." The flowers were dead; it felt like that was what Finn was going to do to her.

"Yeah, you're right. It just got serious. But first, I need to call David. Would you excuse me for a second?" she asked as she sat on her bed and pulled her phone out.

"No problem." I turned to leave, but she stopped me before I got to the door.

"Annabelle, please take the note with you. I don't want the police to see it."

221

"I've already got it along with the tape from the vase." I walked out and was going to head to my room, but I needed some air. I felt like the world was closing in around me and I couldn't breathe.

I pushed through the door and stumbled to the nearest bench. There I sat, my head between my knees, no coat, no make-up, no shoes, no bra, and no idea what to do. I tried to calm the fear that was raising up inside of me and threatening to come out. I lifted my head and looked at the sun, wondering what we were going to do.

"What the hell happened? Was it Kingsley? If he hurt you, I'll kill him," Jason warned as he sat down next to me. I didn't even hear him come up.

"It's not Kingsley, it's Violet. Someone left her a vase of dead flowers and a note." I handed it to him and he took a moment to read it.

"Come with me," he insisted as he grabbed my hand and pulled me with him. "By the way, next time you have a panic attack, grab your coat." He slid his off and draped it over my shoulders.

"Sorry, I will remember that for next time. By the way, how did you know I was here?" I followed him to his room and sat on his bed, like I had a million times before.

"I am stalking you as well."

"Seriously, not funny at this moment."

"Honestly, I just wanted to see if you and Violet wanted to grab breakfast or something. It was a crazy coincidence. I don't know. I just felt like I needed to see you guys. Guess my Spidey Senses knew something was wrong."

Jason grabbed his laptop and took a seat next to

me. "Look, I've been saving this until it was ready because I wasn't sure if I'd be able to do it. Violet gave me the photo and I've been messing with it." He pulled up some computer system and showed me the initial picture of Violet and Berneli kissing in front of the apartment complex.

"Okay, what did you do? It looks the same."

"Patience. Wait for everything to load." He clicked around on the screen and another picture popped up, but I wasn't ready for what I saw. It was Berneli and me kissing. My eyes grew wide and my mouth dropped to the floor.

"What the hell? This never happened. Oh my god, you can't show this to Violet." I was furious. What was he doing?

"You don't get it?" he asked, looking at me incredulously.

"No! Are you trying to screw with me?"

"Did this ever happen?"

"Of course not! I would never do that to Violet. Besides, I'm with Kingsley."

"Exactly. It never happened. But what does it look like?"

"Shut up! You made that?" I couldn't believe it. This could solve her issue with Finn. If we could make the dean think the original picture of Violet and Berneli was fake, then Violet couldn't be blackmailed. We could go to the police and they wouldn't have to know about Berneli and Violet's relationship. "This is brilliant."

"It gets better. Just in case they thought this was fake, I took a picture of the dean and…" He pulled up another picture and sure enough, the dean and

Berneli appeared to be kissing each other.

"But how did you do this? How could you do this?"

"It's not that hard. I'm just a bit of a social media creep. You and Kingsley posted a disgusting kissing photo from that Christmas festival, so I used it here. The dean was kissing her husband at their anniversary party last week. The rest of it was painstaking details that took me forever." He was practically shaking with excitement and I didn't know what to say.

"Jason, this is…"

"I know. I couldn't let him play with our girl like that."

The panic I had felt before was lifting off my chest and I pulled him into a huge hug. This could really work. He held me tight and rested his chin on my head. "I don't know what to say. Earlier, Violet was talking about transferring schools, and I can't imagine being here without her."

"Don't worry, if there is something I can do, I won't hesitate."

"I know, and that's why I love you." Oh shit. I froze. What the hell did I just say to him?

Jason pulled back and looked at me. Really looked at me. I stared back and waited to see what he had to say.

"You know, I mean I love you like a—"

But he cut me off. "Are you happy with Kingsley?"

"Yes," I uttered.

"Do you feel butterflies when he's near you?"

"Yes."

"When he kisses you, do your knees give in?"

"Yes."

"How about now, how do you feel now?"

I couldn't move. I just stared back at him as what felt like hours went by. He reached out and tucked a lock of hair behind my ear. Tingles shot through me and I tried to control my shaking as I took a ragged breath.

"I don't know how I feel."

Jason leaned forward so he was inches from my face. "How do you feel now?"

"I—"

He cut me off with a kiss. Jason's lips were smooth and tasted like peppermint. I leaned into the kiss and then ran my fingers through his hair and it felt wrong. I jumped back and stared at Jason in shock.

"No, you can't do this! We can't do this. You have Janice and I have Kingsley. Why would you even do that? Don't you love Janice?"

Jason stood up and started pacing the room. He started to talk and then closed his mouth again. I just watched as he seemed to be deep in thought. I didn't know what I was waiting for. What did I want him to say?

"Yes, I do love Janice, but I'm just—"

I jumped up and pointed a finger in his face. "Confused, I know. But you know what, I'm not going to be this girl. I won't be the girl who helps you figure out that you're madly in love with your girlfriend. I refuse to let you use me like that. I have too much respect for myself and too much respect for Janice."

225

"You don't even like Janice."

"No, I don't like her, but that's not the point. I won't be this girl again. Kenny tried to play me and I won't let you do it too." I grabbed his computer and turned to walk out the door.

"It's not like that, Annabelle. I just—"

"No, I'm done. We need to get this computer to Violet before she does something she'll regret. We've already wasted enough time." I left the room, still wearing his jacket, and practically ran to her room.

When I knocked, Violet was sitting on the floor, knees at her chest, and tears falling down her face. I put the computer down and turned around to hug her, but Jason was already there.

"Vi, take a deep breath. I found a way to fix everything. Just get up and let me show you on my computer."

Violet nodded and let Jason pull her up and place her in the desk chair. He quickly brought up the pictures and explained to her what he had told me earlier.

Violet threw her arms around Jason. "You're quite possibly one of the most amazing men on the face of the planet. David just called me and said the investigator has a lead as to who the outside help is but he isn't sure of anything yet. We don't know if Trent is the only one helping Finn. I am so scared."

"Well, Vi, let's go to the police. They need to know about all of this and we need to keep you safe. They can probably sort that out a lot faster than the investigator." Jason grabbed her coat off of the back of her chair and draped it over her shoulders like he had done to me earlier.

I looked down and realized I still had no bra or shoes on.

"Um, guys, do you mind if I meet you at the security office? I need to put some clothes on." I crossed my arms to try to cover my boobs. Besides, I could use a minute alone to get over what just happened with Jason.

"Yeah, I got her," Jason said, and we all left. Violet went to pick up the flowers, but I stopped her.

"Wait, get a scarf or something to preserve the fingerprints."

"You already touched it and so did I. Plus, we took the card off," she reminded me.

"But still, you never know what they'll find," I insisted.

"Fine," she said, and went back in her room. Jason and I were in the hall alone. He looked at his feet and I stared at a hole in the wall. It was crushing me to think we'd just ruined our friendship. I should have stopped it earlier or something.

But then a voice in my head said, *You didn't want him to stop.* I pushed that voice away and went in my room to change, leaving him alone in the hallway. I did want him to stop, which was why I pulled away.

***

When I walked up to the security office, Violet and Jason were standing outside.

"What's going on?" I asked, looking at the two of them.

"Look who's at the front desk." Violet pointed to the secretary who was nasty to her when she tried to report Finn the first time.

"So why are you still out here? Let's go in and speak to the chief. He already knows you, and I'm sure he wants to hear about this. If not, we'll call 9-1-1 and get a different set of cops," I insisted, and opened the door for the two of them, not entirely sure if that was how this all worked. But I needed to stay strong. "Let's go," I reiterated when Violet didn't move straight away.

Jason caught on and gave her a little push on her lower back.

We all walked up to the desk and the secretary glared at Violet.

"What do you want? Are you trying to ruin someone else's life?" she asked, snapping her gum.

"I need to speak to Chief Johnson," Violet responded with as much authority as she could muster.

The secretary gave Violet a snide look and snickered. "Well, he's busy. Why don't you all come back later? Don't you have to go to class or something?"

"Listen, you played this game last time and it almost got me raped. So excuse me if I don't give a crap about what you have to say." Violet tilted her head, smiled, and then walked around her desk. She bolted toward the back where the chief's office was.

Jason and I looked at each other, wide-eyed, and ran after her. We caught up in the chief's office. He was standing and shaking Violet's hand. She quickly reminded the chief of my name and then introduced Jason.

"All right, Miss Carrington, what can I do for you? You mentioned my secretary was causing some problems."

"Chief, as I told you last time, I tried to report the incident but your secretary made light of the whole thing and more or less forced me to reconsider talking to someone. I came here with other problems relating to Officer Finn and she wouldn't let me speak to you."

"All right, we can worry about that later. What's going on with Officer Finn?"

Violet explained about the flowers and placed the vase on his desk. Then Violet took a deep breath and handed him the initial note and the picture the stalker had left.

"I was afraid to come in before. I didn't want someone to think anything of this. But he's blackmailing me with this picture."

"Well, relationships with professors are against the school's rules," the chief reminded us.

"Look, Chief Johnson." Jason pulled up his phone and showed him the pictures he had been working on. Before we came to the office, he had emailed them to himself. "He is trying to get back at Violet. I made the same pictures on my computer. Here is one with the dean of students hooking up with Professor Berneli." Jason handed his phone to the chief, who let out a subtle laugh.

"Well, we know this didn't happen." He handed the phone back to Jason but kept the picture of

Violet and Berneli. "We will contact the jail and look into this. Until we get an answer, I need you to report any further communication that might come your way."

"Thank you, Chief," Violet said, managing a weak smile.

"Is there anyone you think could be working with Finn? Is there anyone who may be creating drama or threatening you?"

Violet sat quietly for a few minutes and then looked at the door. "Chief, I think something is going on with Trent, a senior here. He delivered me one of the notes. I don't know about these flowers, but he got physical with me last semester and he was passing—"

"What do you mean he got physical with you?"

"He grabbed my arm and wouldn't let me go. I had a mark on my arm for two weeks. Annabelle was with me. She can vouch for it."

"Did you take pictures of the bruises?"

"No."

"Did you film it, text about it? Any kind of proof? Right now, it would just be your word against his."

"No, I didn't. I didn't want to make a big deal about it."

"Miss Carrington, I cannot do anything about him, then. Did Trent threaten you?"

"Well, no, but—"

"Officer Finn is not allowed to contact you, Miss Carrington. If Trent is delivering messages, then we will sort that out. Let us handle it. Until then, I'd suggest you file a restraining order against Trent.

Other than that, there is not much else we can do."

"I understand," Violet replied. She took a deep breath and I hoped this would help give her some peace of mind.

"I don't want you going to see Finn, understand? Don't worry about the picture, don't worry about any of it. Going to see him will only give him what he wants and continue to perpetuate this obsession he's carrying."

"Right," Violet agreed. I was thrilled she didn't have to go. Nothing good could have come from it.

We talked over some more specifics with the restraining order and went to leave, but the chief stopped us.

"By the way, Miss Carrington, does Professor Berneli know about this connection?"

"No," she mumbled. "I wouldn't have a reason to tell him since we aren't in a relationship."

Chief Johnson looked at her for a minute, not saying anything. At first, I thought he was going to call her out for the horrible liar she was. But instead, he grabbed his phone. "I will contact him for you. However, if I were you, I'd be careful to ensure no other fake pictures are taken. That would not look good for anyone."

"Thank you."

We left and Violet collapsed on a bench near our dorm.

"I feel like I can breathe a little. Finn must have been bluffing about sending in the picture, or maybe the school mail lost it or something. Chief Johnson had no idea about that picture until we showed it to him. That's a relief."

"For now."

Jason and Violet whipped around and looked at me.

"Sorry. It just seems to me this is not gonna be the first time someone finds out about your relationship. I feel like it's time you decide what you want. He's leaving in a couple months, what's gonna happen then and is it worth getting kicked out of school?"

"Annabelle," Jason chastised at me. "I don't think this is the time to be bringing this up."

"Why not? Something could have happened to her. Something could still happen to her. What if someone else finds out? Clearly Chief Johnson knows something is up."

"I know," Violet said softly. She looked up at me, tears filling her brown eyes. "I'm afraid to have that conversation with him. I don't think my heart could take it."

Jason reached down and pulled her into a hug. "Vi, you don't have to deal with this right now. Just relax and try to enjoy the time you guys have left."

"I love the two of you dearly, but I can't keep talking about this. David has become so important to me and I know he'll be leaving. We don't have a plan. Maybe I should just end it with him. Save us a lot of heartache in the future." Tears started streaming down her face and she took a couple deep breaths.

"On top of that, I'm scared. What if Trent tries something? What if he and Finn are teaming up to screw with me"

"I agree it sounds bad, but why does Trent care?

232

It doesn't make sense. It's not like he and Finn were close or anything. I mean, did you notice anything?" I asked her.

"No, I never saw anything between them. Maybe he has some blackmail on Trent or something. I don't know. I just can't keep doing this."

"So what can we do to help you?" I asked her gently. My heart broke to see her so defeated. This was Violet. Anything was possible with her. She always found a way, and that was one of the things I loved about her. Now, she was so deflated, and I couldn't do anything to help her.

"One of you needs to go talk to David. Jason, it'd be great if you did it so you could show him the pictures. And, Annabelle, I need to get to class. Why don't we get our things? I know how you feel about being late."

"It doesn't matter, Violet. I just—"

"I know. I just can't talk about it anymore."

We agreed and Jason stormed off to talk to Berneli. Violet turned and looked at me.

"What?"

"So, Jason showed you the computer stuff. It was lucky he figured all that out. Did you know he was working on it?"

"No, he showed me for the first time today." I thought back to being in the room with him and of when he kissed me. I was completely distracted that I tripped over a root.

"You okay?"

"Yeah, why?

"Where did you just go? It seemed like you went far away. What's going on?"

"We don't need to talk about this now."

"Just tell me what happened. I could use the distraction."

We started walking up to our rooms and I filled her in on the kiss.

"I just feel so guilty. Kingsley deserves better than that. I can't believe Jason made me cheat on Kingsley like that."

"Okay, let's calm down for a second. Jason didn't make you cheat. There is a split second before a kiss that you know it's coming. If you really wanted to avoid it, you could have. Are you honestly telling me that for just one second you didn't enjoy that kiss?"

I opened my mouth to shut her down immediately but closed it again. I couldn't lie to her.

"Fine, I enjoyed it for a second but then I remembered Kingsley and Janice. I also enjoy kissing Kingsley and I hope Jason enjoys kissing Janice. It doesn't mean I want to go out and buy his and hers towels with Jason. It just means I like kissing. Give me more of the drinks Christie makes and I may even kiss you."

"I think you're focusing on the wrong thing. Jason was trying to show you that he has feelings for you."

"Right, and when I asked him if he still loved Janice, he said yes. It's over. I'm not playing games with Jason anymore. I'm going to enjoy my time with Kingsley. It…it just doesn't matter with Jason anymore. He made his choice."

"Why did you ask him if he loved her?"

"Because I needed to know."

"Why?"

"Because."

"Right, so I'll just finish that since you're too scared to say it. Because you wanted him to tell you that he didn't love her. You wanted him to come out and tell you he was in love with you."

"But he didn't.

"I kinda think he did. I notice you didn't talk about your feelings."

"All my feelings are with Kingsley. I stopped crushing on Jason when Kingsley and I got together."

"Then you wouldn't be this upset."

Chapter 14

I was sitting at the coffee stand, waiting for Christie, when Kingsley walked over to me.

"Hey, babe," he greeted, and leaned down to give me a kiss.

"Hi," I replied, smiling, hoping to push Jason from my mind.

"I know you're probably a little upset because of the other day, so I have a plan. Tomorrow night, pack an overnight bag and be ready at around five."

"You don't have to keep surprising me. I promise you, buying me things and going over the top like this isn't necessary. I just want to spend some time with you." I reached out and took his hand.

He kissed my hand and smiled at me. "I have money and it's okay if I spend some of it on you. Just accept it and look beautiful tomorrow. Let me spoil you so you don't have to worry about anything."

How could I say no to that? This was the Kingsley I was falling in love with. This considerate man who took the time to plan excursions with me, who wanted to be with me and only me, who wasn't in love with another woman.

"Sounds great. Is there anything specific I should wear?"

"No, babe. Listen, you always look perfect, though maybe just don't wear jeans. But even if you do, you'll still look beautiful on my arm."

"Aww, you make me blush. You're sweet."

He kissed me on the forehead and then smiled.

"I have to go. I'm meeting up with Karen to talk about her cousin and the funeral."

"Do you want me to come with you to the funeral? I don't mind," I insisted.

"No, no. I don't want you to feel like you have to or anything like that. I don't even know when it is or even if I'll be going. You know, since I wasn't family, I might not be able to go." He got up and waved goodbye before I could say anything else.

I stared at his back as he walked away and couldn't sway the feeling that something about what he said wasn't right. But I couldn't focus on that. He'd given me no real reason to doubt him.

With a sigh, I turned my head and looked out the window. What I saw completely distracted me from Kingsley.

Christie was now Biker Chick Barbie. I watched as she climbed off of some guy's bike and handed him the extra helmet she had been wearing. She shook her hair out and waved goodbye to him, giving a whole lot of shake to her walk as she headed into school.

I waved as soon as she saw me. Christie held up

a finger and went to order a coffee. While I waited, I texted Violet to see how she was doing.

Armed with her drink, Christie sat down across from me. "So, what's going on?" she asked, feigning innocence.

"No, no, explain to me what you were doing climbing off some guy's bike. Is Rob in town or something?"

She turned red as her lipstick and smiled awkwardly. "Okay, so, it really isn't that big of a deal. I was parking my car to go to my first class and it was, like, the day from hell. My bag ripped and my laptop fell out. It smashed and then I cut my hand trying to pick it up." She held up her bandaged hand and grimaced a little.

"Are you all right?"

"Yeah, I'll live. It isn't really deep. But anyway, I didn't have anything to wrap it up with, and the rest of my stuff was still everywhere, so I just sat down on the ground for a minute, cringed, and then took my jacket off so I could wrap my hand and get all my things. As I was about to do that, Shane, the guy who tried to steal my coffee, walked up and handed me a white t-shirt. He was like, 'It would be a shame to ruin such a nice jacket.' Then he wrapped my hand up tight and grabbed the rest of my things."

"Aww, how gentlemanly. Then what happened? I still don't see how you ended up on the bike."

"Well, I thanked him, obviously, and started bitching about how shit everything was and then I decided I just didn't want to go to class. I was over today. So he suggested we go for a ride. Shane told me that nothing relaxes you like taking a ride or driving fast. And I don't know what happened, I just jumped on the bike. I held onto his waist and his abs were tight as anything and I don't know. I felt a hum go through me as we flew down the road."

Christie was staring off as if she was still on the bike. I had never seen her like that. It was as if she were in a different world. One that left her without sarcasm or a witty retort. Instead, she looked happy.

"And that's it? He let you off the back of his bike and nothing came of it? Really?"

"What do you want me to say? My boyfriend is down south, but that doesn't mean I'm going to cheat on him with Shane. I just wanted to have some fun every now and then."

"Shouldn't you and your boyfriend have fun?"

She looked at me and was filled with sadness. "We have fun. It's just more adult fun. To him, talking about the wedding and baby names is fun. And sure, thinking about that stuff is fun for a while. The problem is, it's really close. Like, I won't be able to drink at my bachelorette party soon."

I took what she said under consideration and thought about Kingsley. Maybe I was a little too hasty in thinking he was the one for me. I should probably ease off that a bit and just enjoy being with him. I should be a bit more like Violet and live day to day.

"Well, you looked good on the back of that bike, very *Sons of Anarchy* Barbie. Did you decide to go to class after all?"

"Oh, no, that class was over a while ago. I just wanted to meet up with you."

"Good, I could use a favor."

"What's up?"

"EET is having the karaoke competition tomorrow and I'm supposed to help and take attendance as to which volunteers show up. But…Kingsley invited me out tomorrow night, and after the fight the other day, I really want to spend some time with him." I smiled and tried to give her my best begging eyes.

"No problem. Will Violet be there?"

"She should, since this is one of the events that she helped organize. Some things have happened with the guy who attacked her. He has someone leaving her creepy notes about watching her and stuff, so she may be a little upset about that."

"Oh god, yeah, I'll be there. No stress. I mean, I hope she's there, because that would mean everything is fine, but I can definitely help if it isn't. Though, I might drag her there. She's always going on about how she needs distractions. Watching someone sing a Britney Spears song would certainly fit the bill."

"Please make sure someone records it if you guys perform."

"Oh, hell yes. We're going to need it for her wedding video one day."

"I like that twisted mind of yours." We toasted to that and took a big sip of coffee.

We talked a bit more about EET and then parted ways. I needed to get back to my room and pack for tomorrow. Plus, I wanted to check on Violet again.

Turned out, she definitely didn't need my help.

"It all just became too much," she told me on the phone. "I took a cab over to David's and we're just enjoying each other's company."

"Ew, I know what that means."

"Shut up, that's not what I meant."

"Yeah, it probably is exactly what you're talking about, you nympho. Are you planning to go to EET tomorrow?"

"So far. I mean, it would look bad if both David and I weren't there, so we are definitely going to make an appearance."

"Great. Kingsley planned this whole thing for me so I won't be able to go, but Christie is going to stop by to help."

"Aww, but what about our love song duet?"

"I was never getting up there to sing anyway."

"Fine, but don't get jealous when Christie's and my relationship gets serious. Backstreet Boys ballads have a way of bringing people together."

"I'll plan the wedding."

We said goodbye and then I tried to pack with the lack of direction from Kingsley. We definitely needed to talk about his inability to consider my packing problems. I overpacked on a good day, not knowing where we were going, what we were going to do, or anything else totally made it worse. All I knew was that we'd be spending the night.

***

Kingsley sent me a text saying he would pick me up around four, so I had a lot of time to do some of my homework. At around noon, I grabbed some lunch and brought it back to my room so I could finish.

I was wrapping my sandwich up in a to-go box when I heard someone call my name. Jason was standing there awkwardly.

"Hey," he mumbled, looking down at his feet.

"Hi," I replied, and focused on the fact that I couldn't close the freaking box.

He reached out and took it from me, closing it in one swift motion. "Look, I texted Violet to see where you were, and she told me you were in your dorm. I went there and, obviously, you weren't home so I took a shot that you'd be in here. I want to talk about yesterday."

I almost instantly closed off and held my hand out, stopping him. "I get it. It was a mistake and it shouldn't have happened. We don't need to talk about it at all. I won't tell Janice or anything, so let's just try to be friends and move on."

"The truth is I can't just be friends with you anymore. That's not what I want. I decided."

I felt as if the wind had been knocked out of me. I needed him as a friend. God, I was such an idiot. I knew if something like this happened, it'd ruin our friendship. "You can't just spring this on me in the cafeteria while you're holding my takeout box."

"Why not? Do you want me to scream it to everyone in here? Should I take you to an expensive dinner and have them spell it out on a cake? Tell me what I need to do and I'll do it. I want to be with just you, and not as friends."

He took the hand that wasn't holding the food,

242

and stroked the back of it with his thumb. "Come on, Annabelle, let's give this a try."

"I'm with Kingsley. We're going out tonight. What do you want me to do? Cancel with him and be with you?"

"Yes, that's exactly what I want you to do. I want you to look me in the eyes and tell me this isn't what you want too. Come on, Annabelle. We've been dancing around this for months now. Let's just be together."

"It doesn't work like that for me. I don't bounce around. I'm with Kingsley and I'm not trying to hurt him. He cares about me. You've been with Janice forever. This is probably just some phase you're going through."

Jason let go of my hand and shoved his in his pocket. "Listen, I know this isn't a phase. Violet even knows it's not a phase. I'm sure she's been nagging you about this as much, or even more, than she's been bothering me. After the kiss, I thought about what I really wanted and it wasn't Janice. To be honest, it hasn't been Janice for a while."

I stared at him. This was what I wanted to hear the other day. I wanted him to tell me all these things but something was stopping me. I didn't have a label to put on it just yet, but it didn't feel right. Something about this seemed off. Maybe it was too late. I did have feelings for Kingsley.

"Jason…"

"Look, it took me some time to sort all of this out for myself. I want you to be happy, and if he is what makes you happy, then that's fine. But my feelings for you aren't just going away. I'll be here when you realize we were made for each other. I don't even care how long it takes."

I thought about Christie's conversation earlier and my heart started to race. I didn't want a soul mate just yet. It was all becoming too much.

"Jason, I can't do this right now." I started to walk away, attempting to control my body from shaking. Why was it when the girls in movies got the dramatic declaration they always seem so happy? What about the day after the declaration? And the day after that? What happened when Jason realized I wasn't Janice? I'd lose one of my best friends. If Violet sided with him, I'd lose her too. No, I couldn't do it.

Jason grabbed my arm before I could make it out of the cafeteria.

"What, Jason?" I asked him, completely deflated.

"You forgot your food." He handed me the box and grazed my fingers in the process. I felt a surge of something flow through me and I looked up into his eyes.

I opened my mouth to say something but nothing came out.

"Shhh," he said, putting his finger to his lips. "You don't need to speak just yet. Think it all over. I'll be here if you change your mind. Will I see you tonight at the karaoke party?"

"Uh, no. I told you, I'm going out with Kingsley tonight." I looked down and shifted my weight, a little embarrassed.

"Right, sorry. Well, have fun. You know you can call me if you ever need anything."

"I'll keep that in mind." I nodded and then

headed back to my room.

***

I didn't know what to say about Jason. I could barely concentrate on my homework. Eventually, I gave up and went to take a shower and get ready to see Kingsley. I grabbed my shower stuff and then looked out the window to think about what I was going to wear. A small smile spread across my face. The smallest flakes of snow were beginning to fall. I always felt good about snow. It was like a sign that I made the right decision to stick with Kingsley. I was reminded of our winter festival date and all the gushy feelings I had that day came rushing back to me. Then I thought of the blindfold. I grabbed one of my darker scarves and tossed it into my bag. Maybe this would help to excite things.

I got out of the shower and got ready. Kingsley texted me saying he was running a little late. I sat on the bed and tried to wait. Waiting was awful. I didn't want to sit and have time to think. Before I could help it, I was making a list of Jason's flaws and Kingsley's flaws. I couldn't figure out why I started with the flaws. It may have had something to do with the fact that their attributes were almost constantly on my mind. Kingsley was so tender whenever he touched me and it felt so good. But then again, Jason's eyes had the ability to stop me in my tracks. Kingsley was spontaneous and always up for an adventure, while Jason was sturdy and reliable.

The more I thought about it, the harder it was for

me to actually make a decision as to what I wanted. Kingsley sent me a message and told me that he was here so I left my room and that decision behind me. Maybe this date would help answer some questions for me.

I climbed into his SUV and he gave me a little peck on the cheek.

"You look beautiful," Kingsley told me as he looked over my dark peacoat, burgundy dress, black tights, and black boots. I had wanted to look nice for him and it seemed I'd made the right decision. He looked like he'd stepped out of a catalog for men's wear and I fought to keep from swooning. Under his stylish jacket, I could tell he was wearing a nice green button-down and black slacks. His hair was gelled in front and he was clean shaven. When he gave me a light kiss, I inhaled his cologne. The intense evergreen smell was intoxicating. But it was the expression of adoration in his eyes that really did me in. I'd never question whether or not he cared for me.

"Thank you. I wasn't sure what to wear, so I just settled on this. Where are we going?"

"Well, I thought we could have a nice dinner and then a little something else." Kingsley reached behind him and pulled out a box wrapped with a beautiful bow. "I got this for you, babe."

"I told you, you didn't have to get me anything," I cooed while I quickly opened the present. As I lifted the lid, I blushed from head to toe, but I was really excited. A crimson pair of panties and matching bra were sitting in the box. It was almost the same set I had worn the other night.

"You told me your other set made you feel confident, and I said I'd buy you more. This is just the first of many to come, I hope."

"But how did you know my size?" I asked after looking at the tags.

"I called Violet. She had a good idea, so I hope it fits. If it doesn't, then we blame her."

"No," I said, and reached out to stroke his thigh. "This will make tonight perfect." I bit my lip a little and felt the fabric between my fingers. It was silky smooth and I was kind of itching to put it on. I actually thought about climbing into the backseat like I did with Christie but I couldn't bring myself to do it. I could always change later. Or maybe I could just do it now.

Kingsley started the car, and was about to pull out of the parking lot but I stopped him. "I want to run back up to my room and put this on." I reached to open the door, but he stopped me.

"Actually, now that you said it was the right size, I would like to get to the restaurant. You can just put it on for me later." He drove out of the parking lot and that was that. I closed the lid on the box and placed it in the backseat.

"So, did you get called in yesterday?"

"Yeah, but luckily it was just a very minor thing. We finished quickly."

"Oh, that's great. What else did you do?"

"Well, when I left you, I went back to campus and hung out with Karen because we still had some things to do."

"What were you guys doing? Should I be worried?" It felt a little ridiculous for me to feel

247

jealous. Jason had just asked me to be with him, and here I was trying to act like that never happened and judge Kingsley for doing the same thing. "No, you don't need to tell me. I understand that you and she had a lot to worry about with her cousin's death. I trust you."

"Aren't you the mature one? I like you like this." He took my hand and kissed the back of it. I smiled from ear to ear and listened to him continue to talk about how influential he was in stopping the fire last night.

When we got to the restaurant, Kingsley helped me out of the SUV and we walked inside hand in hand. It looked fancy, really fancy. The kind of fancy that made you want to stand up a little straighter, check your teeth for lipstick, and be on your best behavior. I had never been to a place this elegant before and tried to make a mental note to hold my pinky up when I drank.

"Mr. Kingsley, it is so nice to see you again," the maître d' exalted when we walked in.

"Thank you, Peter. This is my girlfriend, Annabelle."

He took my hand and made a show of kissing my knuckles.

"Nice to meet you," I replied delicately.

"Your table is ready, and the chef has already started your order." Peter took us to a dramatic booth with red plush seats, a strong oak table, and crystal glasses. The cloth napkins weren't wrapped around silverware, they were in a dramatic fold design that looked nothing like a cheesy swan and everything like an elaborate flower. The several

248

pieces of silverware were placed around the plate and I felt a little like Vivian in *Pretty Woman*, but I didn't even know which one was the salad fork. I was completely impressed and slightly uncomfortable.

We took our seats and Peter filled our water cups before leaving.

"I hope you don't mind that I ordered for us. I just love this one dish and I'd hate for you to miss out on it," Kingsley insisted, practically bouncing with excitement.

"How does everyone know you here?"

"My dad worked as their lawyer when there was a huge scandal here. After that, my family stops by every now and then. They always treat us like royalty since we kept the owner out of jail."

"Well, who doesn't like being treated like a princess?" I grabbed my water glass and took a sip. To be honest, all of this special treatment made me feel a little sleazy. Why was the owner almost in jail? Was this restaurant a mob front? It seemed awfully nice to be catering to two college kids. But I was probably just trying to displace my agitation. This was definitely something I hoped I could get used to when I wasn't so frazzled.

"So, this dinner, we're going to have the most tender steak you've ever tasted, with some delicious steamed vegetables, a baked potato, and this amazing sauce. I don't even know what's in it, but seriously, it will change your world."

"I am not the biggest steak fan, in all honesty. I think I mentioned it on our first date." I felt terrible but it was the truth.

249

"I know, but you haven't had *this* steak. When you said that, I knew I had to take you here and prove to you that you actually *do* like steak."

Forcing a smile, I took a big sip of water and tried to bite back my retort. How could I change my tastes? That just didn't seem to make sense. But for Kingsley, I could at least try it. Besides, I didn't want to waste the food.

We talked a bit more about classes until dinner came. I was nervous as I tried the steak. It was awful and crazy chewy. I took a few more bites but I just couldn't stomach it anymore. Instead, I switched to the vegetables, which were a little mushy. I did manage to get those down. The saving grace was the baked potato—it was amazing. As I inhaled it, Kingsley seemed to notice the giant piece of steak sitting alone on my plate.

"Seriously, you've barely touched it. How can you even tell that you don't like it if you don't give it a chance?"

"I gave it a chance. I had, like, three bites and it's just too chewy. I can't take the consistency. Really, I can't eat it."

"That's such a waste."

"I know, but I told you I didn't like it," I insisted.

"I don't want to fight with you. Let's just take it with us and maybe you can try it again later."

I sighed and let it go. We ordered some dessert, but the table was pretty quiet. I wasn't fond of how he was kind of ignoring my opinion but I didn't want to make a big deal about it and ruin the night. Instead, I forced a smile and looked over at him.

"Babe, I don't want to fight anymore. We're just

not going to get into this now. I have more of a surprise for you. Would you like to hear about our night?"

"Sure," I replied, trying not to be so nervous.

"How does a hotel suite with a hot tub bath, a fluffy bedspread, and pillows that make you feel as if you were sleeping on a cloud sound?"

"That sounds amazing. I feel like I can put the gift in the car to good use."

He smiled at me and gave me a little wink. "Then let's get the check and head out."

Chapter 15

I was standing in the hotel bathroom, in my new underwear, practically shaking. I wanted to go out there and seduce him, but something just didn't feel right. The more I thought about what it could be, the more my nerves took over.

It must have been a while, because Kingsley knocked on the door.

"Are you doing okay in there, babe?"

"Yeah, I'm just…" I looked around and grabbed my toothbrush out of my toiletry kit. "Just brushing my teeth." I turned the water on and then grabbed my toothpaste.

The door opened and Kingsley walked in, wearing only his boxers. His taut muscles captured my attention and I missed my mouth with the toothbrush and smeared toothpaste on my cheek. He walked to me and wiped his finger across my face to take care of the mess.

Kingsley took my toothbrush out of my hand and tossed it into my toiletry bag. "I don't think I can wait anymore. Not seeing how amazing you look in that." He threaded his fingers through mine and pulled my arms out to keep me from trying to cover up myself.

"It feels amazing on me." I stood up a little straighter, trying to get that confidence I felt in the other set back.

"I bet. It feels even better on my end." He let go of my hands and pulled me into a kiss. It was long and filled with passion and the promise of more. "Last time we were together like this, it didn't go well. I thought it might be time to give it another try. Maybe with me taking the reins since I'm more experienced."

I nodded and wrapped my hands around his neck. Kingsley picked me up and placed me on top of the counter. He pulled me in for another kiss and gave my hair a little yank. I moaned into him and wrapped my legs around his waist.

He slid his hand up my thigh and tilted my torso forward so my head was up against the mirror. I dug my nails into his back, not too hard that I'd leave marks, but hard enough to get his attention.

"You're getting feisty, I like this." He bit my neck and started to suckle at my collarbone. He slid his palm up my stomach and onto the lacy fabric of my new bra. He stroked and groped as I practically panted in excitement. I finally couldn't take the teasing and reached behind myself to unhook the bra. Then I chucked it behind him and thrust my chest into his hands.

Kingsley placed one hand on my lower back and pushed my boob even further into his palm. He grabbed my nipple and started to twist it gently. The noise that burst from my mouth could only be described as animalistic. I gripped my legs tighter around his waist, trying to ease the throbbing sensation I felt there.

"Now, now, calm down. We've only just started."

I grabbed Kingsley by the hair and pulled his head up from my chest so that we had direct eye contact. "No, none of this 'just started' shit, I need it now. Grab a condom and take me to the bedroom." The sexual tension I'd been feeling over the last couple days was pouring out of me and I felt like I'd explode if it wasn't eased. I ignored the feeling in my gut and decided to go through with it. I wanted it to feel like the first time but I wanted to play a bigger part. Since he was already hard, maybe I could get it together and please him too.

"I brought one in my shower bag, why move?" He unwrapped my legs from his waist and went to move to his bag, but I stopped him. "What's wrong?"

Blushing, I looked up into his eyes. "Before you get that, maybe I could try something else first? I don't want to take control from you, but I want to make this work." I hopped off the counter and grabbed his hips. Pushing him against the wall next to us, I went to my knees and slipped a finger in the waistband of his boxers. I pulled them down and took hold of him, grasping tightly.

He growled and his head fell back against the wall. Unlike last time, he was firm before I took him into my mouth. I heard a deep intake of breath from Kingsley, and it encouraged me to take him deeper. I tried to imagine my throat opening as wide as I could possibly make it, and I forced myself to go as far as I could. Then I slid back and repeated the process, slowly at first and then with gathering speed. I sucked hard as I got to his tip and flicked my tongue across it.

He raked his fingers into my hair and forced me a little too deep. I had a moment of panic as I struggled to breathe. But tonight was about pleasing Kingsley, so I took several deep breaths through my nose and continued until his breathing was almost as labored as mine. I took him in deep again and as I was sliding up, Kingsley removed himself from my mouth and picked me up, laying me on the counter again. He grabbed the condom and had it on in a ridiculously long second. Then he reached for my panties, yanking them off, and was inside me, awakening the sex goddess I longed to be.

Grabbing ahold of my shoulders, Kingsley began to bang out a fast and rough pace that left me practically shaking at the sensations flowing through me. A moan escaped my lips as I felt an orgasm building up inside me. Then it hit me, hard and fast, and I shuddered underneath him. My hands pulled at his hair while I tried to hold on to the last of the aftershocks.

Kingsley grabbed my hips and pulled them closer to him, increasing his already rampant pace. I tried to look into his eyes as pleasure overtook him, but they were closed tight. Breathing as if he'd run a marathon, Kingsley pulled out of me and quickly dealt with the condom. Then grabbed his boxers off the floor and started towards the door.

"I'll let you clean up, or whatever it is girls need to do."

The door closed and I was left feeling a little empty. I didn't know what I was expecting, it wasn't like we could cuddle in the bathtub or anything like that. I brushed the feeling aside, realizing it was ridiculous, and also realizing that I didn't think to grab pajamas.

I opened the door in my underwear, trying to cover any lumps I was ashamed of, and smiled at Kingsley lying in the bed.

"Sorry, I forgot pajamas. Maybe I could borrow your shirt or something?" I wanted to die of embarrassment.

"Why? You have that beautiful underwear set, why would you cover it up?"

"Um, I'm not really comfortable with that."

"Listen, Annabelle, you're beautiful. I wouldn't be with you if you weren't, and I don't want you to feel like you need to cover yourself up and hide. In there," he pointed to the bathroom, "I saw all of you and it was amazing. Why would you take that beautiful view away from me? Frankly, I think it's a little selfish," he teased with a smirk.

Biting my lip to keep the huge smile off my face, I crawled under the covers with him and laid my head on his shoulder.

"See, this is nice. Actually, it's more than nice. It gets me excited for round two." Kingsley started to stroke the top of my breast where the lace of the bra met my skin.

I brushed his hand away and fluffed my hair a bit. "If you're lucky," I told him, and gave him a little nudge.

"So, what were you up to yesterday? You mentioned that things were a little crazy."

"Things with Violet took a weird turn when the guy who attacked her tried to threaten her so we were trying to make sure she was okay."

"Did everything turn out okay?"

"Yeah, no need to worry about it. She went to the cops and they are looking into it. We were just really worried about her. I guess it's just a little terrifying to think of anyone trying to hurt her."

"Right…" Kingsley pulled his arm out from underneath me and turned to look at me, and it was menacing. "I tried to give you the benefit of the doubt that you had misspoken, but you just said 'we' twice. I'm only going to ask you this once. Who was 'we'?"

"Well, it was Jason and me. Listen, he and Violet are best friends and she needed us both. We were only alone for maybe half an hour. While we were trying to figure—"

"No," Kingsley screamed, and climbed out of bed. "I told you I didn't want you alone with him. Why would you deliberately do that? Where was Christie? Why couldn't she go off with Jason? Why did it have to be you?"

I climbed out of the covers and crawled over to him, stopping just before where he was standing. "Christie lives off campus and wasn't there. Some creep left Violet dead flowers and threatened her, we had to handle it right away. What did you want me to do?" I begged him.

"You could have called me. If someone is

threatening Violet and you're with her all the time, did it ever cross your mind that just maybe you might get stuck in the crosshairs? I could have called out of work and stayed with you so this wouldn't happen." He reached out and held my face between his hands.

"You're right. I should have come to you, but I didn't. But I'm here now. Let's not ruin the night." I touched his arms and gently stroked him.

"What happened when you were alone together?"

"I can't tell you the particulars, since it involves Violet's case." I looked down, wishing I could tell him about Finn, and Berneli, and how Jason had shown me the pictures, but I couldn't do it. It wasn't my secret to tell.

He dropped his hands from my face and I watched the anger return. "I think there may be another reason you won't tell me. I see it in your eyes, Annabelle." Kingsley stalked away from me and leaned against the window frame.

Quickly, I slid off the bed and rushed over to him. I was terrified of losing him and all of a sudden felt panic building up inside of me. I couldn't not tell him, but he was going to freak out when he heard. Maybe if I did tell him, he'd trust me. This was what I wanted, or at least what I decided I wanted two seconds ago.

"Kingsley, listen, something did happen. Jason was acting weird and he kissed me, but I pushed him away. I told him that I was with you and I wanted to be with you."

Kingsley wouldn't turn to look at me, but I saw

the muscles in his back contract and his frustration became evident. "You pushed him away?" he asked the window.

"Yes, I pushed him away."

"Good, but now I need to kill him." Kingsley rushed through the room in long, fast strides and grabbed his bag. He went to the bathroom and slammed the door shut.

A million different things were rushing through my mind at that moment. I didn't know what to think. Kingsley was who I wanted. When I kissed him, it felt amazing. My stomach exploded with a million different sensations and it was…erotic. I kept telling myself this was what I wanted. The inky feeling inside of me that kept trying to contradict it was just because I was scared of what he and I could have. That had to be it.

I heard a loud crash in the bathroom and I was scared. Kingsley looked furious and a dreadful thought passed through my mind. What if Kingsley really did hurt Jason? It would all be my fault. Kingsley could get in trouble and possibly ruin his chance at becoming a full-time firefighter. Jason…damn, I didn't know what would happen if Kingsley tried to hurt him. I couldn't be responsible for ruining both of their futures.

"Kingsley," I called as I ran to the bathroom and pounded on the door.

"Annabelle, not now. Let me be for a few minutes."

I ran back next to the bed and grabbed my clothes from my bag. I shoved my legs into my tights and yanked the zipper up on my dress.

Gathering the rest of my things, I waited at the bathroom door for him, ready to chase after him if need be.

Kingsley emerged from the bathroom, glassy eyed and furious. He was shaking and rushing around the room, throwing his clothes on fast.

"You don't need to do any of this. Nothing is going on between Jason and me. Didn't that moment in the bathroom prove anything to you?"

"You mean when we fucked? That's not making love. I would have shown you what making love was later tonight. I would have held you in my arms as I was inside you, professing my feelings through my eyes as I watched ecstasy overwhelm you. Then, when you reached your ultimate level of pleasure, I would have pulled you against me and fallen asleep to the beating of your heart pressed against mine. That would have proved something to me. Instead, you proved nothing earlier except that you can give an adequate blow job. So please, don't try to stop me. You're mine and this guy needs to back off."

Tears rushed down my face and I stood for a moment, watching him tie his shoes. I was horrified at what he'd just said to me. Was that really what he thought of me? Then again, I'd basically said I cheated on him. He stormed past me and headed toward the door. I reached out, just barely managing to grab his sleeve.

"Kingsley, I did tell him to back off. Earlier today when I saw him, I told him I wanted to be with you."

He closed the door and turned around, glaring at me in such a way that I was left frozen. I'd never really been scared before, but at that moment, I could have fallen over from fright.

"You saw him again today?" he asked me slowly and quietly.

Goosebumps stood up on my arms as I nodded. "It was an accident. We were both in the cafeteria at the same time. It's going to happen. We go to the same small school."

"There you go again with that 'we' crap. Annabelle, I've had enough of this. *We* are leaving and I'm going to teach that jackass a lesson." He grabbed my hand and pulled me all the way to his SUV.

People kept looking at us, and I thought a few of them wanted to help me, but I shook my head at them. This was my mess and I had to think of a way out of it. Kingsley unlocked the Range Rover and we both climbed in. He pulled out of the parking lot and the silence became too much. I had to talk him down.

I reached out for his hand that was resting on the gearshift. He quickly pulled it away and glared at me. Again, I couldn't help but notice how glassy his eyes were. Maybe he had been crying or something. This was how he looked when he'd found out his friend was dead. It made sense. He didn't want me to see him weak again.

"Please, Kingsley, you don't need to do this. I'm trying to think of you. Violence isn't going to help you become a better firefighter. Isn't that what you want?"

"'Course that's what I want," he said, slurring his words a little. "But you know what? I will get there without your input." The slurring continued and a different thought crossed my mind. He looked wrong. Something was not right.

"Kingsley, I'm just trying to help."

"I don't need your help. I'm going to pound that guy's head into the ground until he bleeds all over the grass. It'll be like Christmas, the green and the red. What do you think about that? I know how much you fuckin' love Christmas."

My pulse quickened as he shot me a quick glance. Kingsley was unrecognizable as pure hatred had taken over, but he wasn't done, and neither was the slurring.

"I'm going to take those chicken arms and break them so he can never hold a woman again. And then I'm gonna fuckin' pull his tongue out. Screw that if he thinks I'm going to give him a chance to touch my woman again."

"Kingsley, you can't do these things," I begged, shivering at the thought of it all. Maybe before he was just upset and exaggerating, but now, I didn't know what he was capable of. I was shaking, more terrified now than of anything I'd ever experienced before.

"I will do whatever I want. He shouldn't have touched another man's girl. Besides, why do you care? Huh? You're mine, so what the hell does it matter if he's dead?"

"Because I love him!" I screamed, barely registering what I was saying.

Chapter 16

As soon as I said it, I knew it was true. I knew I'd been afraid to mention it before, but now that I had, I realized the only reason I'd been trying so hard with Kingsley was because I was afraid of what would happen with Jason. What Kingsley and I had was nothing compared to the way I felt when I was with Jason. Violet was right again, I had been afraid of it all.

But now I was afraid of what Kingsley would do. I risked a look at him. Sweat was practically pouring off of him and he was white knuckling the wheel.

I opened my mouth to say something and Kingsley put his hand up. "No, you've done enough talking." He stepped on the gas and the SUV started flying down the highway.

I gripped the seat tight, horrified at what was going to happen, but I figured I could warn Jason. I took my phone out of my bag and started to send him a message. Kingsley reached over and grabbed my phone. But I pulled it out of his grasp.

263

"Don't you dare text him when you're with me!" He reached for the phone again, but this time when he leaned over, the steering wheel went with him. Kingsley wasn't able to correct the spin, and I closed my eyes tight. I could feel my stomach flipping as the SUV continued to spin until we slammed hard into something. I felt a shot of pain as my head connected with glass.

Barely conscious, I kept my eyes and mouth closed, afraid of glass falling into them. Instead, I focused on breathing. In and out. This was a very populated highway. Someone had to see us and call for help.

"Annabelle," I heard Kingsley say.

I still didn't want to say anything so I tried to reach out to him but couldn't quite make it.

"Annabelle, seriously, are you okay?" He reached over to me and took my hand. I squeezed gently and I heard him sigh. "Good, you aren't dead. Listen, I'm gonna call my dad and he'll handle all of this. I don't want to call the police. Just sit still."

I listened to him call his dad and tell him what was going on. And then he said something I couldn't grasp.

"I told her not to do drugs. I tried to take the pill bottle from her and that was when I crashed." He listened for a few minutes as I sat there seething. How could he lie like that? But it just kept getting worse.

"She put something in my drink too. I feel really weird."

Then I heard sirens, and they sounded close. I

doubted his father had called them so I was gracious for some good citizens. As soon as they cut me out of this car, I was going to tell them everything, especially about the drug use.

"Oh shit, Dad, the cops are coming here. Someone must have seen the accident and called." He listened for a few beats. "Right, I won't say anything until the lawyer gets to the hospital and I'll make sure my girlfriend doesn't either."

Kingsley started talking to me directly, but I couldn't focus on his voice anymore. The pain in my head was beginning to get to me and I was fighting losing consciousness. I needed to stay awake. I needed to report this to someone before Kingsley's lawyer blamed me for the whole thing. Most of all, I needed to talk to Jason.

Kingsley started to shake me and I moaned in pain as the glass seemed dig deeper into my head every time I moved. But he just wouldn't stop. I swung my arm as best I could in his direction and finally connected with something on my third swing. That seemed to stop the shaking, at least until the firefighters showed up.

With all of the commotion, I could just make out that they were converging on the SUV. Hopefully, they'd get Kingsley to leave me alone. I heard some yelling and thuds coming from the driver's seat. If I had to guess, I'd say Kingsley was out of the car. Thank God. Then I heard someone else's voice.

"Excuse me, miss? I'm going to get you out of here. Hold on tight to me." He gently took hold of my head and moved it from the window to an upright position. I felt a rush of nausea as the world seemed to spin. I risked opening my eyes, hoping that would stop the world from turning, and saw the firefighter. He smiled and showed me the neck brace before securing it.

My neck didn't hurt, so I was assuming that meant it was broken. Gingerly, I wiggled my toes and felt them move. I let out a sigh of relief. On the bright side, I wasn't paralyzed. On the down side, I must have had a giant gash on my head, as I felt a wet substance, probably blood, hopefully not brains, fall down my cheek. I forced my mouth closed even tighter to avoid tasting it.

"All right, miss, I'm back with this half back brace. I'm going to slide it behind you and then maneuver you out of the car. Stay extremely still."

I felt the stiff board slide down my back and I focused on his voice as he talked me through every movement before he did it. Nothing surprised me and this helped me stay still and maintain a semblance of calm. Once out of the car, they put me on a stretcher and I opened my eyes. There was a paramedic putting me in the back of an ambulance before another one drove like a maniac.

I felt the liquid being wiped away as we rode to the hospital. Now that it was gone, I was desperate to tell my story.

"Listen to me, the boy I was with is going to claim I was on drugs, or brought drugs, or spiked him with drugs. I never touched them. Please do a test and prove it. I have nothing on my hands or anything. I heard him talking to his dad, claiming he was going to lie."

"Okay, I hear you, honey. Don't worry. I'll tell

the doctors what you said and I'm sure they'll do all those tests," the paramedic said in a motherly voice. "Let's forget about the drugs, those tests will prove you right, and just focus on this cut on your head."

She continued to treat my head and I tried to ignore the pain that was almost dragging me into unconsciousness, but then I heard my mother's voice in my head.

"If you fall asleep when you have a concussion, you could end up in a coma." She was a nurse and liked to ruin playtime with warnings like that. You try sledding down a hill head first when all you can think about is falling off, hitting your head, and falling into a coma. It wasn't that easy.

Instead, I focused on what I would say to Jason when I saw him. I needed to apologize first. If I had just listened to my heart in the first place, I wouldn't have been with Kingsley, we wouldn't have crashed, and I wouldn't be at risk of being arrested for drug possession. I was responsible for it all and who knew what Kinsley's family was going to blame me for. My parents didn't have anywhere near the money his did. In a legal battle, we'd sure as hell lose.

I forced myself to ignore that for now and continued to think about Jason. Assuming he forgave me—I was thinking positively—I'd tell him that I wanted to be with him too. That he didn't need to wait for me to see what he already figured out. We were perfect for each other. Then we'd share our first kiss—well, technically, it would be our second kiss, but our first one since being honest with the other.

I imagined how magical it would be when those blue eyes stared down at me as his soft lips caressed mine. Once we kissed, I'd fall into his embrace, run my fingers through his out of control brown hair, and hold on tight as we started this crazy rollercoaster together. I was almost relieved. We couldn't go back to being just friends because I didn't think we ever were truly just friends. Now, we could only move forward together.

This made me smile and I opened my eyes again. I was being moved. When I tried to look around, I couldn't because I was still strapped to a board. I could only look up. Luckily, it wasn't long before a doctor was there, shining a flashlight in my eyes and asking me questions.

No, I wasn't allergic to any medication.

No, I didn't have any medical conditions.

Yes, I could feel the needles being stuck into my toes.

I screamed my mother's number at least three times. I wanted to make sure someone called her. She was a force to be reckoned with and would make sure I got the best care possible. And maybe I wanted to see her. Maybe I needed to see her.

After what seemed like hours, they were done doing tests. I hadn't broken my neck, and there was no bone damage in my skull. Everyone kept insisting I was very lucky to have such minor injuries. As my head was pounding, my shoulder throbbed, and my hip felt like it had been crushed, I begged to differ.

The pain medication they gave me helped, but it upset my stomach. At this point, I wasn't sure which was better, the pain or the nausea. But then I heard the best sound ever.

"Well, you tell me what room she is this instant!" It was my mother's shrill voice. She had found me and was already wreaking havoc. A laugh managed to escape my lips before I was smothered by my intimidating, four foot nine mother. "Oh, Annabelle, I've been so worried about you."

"I know, Mom, but I'm okay."

"Yes, that's what the doctor told me when I first got here. Then they started playing games with insurance, but I just wanted to see you so your dad took over with those money grubbing insurance jerks."

"Good, I'm glad you both are here."

"Yes, but, honey, there are some police who want to talk to you. Are you up for that? If not, I can make them go away for now."

"No, I need to talk to them ASAP. It's fine." My pulse sped up and panic began to take over. I hoped they believed me. They had to. The other option was too crazy to think about.

"Miss Lewis, my name is Officer Stein," the cop said as he walked into the room. "And this is Officer Korey." He pointed to his partner.

Stein had a bit of a potbelly that was probably once a set of rock hard abs. His black hair was slicked back and he seemed to have kind eyes. Korey was a younger guy, maybe five or six years older than me. His wired glasses hid a pair of deep brown eyes. His dark hair was cropped short, his smile was nonexistent, but his muscles were apparent. He was the bad cop out of the two.

They sat down in the chairs across from the bed and took their notepads out.

"Officers, I'm glad you're here. Kingsley tried to tell a bunch of lies about me. He's going to tell you all about how I've been involved with drugs, but I never touched them. Check my lab reports. And I would never give him any drugs," I explained very quickly, ignoring the shocked gasps coming from my mother. But to her credit, she stayed quiet.

"Miss Lewis, we know your lab results are clear. The pill bottle that was recovered from the SUV was dusted for prints. The only ones on it belonged to Mr. Kingsley and a woman named Karen Yackey. Mr. Kingsley has a history of drug use, and Yackey of distributing," explained Stein.

"Oh, thank God! I heard Kingsley telling his father they were going to blame the whole thing on me." I took a deep breath, relieved they weren't coming after me.

"With the drug levels in Mr. Kingsley's system, he's been using for quite some time now. Why did you get in the car with him if you knew he was using narcotics?" Stein asked.

"Well, he told me that he only used Ritalin when he was fighting fires because it helped him focus. He promised he'd never use around me but...wait a minute." I looked at them, confused. Ritalin wasn't a narcotic.

"Miss Lewis, Mr. Kingsley was under the influence of a narcotic. If I had to guess, I'd say it was probably oxytocin. From the levels in his system, I'd say he's been habitually using for a while."

My mouth fell open. "He took some pills and then got behind the wheel?" This was obvious, but I was still shocked. I thought he cared about me. True, it was not the right kind of caring, but he put my life at risk. I wasn't sitting in the hospital because of anything I'd done. Screw that. I was in the hospital because he was an addict.

"Do you recognize this woman?" Korey asked me, holding up a picture.

I laughed, shaking my head as the pieces all seemed to be coming together. "That's Karen Yackey. The woman you said was known for distributing. She goes to Elton Hall with us. I've seen her with Kingsley a lot. He said they were childhood friends, but it makes a lot more sense that she was his dealer."

Right before we got in that big fight over my poor performance, she had left his room. I wondered if performance issues were a side effect of prolonged pill abuse. If he took something in the bathroom, maybe that would explain the blind rage he felt towards Jason. It also probably explained the slurring.

The officers asked a few more questions about the accident and I answered them to the best of my ability, but my eyes were becoming awfully heavy.

"Okay, Officers," my mother said. "I think it's time we let Annabelle rest. We can call you tomorrow if anything else comes up."

"Thank you, Mrs. Lewis," Stein replied, handing Mom a card. "If you need anything, please feel free to call."

"I will." Then my mother turned to me. "All

right, honey, why don't you try to get some sleep. A doctor is going to be coming in to check on you in about forty-five minutes. You can get a nice nap in between now and then."

"Seriously, they aren't going to leave me alone? I thought they said I didn't have a concussion."

"They just want to make sure. There will be someone coming in every two hours or so."

She settled herself into one of the chairs and covered herself with her jacket.

"Mom," I said, and she looked at me expectantly.

"I'm sorry about all of this."

"No, baby, it sounds like you just trusted the wrong boy. It happens. One day, I'll tell you some of my stories before I met your father."

I smiled at that. My mother was about as straight laced as they came. How could she have had a past? I fell asleep imagining my mother in her pink frilly apron, dancing at a frat party.

Chapter 17

"It looks fine. It's so close to your hairline that I doubt anyone will notice," Violet insisted as I complained about the cut on my head for the twentieth time. I had taken a look at myself in the mirror about fifteen minutes ago when Violet had come in to visit and that was the first time I'd seen it.

Well, it was still wrapped with gauze, and underneath it was stiches, so I didn't really see it, but I saw how big the bandage was. The doctors said it wasn't too deep but it was pretty long, going from my temple to just above my ear. Violet was right, though, it was right next to my hairline, so probably no one would notice it when it healed, and there was always make-up. I was sure she could hide it if I asked for help.

"I just can't believe he freaked out like that," Violet insisted.

"I know. I was doing some research, and one of the side effects of oxy is, like, this crazy rage that bursts out of you."

273

"Well, I guess that plus macho entitled asshole equals this accident."

I had explained everything to her, just not the part where I expressed my love for Jason. I only told her I was warning him. It didn't seem right to tell her first. I needed to see him. Frankly, I was a little surprised when he didn't walk in with her.

"So what's going on with Finn? Anything new?"

She smiled big. "You'll never guess. The investigator came through. Apparently, Finn and Trent are cousins. After Trent told Finn he was interested in me, it became, like, this competition that turned into obsession. Anyway, Trent visited him in jail and that's how the whole crap started. Trent wanted to get back at me for putting his cousin in jail and Finn is still a little obsessed."

"Are you serious?"

"Dead serious."

"I don't even know what to say to that." I was shocked. But it made sense. That kind of behavior ran in their family, so naturally they were both jerks. "What happens with all that now?"

"Well, now we know. Trent still hasn't technically done anything wrong but at least I'm not waiting for some ridiculous shadow to pop out anymore. I know what to look out for and I got this little hot pink pepper spray bottle," she said as she fished her keys out of her bag. Sure enough, a small pink canister hung next to her dorm room key.

"What about you and Berneli and your relationship? What's going on with that?"

Violet looked down at her feet and spoke softly. "I made a decision about that. I'm going to study

274

abroad next semester. I'll be going back with David as soon as I take my last final. I applied for a couple schools, and as long as I get in, I'm going to take them up on it. I just think it might be a good time for me to get out of town. Trent will be graduating at the end of this semester and Finn still has a few more years in jail. I don't know, I feel like if I leave, then when I come back, it can be like a fresh start."

"Yeah, I'm sure he doesn't like the idea of not seeing you when he returns to England at the end of this semester." I tried to keep this conversation light, but my heart was breaking. I was really going to miss her. If I was being honest with myself, I kind of knew she'd make this decision. A small and selfish part of me wished she wouldn't, but she deserved to be happy. "But it's just for one semester, right?"

"So far. I just applied for the semester program. They have a year one but I don't think I'm ready for that just yet. I still love it here. I'm just gonna keep playing it one semester at a time."

"You're lucky that you can dream this big."

"You can too."

I smiled at her, thinking about everything that had happened. Applying a little more of Violet's boldness with Kingsley had felt good. While it didn't exactly turn out well, I had lived. Maybe it was time I started dreaming a bit bigger.

"I really hope you get into the program."

"Me too. David said he wasn't ready to give up on us yet. We fell in love in England over winter break and I really enjoyed it there. I think it will be a good move. He asked me to move in with him." She looked up at me weakly. It was like she was waiting for my response. Like she needed me to be okay with all of this as well.

I put on a fake smile and forced some enthusiasm. "That's so awesome."

She tilted her head at me. "How do you really feel?"

I laughed a little. She really knew me. "Okay, I'm bummed. You're my best friend and I don't want to see you leave. But I agree with why you're going. It will get you out of the country and away from Finn and Trent. It's more than that though. Berneli looks at you with so much love, I'm surprised no one else has noticed it. You guys need to give this a chance. And besides, he could always get a job at another university here. In fact, I highly suggest this plan of action."

"Yeah, he has to finish his contract in England first, and then we can talk about it. But...David did tell me that you can visit whenever you want, so start saving up for that flight!"

"Definitely. I'm going to need a break after all of this crap," I said, and smiled at her.

"I'm glad you're all right. You really gave us all a scare." Tears filled her eyes as she gently stroked my hand.

I gave her fingers a little squeeze and smiled up at her. Our beautiful best friend moment was interrupted when three new people walked into the room.

There was a doctor, Shane, and Christie. Shane was wearing a dress shirt and khakis, looking like quite the professional.

"Good morning, Miss Lewis, I am Dr. Choi. This is my son, Shane," a new doctor said. "Your friend, Christie, and Shane go to school together and they insisted I come check you out. I'm the neurologist on call today so I knew I'd be here eventually. I hope you don't mind me coming a little early?"

"No, not at all," I said, trying not to laugh. Christie must have worked her magic to get the doctor here. Well, looking at Shane watching Christie, it might not have been magic after all.

"I hear you'd like to be discharged," he commented while looking at my chart.

"Yes. No offense, but I'm not the biggest fan of hospital."

Dr. Choi laughed and examined my cut, my head, and my vitals. After another glance at my chart, he sighed. "Well, it looks like you can go home. But you shouldn't be left alone today."

"Don't worry," Violet assured him. "We'll bother her for the next two days nonstop."

"Perfect," he said, chuckling.

The doctor gave me some more instructions about caring for my wound and then said a nurse would be coming in soon with another prescription for pain meds in case I needed them. He and Shane bowed out, but not before Shane and Christie shared a longing look.

"How did you find him?" I asked Christie when she closed the door.

She giggled a little and blushed brightly. "We were in the waiting room almost all night, scared you'd fall into a coma or that something would happen. The doctors told us that head injuries were tricky. Anyway, I got up to get some coffee and he was at the machine."

"Are you sure you aren't following him?" I asked her.

"No, but I was a little worried he was following me. It was just a coincidence. I don't even have his phone number. Well, I didn't until earlier. He's interning here with his dad on the weekends. When he told me that his dad was in neurology, I practically dragged him to see his dad. He said his dad was the best and you obviously need the best."

"I knew you insisted on the rush. So thanks, I really do want to get out of here." We were quiet for a minute and I tried to build up enough courage to ask what I'd wanted to know since Violet walked in twenty minutes ago. "Um, you guys were in the waiting room all night. So you would have seen everyone who was there, right?"

Violet and Christie exchanged glances. "Kingsley wasn't there," Violet told me.

I waved my hand at that. I didn't want to see him anyway. "He's not who I was thinking about."

They both smiled, apparently knowing exactly who I meant. "He's been in the waiting room all night," Violet said. "When Kingsley went for your phone, one of you hit the call button. Jason heard the car accident and called us. He didn't know where you were so he called me and I called your mom. That's how we found out about this."

"Well, why isn't he in here with you guys?"

"Oh, honey," Violet started. "He's blaming himself for the whole thing. He doesn't think you want to see him."

"That's insane. This whole thing is Kingsley's fault. I need to see Jason. Can one of you get him?"

Violet nodded and headed out the door.

"So you got his number?" I asked Christie, trying to distract myself before my big romantic declaration.

"Yeah, it's all innocent though. He just thought I might want to go for a ride or something. You know, blow off some steam. Apparently, he has this badass car he races illegally on back streets."

"Wait, that kind of thing happens in real life?" I knew it was super popular in movies, but I'd never actually heard of anyone doing it.

"I guess. I've never seen it either. I kinda want to check it out though. It sounds like a lot of fun."

"Definitely," I responded with a lot of trepidation. Illegal street racing wasn't really my scene, or a scene I wanted anything to do with. It sounded even crazier for Christie. But then again, this was the same gun totting mamma who threw back whisky like a pro. Maybe it was more her scene.

She looked giddy, like a girl just enjoying time with a new guy. This could possibly create problems with her relationship with Rob, but I wasn't going to say anything yet. She was just having fun for now, and like she said, it was all innocent.

Jason and Violet walked in a minute later. I smiled weakly at him and tried to control my heartbeat. Violet and Christie snuck out of the room and Jason looked at me but wouldn't make eye

279

contact. Instead, he was focused on the bandage over my scar.

"I'm so sorry, Annabelle. I should have never said anything to you about my feelings. You're with Kingsley and I know this. I just couldn't accept it. Then when I heard you screaming in the car, it almost ripped my heart out. If I hadn't done that, then he wouldn't have gotten mad at you. I'm just so sorry about it all." He sat down in the chair next to the bed and dropped his head into his hands.

I swung my feet over the side of the bed and walked over to him, dragging my IV pole with me. I sat down next to him and rubbed his back. "Just listen to what I have to say and don't comment. I need to get this out. I've been afraid to admit my feelings for you. I didn't want to ruin our friendship and I didn't want to be a homewrecker. But when I heard Kingsley was going to hurt you, I just knew I couldn't let it happen. When he asked me why not, it just came out. I fell in love with you a long time ago. It's just taken me some time to be brave enough to allow myself to admit it." My heart raced as I waited for him to respond. He had to forgive me for leaving him like that. I would completely fall apart if he didn't.

Finally, after what seemed like forever, he nodded. "Annabelle, I think I've loved you since I saw you that first day in the EET classroom. At the very least, I knew I could love you. After that, everyone else, including Janice, was like a dim light in my eyes." He started to lean in to kiss me.

I pulled back for a second, needing to know one more thing. "Are you still with Janice?"

"No. After I kissed you the other day, I spent that night trying to figure out what I wanted. You were right, how could I say I wanted you but still be with Janice. I was just afraid. Janice and I had been together for so long that it was comfortable, but it wasn't love. I was settling. Looking at you now, I feel more fire and passion than I ever felt with her. This feels right."

I couldn't help myself and pulled him in for a kiss. It made me a little dizzy but I held on anyway. With Kingsley, my stomach did little flips. With Jason, it was as if the small butterflies turned into giant eagles. Kissing Jason sent a sensation through me that could ignite a city, while when I was with Kingsley, it was just a slow burn. It felt good, but not right. With Kingsley, I wanted to make it work. With Jason, I knew it would. That was the difference.

Jason brought his hand to my face, and the other weaved through my hair, resting on the back of my neck. My senses were heightened, my body was buzzing, and I felt heat radiating through me that didn't just excite, but it comforted me as well. For the few minutes I was kissing him, I forgot my pain.

Chapter 18

Jason left right before my mom came back, thank God. I wasn't ready to explain that to her just yet. And with some nagging from her, and a little bit of luck, I was out of the hospital in about two hours. My parents wanted me to come home for a few days and I had tried to fight it. But it was only a matter of time before she wore me down. The doctor wanted me to rest for at least a week so, much to my dismay, I spent the next five days in a fog.

Once the IV was taken out of my arm, the pain really sunk in. The right side of my body was more or less black and blue. My friends constantly insisted I was more interesting now that I had a giant gash on my forehead.

"Scars are beautiful," Violet insisted on the phone one day. "They mean you survived."

"It was just a cut on the head, let's not be overdramatic," I reminded her.

"But it could have been a lot worse. You spun out on a highway while going way over the speed limit. There's a good chance you could have died.

Maybe you should be a little more aware."

What she said stayed with me. I felt like I may have been trying to brush the severity of it all under the rug. I could have fallen into a coma, or I could have broken something or several somethings, but I came out the other end. It was probably time I celebrated that instead of acting so frustrated that my mom had me practically bedridden.

Even with my new way of thinking, I still didn't have enough to do. I got up, had breakfast, took my pain pills, and watched daytime soap operas as I drifted in and out of sleep. My professors insisted my school work could wait until I got back so I couldn't even be focused on that. My mother fussed over me at my check-up appointment, and my dad tried to save me by taking over for a few days so she didn't have to keep taking leave. We hadn't spent a lot of time together lately, so that was nice. But he did make me watch a couple boring war documentaries, so there was a positive and a negative to everything.

Violet and Christie stopped by a few times, but I hadn't seen Jason. He wanted to come by, but I wasn't ready for him to meet the parents, walk into my childhood bedroom, and, to tell the truth, I still wasn't sure it was all real. I wanted to believe it, but I needed to see him again.

Ignoring my mom's protests, I left home on Friday and went to my classes. I expected everyone to ask a lot of questions, but no one seemed to know what happened. I was a little surprised. Frankly, I had expected Kingsley to start spreading rumors about me being a druggie or something like that.

As I walked into the cafeteria for lunch, I saw Jason sitting at our table next to the windows.

I smiled and gave him a little wave. On my way toward him, a man in a suit stopped me.

"Are you Annabelle Lewis? I'm Frederick Mason."

I nodded and looked him over. His three-piece suit screamed money, and his watch confirmed it. But he didn't fit in at the school. He was in his early thirties, with a touch of salt and pepper at his temples.

He extended his hand and I shook it firmly. "Is there someplace private we can go?"

"No. I have no idea who you are. I'm not going anywhere with you," I spat at this creeper.

"My apologies, I was told you'd be expecting me. I am one of the attorneys for the Kingsley family. They'd like me to speak to you on behalf of Thomas Kingsley III and the unfortunate accident from the other night."

It started to make sense but I pursed my lips. I didn't want to be alone with him. What if he tried to bully me? Obviously, I didn't have a lawyer, or anyone on hand. There was only one person I could feel comfortable to have sitting in the room with me. I checked my watch and smiled. I knew exactly where he was at this time.

"Follow me," I said to Mr. Mason, and headed upstairs. He continually tried to start small talk, but I didn't want to give anything away. Anything you said could be used against you, right? Wait, maybe that was only with cops. I probably needed to take a law class.

The door was open, so I knocked on the frame.

"Excuse me, Professor Berneli?" I asked lightly. He whipped around at the sound of my voice and looked at me, brows raised with concern. "This is Frederick Mason, he's the lawyer for Kingsley's family and he'd like to talk to me. Since my parents are an hour away, and I don't have a lawyer, do you mind sitting in with me while he speaks? I'm not looking for lawyerly advice but…"

"Say no more, Miss Lewis." Berneli got up and extended his hand to Mr. Mason. "I am Professor David Berneli and I am the staff member in charge of the Elton Entertainment Team that Miss Lewis is a member of. I know her well and I'll sit in with her. I trust you'll treat her fairly, but also understand that whatever deal you offer, she will not be accepting until her own solicitor looks at a written contract." He pointed to the chairs in front of his desk and offered one to me and then one to Mr. Mason.

Berneli eased into his chair. "What does the Kingsley family have to say for the actions of Mr. Kingsley? Driving under the influence of anything is certainly not a proud moment."

"I have spoken with Mr. and Mrs. Kingsley and they have decided to offer a number of things. First, any medical bills that your insurance hasn't covered, the Kingsley family will pay in full. No matter the amount." He paused as if to gauge our reaction.

Berneli's face didn't change and I stared forward at him, afraid to say anything that might be deemed a commitment.

"In addition, they wanted to assure you that they are taking what happened very seriously. Kingsley has been pulled out of school to take care of his personal issues. You don't need to worry about him bothering you anymore."

"Their assurance is not enough. I am sure Miss Lewis is sufficiently frightened and we would like to seek a restraining order. Her solicitor can work out the details, but this is not negotiable, isn't that right?" he asked, shifting his attention to me.

I nodded, holding eye contact with Berneli.

"I will bring that up with my clients. Out final issue is that the Kingsley family has a very proud reputation and we'd like her to sign an agreement to keep this issue quiet. In return for her silence, we'd be willing to put together a scholarship for the remainder of Miss Lewis's education."

"That is considerate of you. Miss Lewis and I will bring these terms to her solicitor and someone will be in contact with you." Berneli stood up and again offered his hand to Mr. Mason, indicating that the conversation was over.

"The Kingsleys were hoping to get this taken care of quickly," Mr. Mason informed us, not moving from his chair.

"I'm sure you would. That's why you chased an eighteen-year-old down at her university. She doesn't have a solicitor and her parents can't advocate for her. I think the Kingsleys should be more concerned about Miss Lewis sharing this with the media. They sure would be gutted to hear the media portraying the family as a bunch of bullies."

"We are by no means trying to bully Miss Lewis,

we are just interested in protecting the Kingsley name." Mr. Mason's face was turning bright red and his jaw was locking.

"As Mr. Kingsley is the one responsible for the accident and Miss Lewis's medical injuries, it is not *her* you should be concerned about ruining their reputation. Now, I do believe this conversation is over until proper representation can be obtained." He opened the door for Mr. Mason.

"Just one warning. I may not be able to come back with such a good offer." Mr. Mason had stood up, but hadn't moved toward the door.

"I repeat, we will not speak with bullies. Kingsley put Annabelle's life at risk and you will not take more from her in this manner. You will exit the premises or I will have security escort you off."

Mr. Mason adjusted his ugly watch and walked out of the room without a backward glance. I slumped in my chair and started to breathe again.

"What a tosser," Berneli muttered, and closed the door. "Are you all right? Fancy some water or something? I have some in a cooler back here."

"Yeah, that would be great." I looked up and he handed me the bottle. I took a long swig and closed my eyes, shaking my head.

Then there was a knock on the door. Berneli jumped up to get it.

Mr. Mason stared back at Berneli with his hands up.

"I apologize. I meant to give this letter to Miss Lewis. It is from Mr. Kingsley III and he is not promising anything that involves a lawyer so you can look at it without my presence. Feel free to read this whenever you want and know that nothing further is expected as it pertains to the letter." He handed it to Berneli and then turned the other way, practically running down the hall.

"Do you want me to ring Violet? You probably shouldn't read that alone." He closed the door and returned to his desk.

"Uh, yeah. That would be great."

He took his phone out and quickly asked her to meet us in his office.

"Thank you for all of this, by the way. I know I kind of just dropped this on you."

"No, no. Honestly, I think you did what's in your best favor. You were right to think something was off about all of this. And I don't mind helping. You're more than just my student. You're my girlfriend's best friend and I'll do whatever I can to help you."

"If I got up and hugged you, would it be weird?"

"Most definitely, but you should do it anyway."

I gave him a bit of a side hug. As he wrapped an arm around me, I placed my other arm around his waist. He then added his other arm and the hug was full on. As I stood there, the tears started to fall.

The weight of it all was too much and I was finally breaking down. The breakdown my mother was tiptoeing around was finally happening and it was completely at the worst time. The door opened and I jumped. Violet was standing there, white as a sheet.

"Oh god, what's happened now? Is everything okay?" She closed the door and walked over to me, pulling me into a hug.

"A solicitor came to see Annabelle about the accident and tried to browbeat her into accepting a bunch of loaded things. Then he handed her a note from Kingsley."

"Well, let's just take a look at it," Violet said, and she led me back to the chair.

With shaking hands, I opened the note.

Annabelle,

I know what I've done can only be considered terrible, but you have to understand where I was coming from. I wanted to be perfect. Get perfect grades, be the perfect firefighter, and be the perfect boyfriend. I've watched the way my father treated my mother and she always seemed so happy. I tried to do the same with you. I'm sorry you thought someone was better suited for you than me. Frankly, he has nothing on me and you've made a huge mistake.

Anyway, the drugs weren't as intense as everyone is going to tell you. Karen and I just needed to relax every now and then. Sometimes I couldn't come down from the intensity of the Ritalin and I needed to take something else to relax. It was under control until I heard about you and Jason. So, I guess I hope you'll be happy, but just know, I won't be here when you realize you should be with me.

Sincerely,

Thomas Kingsley III

"The nerve of this crap. Doesn't he realize how much of a douche he is?" Violet asked as she read over my shoulder.

"Sadly, I don't think he does," Berneli commented. "Men like this suffer from such a level of entitlement that they don't realize these things. Kingsley has probably never been properly chastised for anything, and still, he doesn't accept responsibility in this letter."

I looked at the paper and quickly ripped it up. As much as I thought I cared about him, the truth was I wanted to care for him more than anything else. He was the crutch that kept me from acknowledging my feelings for Jason. Now that it was out in the open, I realized how I was almost forcing things to work with him.

"It's all right. He was your first, that has to mean something," Violet said, picking up the stray paper that had fallen out of my hands.

"Actually, I think that's why I'm so upset. It doesn't mean anything. At the end of the day, I fell asleep dreaming of Jason. I woke up wondering when I would see him. My first time should have been Jason and I wasted it on Kingsley." My leg was bouncing as I fought to keep it together. Regret washed over me as I really took that in. I'd thrown away my first time with a guy I barely knew in a freaking supply closet. Who did that crap?

"David wasn't my first and I wasn't his. That doesn't make our time together any less special. Yes, technically, you won't get your first time back, but you two will have a first time together one day. And then it will be special."

"Right," I replied, and nodded. "I need to find him." I got up and ran out of the room. Looking at my watch, I figured Jason was probably in class, but I could wait. I sent him a text message to meet me at my room when he was done. Then I rushed to make sure it was picked up. While waiting for him, I had a chance to make myself presentable. Or as presentable as I could be with the giant cut on my forehead.

Half an hour later, I got a text from him saying he was on his way. I grabbed a new water bottle, since I'd left my other one back in Berneli's office, and started searching for information about Frederick Mason, just to kill time so I didn't spend the next few minutes panicking. As I was knee deep in reviews for the law firm, a knock on my door sounded.

Bounding off the bed, I hurtled to the door. But

then I stopped suddenly and took a big breath. Jason was there with a beautiful bouquet of yellow daisies when I opened the door.

"I got these this morning. I was hoping we could talk, and I know yellow is your favorite color."

I accepted the flowers, and with nowhere better to place them, I got the vase Kingsley had given me, making a mental note to buy a new one as soon as possible.

"They are beautiful. I love them." I bit my lip and busied myself with pouring a water bottle into the vase and adjusting the flowers.

"How are you feeling?" he asked, and sat down in my computer chair.

"Um, I don't want to talk about this now. Let's just, uh, let me finish."

Jason nodded and I took a deep breath. I messed around with the flowers a little longer, not really needing to arrange them, but trying to build up my nerve.

Finally, I leaned forward and kissed him. Holding his head in my hands. I let go slowly and smiled at him. "Are we together? Because I want to be together. Can we be official?"

"Annabelle, that's all I want." He pulled me in and kissed me back. It wasn't like the kiss in the hospital. That had been sweet, and dare I say, maybe even loving? But now, there was something else behind the kiss and it sent chills down my spine.

Jason pulled me onto his lap and I straddled him. He grabbed my ass, squeezing and lifting up a bit. Our kiss deepened and his tongue took over. In all the time I'd imagined kissing Jason like this, it never occurred to me to wonder if he'd be good at it. He and Janice almost never kissed in front of us, and certainly not like this. But as he nipped at my lip, explored my mouth, and lightly pulled at my hair, I found myself purring in his lap, batting at him.

Jason picked me up and placed on the bed. He moved over me but stopped. "Are you okay with this? You're not in pain or anything, right?"

At that moment, I wasn't. I pulled him down by his neck and kissed him again. I felt a little dizzy, but I didn't think it had anything to do with my injury.

He climbed on top of me, supporting himself on his forearms. It was endearing that he was so careful not to put too much weight on me. It made me want him more. Reaching for the hem of his shirt, I slid it off and admired his chest. Lean muscles surprised me, as I always thought he was so skinny. But the definition in his abs overwhelmed me as I felt every inch of him.

Then Jason inched my shirt up and caressed my boob through my bra. It was a plain one with no lace, no eye-catching color, and no matching panties. But I didn't care. I wasn't intimidated as he eased my shirt off and saw the old bra or my tiny boobs. In fact, I was proud of them for quite possibly the first time in my life. I fit perfectly in his hand and I shook almost uncontrollably as my body responded to him when he took my bra off and his warm hands caressed me.

My nipples grew hard as he slipped one into his

mouth and sucked. I moaned loudly, running my fingers through his hair, not caring that it was messed up to begin with. There was no gel residue making my fingers sticky, and as I inhaled, I smelled wood, trees, nature, and just a natural musk. It was refreshing and intoxicating at the same time. Then I noticed why I loved that smell. He was still wearing my cologne.

I gently pushed him so that he was lying beside me and I rolled onto my elbow. I sent him what I thought was a seductive smile and reached for his belt, undoing it and sliding it out of his jeans. Then I made quick work of his button and zipper as his pants quickly joined my shirt on the floor.

As I reached for Jason, I couldn't help but compare him to Kingsley. Not necessarily the size and everything, though Jason was bigger, but in the way I felt when I held him. All I wanted to do was please Jason. And not because it affected my self-esteem, not because I needed to prove to him I was good at it. I just wanted him to enjoy being with me because I was enjoying feeling his hands on my body.

I slid up and down his shaft and he grew even harder. A small drip started to form at his tip and I leaned down to taste it. Jason, watching this, lost it. He almost ripped my jeans off my body and had my panties down in a matter of seconds. Then he paused and looked me in the eyes, giving me a long and slow kiss.

"Are you ready?" he asked honestly, caring about my answer.

"Yes, I'm ready to be with you." I grabbed the

condoms Christie bought me when we got the lingerie. She'd snuck them in the bag and I almost didn't see them. I stashed them in my bedside drawer just in case. Now, I was glad they were there. I was pretty sure Jason didn't have one.

I bit my lip a little as I anticipated his next move. But he took me by surprise. Jason brushed a stray hair out of my eyes and kissed me tenderly as he slid inside of me. Letting go of the kiss, he leaned back a little so we could see eye to eye.

I started to close my eyes but he quickly reached for my hand and held it above my head.

"No, let's do this together."

He watched as pleasure washed over my body and started to bring me over the edge. I saw his eyes go from longing to passionate. As my climax took me over, Jason held my eye contact and I gazed at him when it all overtook him.

It was the most intimate moment of my life, and all I wanted was to do it again. But as Jason dealt with the condom, I had to admit I was feeling a little pain now that the adrenaline was gone. He turned on the TV and held me as we lay there and watched the reality dating show he hated but knew I was addicted to. That night, I fell asleep in the arms of the man I was truly falling in love with and nothing had ever felt more right.

Elton Hall Chronicles:

THIRD WHEEL

Chapter One

Christie

It was the day of the spring concert, and I had finally convinced Rob to come up and see me. He hopped a plane from South Carolina and showed up just in time. But now that the band was playing, he was sitting off to the side in the bleachers. He could have been dancing with Violet, Annabelle, Jason, and me. However, he said the music was too loud right by the stage and backed off. It was like he was already an old man.

I looked over at Violet. She was putting on a show for Professor Berneli, who was also off to the side and pretending he wasn't captivated by the way she moved. He looked at her as if they were the only two people in existence. Then I turned to Annabelle and Jason. He had his arms wrapped around her as they swayed awkwardly out of time with the music. They were so in tune with the other that it was hard to watch. I shook my head at them, trying to ignore the pit building in my stomach whenever I saw just how happy they were together.

Rob and I were happy, I told myself for the tenth time that day. It was something I was reminding myself of more and more. At the end of this year, Rob wanted to propose. He would be graduating next May and the military offered an awful lot of benefits if you were married. Since we had always planned to get married in the future, he didn't see the harm in doing it sooner rather than later.

However, at nineteen, I wanted to have a little fun before I settled down. Rob wanted me barefoot and pregnant. But I wanted to be barefoot on the beach with a drink in my hand and a sexy man on my arm. Too bad I wasn't given a hall pass to sow my oats before I was coerced into matrimony by higher wages, a beautiful house, and the promise of forever. Homemaker Barbie would have to wait until Clubbing Barbie had some fun.

About the Author

Always the avid reader, Sarah Fischer found it frustrating that there were so few books following the struggles and joys that a typical college student faces. While recovering from surgery, she decided to write one. *Elton Hall Chronicles: First Semester* is based on real events that happened to Sarah and her friends over the years. When she isn't unveiling long held secrets or working as a government drove, Sarah likes to go to the movies with her husband and spend time with her three furbabies.

Facebook:
https://www.facebook.com/sarah.elizabeth.129

Twitter:
https://twitter.com/SarhAlexander7